Death in Saigon

By

Ron Steinman

KCM PUBLISHING
A DIVISION OF KCM DIGITAL MEDIA, LLC

CREDITS

Death in Saigon by Ron Steinman

ISBN-13: 978-1-939961-46-4
ISBN-10: 1-939961-46-7

Second Edition

Publisher: Michael Fabiano

KCM Publishing
www.kcmpublishing.com

Other books by
Ron Steinman

Inside Television's First War
The Soldier's Story
Women in Vietnam

Contents

Death in Saigon

Ron Steinman

Prologue

Saigon, January 4, 1967. I sit in Givral on the corner of Le Loi and Nguyen Hue, trying to get sober by sipping my second double espresso of the morning. It is four days after the Western New Year, and three days after the annual "light at the end of the tunnel" celebration that lasts twenty-four hours or more, depending on your capacity for food and drink. Most drink more they can hold, smoke too much pot, and have little success getting laid. The party has its share of journalists like myself, CIA agents, United States Embassy officials, spooks from every country imaginable, including the Soviet Union, officers from the United States military, but no Vietnamese who mattered, at least on the surface, except those who could sneak in under the so-called wire. Through that party and now four days later into the New Year, we still have little or no hope of the war ending anytime soon. I have no assignments, none that I want to cover. My head feels as big as a Vietnamese watermelon. I drank too much cheap Algerian wine and I smoked too many doses of harsh Laotian hash.

I sit, smoke my Camels, drink my coffee, and tear off chunks of French bread, stuffing the crust with delight into my maw-like mouth. I enjoy where I sit, watching life pass by and I plan to sit here all day until my head clears or I am safe enough in my mind to sleep. Into the café walks a Vietnamese photographer named Lee, who also works for the AP as a freelance. He has three cameras around his neck, and on his shoulder, his bag of supplies. He wears an American-issue army fatigue jacket. I know the day is changed.

"Hey, man," he says.

I half get up from my chair with the wire back and we shake hands the way the Vietnamese learned from the French. Two quick pumps, and end it.

"What's happening?" I say.

"Going to a funeral," he says. "Want to come?"

"Why? What's different? Once you've seen one funeral, you've seen them all." I laugh, thinking myself clever, knowing how cynical it sounds, even to a Vietnamese who, like most Vietnamese, doesn't appreciate cynicism.

"A Buddhist monk I know came to visit my home. They burying a dead girl with no name. Maybe you get the story. Get off your fat ass. Make a buck. " He laughs again.

The many strong coffees had already affected me. I am sharper than a few hours earlier. I think quickly. What the hell, I might better take a short trip than sit here continuing to wallow in boredom.

"Are you getting paid?"

"No, I'm on spec. You too, come. We'll have lunch later. I know a good place. Great pepper crab. Maybe we get lucky in meantime."

I finish drinking my coffee, stub out my cigarette, pay my bill and exit Givral into the late morning sun. Lee's Honda scooter waits and I jump on the back, wrapping my arms around his slender body and we are off. Story or no, the trip will fill my day.

After we watch the funeral, I file a lengthy story for the Associated Press that they send around the world with Lee's heartfelt photos. Many countries pick it up, edit it to the size they want, and, surprisingly, it plays prominently in newspapers in the United States, Scandinavia, and Western Europe. Lee is right. I make a few bucks, enough to get me through several more weeks of careful living in Vietnam.

I write the following version that AP mostly keeps intact. The night editor in the bureau calls the story, "Another Casualty of War."

Saigon, January, 4, 1967. In a Buddhist funeral service held today, Wednesday, in a section of Saigon's most prominent cemetery, authorities buried a young woman, thought to be no more than sixteen, in a quiet, dignified ceremony where they bury other poor and unknown dead. They held the funeral at noon, according to the Buddhist calendar, a safe time for the presumed and approximate date of birth of the dead woman. Without knowing exactly her age and when she died, the monk who conducted the service said he hoped he guessed correctly or else the young woman's soul would wander between life and death for eternity. When asked where we could find this lesson in the Buddhist liturgy, the monk shook his head vigorously and told us it was a theory, more like a local belief based on how families lived and thought, rather than pure Buddhist custom and ritual.

The twisted body of the young woman had been found at dawn behind the Central Market January 1, raped, brutally beaten about the head and strangled. Wearing a miniskirt and a blouse cut low and tight, Saigon police assume the young woman had been a prostitute recently arrived in the city from the countryside. No mourners or family members were present and no one has come forward to claim the body. But two elderly people, old enough to be a grandfather and grandmother, were standing to one side and twenty feet behind the hastily dug grave. Observers saw them weeping throughout a ceremony filled with the sound of clicking sticks, small, chiming bells, and Buddhist prayers. When the praying ended and the coffin went into the earth, the few mourners paid by the cemetery, and the elderly couple, passed by the open grave and dropped fake paper money onto the thin, wood coffin. This is ghost money. When someone dies, you burn it in an urn. The smoke from the burning money appeases the ghost. At the grave, the money is for the departed soul and serves to pay for whatever the dead person needs on the other side. After the diggers dropped dirt on the grave and started to close it, we looked for the elderly couple but we could not find them. They had disappeared, and like the young woman, they too, had no identity.

The police have no suspects, and like many deaths of a similar nature, the police believe this, too, will go unsolved. A young National Police officer said, "This is only one death among many. We are fighting a war and really have more important things to do than to look for a murderer."

Walking away from the graveyard, I cannot help thinking, I had just seen another dead South Vietnamese, a young woman, a girl, really, and one not because of the fighting, yet a casualty of war as sure as I know my name. Would she have died that way had there not been a war? Would she be in Saigon had there not been a war? That's about all the thought I give her death, an unknown woman gone and probably soon forgotten, especially by me.

In December 1966, there were heavy bombing raids over many parts of North Vietnam. Most attacks are against fortified positions near Hanoi, including blowing up fuel dumps and destroying railroad yards. Everywhere in South Vietnam terrorists strike, assassinating high government officials and lowly village teachers. By the end of the year, several weeks after the young woman's funeral, the Pentagon reports 5,008 United States troops killed, bringing the war's total to 6,664 dead and 37,738 wounded since 1961. At the start of 1967, Saigon's population, once less than 300,000, had jumped to more than 3,000,000.

The crowded city, previously an enviable place to live for Vietnamese and foreigners alike, had become difficult and treacherous. Danger is everywhere, from the Viet Cong tossing grenades and satchel charges at soldiers guarding government installations, to everyday crimes of robbery and murder. People care less about everyday crime because life has to be lived despite the harsh reality they see in their day-to-day battle to survive.

One

My name is Adam Berg. My father thought Adam a good name for his first-born. Truth is, it's a name I didn't like growing up. In the world I'm a part of now it just doesn't seem real. I'll start from the beginning and I'll be brief. I grew up in Brooklyn and lived there for most of my first twenty-five years. We had four seasons, including winter and snow and freezing temperatures. Four. I count them every day in Saigon. In Vietnam, we have one season, with minor variations. Hot and hotter. Rain and less rain sometimes, and at other times, more rain. Rain or no, it is always wet. I'm never dry. Worse, I sweat in Saigon, the way other Americans do because of the damn heat. The damn humidity, though often not long lasting, lasts long enough to do its damage. I choose to be there, so I will not gripe. Sweating probably saves my life, saves me melting away to nothing. No matter how long I stay in Saigon, I know I will never get used to the extreme heat, especially at noon. My shirt always clings to my back. Each day the city stops at noon to three, when people flee home or to bed or to anyplace cool to escape the overpowering sun. The Vietnamese never look like they sweat, though I often see beads of perspiration above their lips or on the bridge of their noses, but little more than that. I know they get hot. They have to. They would not be human if they stayed dry. They, and then we, live in a brutal climate, especially in the south and along the Mekong River. In some ways, during my moments of bitterness when I assume my life has no purpose, I resent their cool demeanor. I have problems with their being shy, and I often mistake it for aloofness. My upbringing might ring with the sound of complaint, which the Vietnamese ignore in my life and their own. They live a life of stoic acceptance, enough to make an ancient Greek jealous.

When I walk the streets, my nostrils sting from the odors of fermented and pickled foods, the hot soups and fiery noodles, the gas and diesel oil fumes, the homemade, ersatz fuels used by motorized cyclos and motorcycles, all clinging to the ground like a protective net. I do not have the grace of the Vietnamese and think of myself more like a lumbering elephant or a plodding water buffalo, especially when crossing a tar-covered street clogged with traffic, when I dodge every kind of motorized vehicle through an endless, deafening roar. I trudge over unpaved streets, past piles of debris, mounds of garbage taller than two men, and heaps of rubble lying near half-built buildings. I plow past monks, their heads shaved, their arms entwined inside their dirt-encrusted saffron robes that drag along the street. Most of the monks I see, and there are many, never look me directly in the eye. When they do, they will give me a sidelong glance and an insincere smile, almost snide, from the corner of their mouths. They do think I am inferior and they know, somehow, they will outlast my kind and me.

I walk past government buildings with soldiers out front, though moderately safe behind sandbags, their M 16 rifles at the ready protected by strings of barbed wire. Oddly, along with those military installations that really need barbed wire, nightclubs, too, ugly and plain in the day, have barbed wire across their entrances to protect the guests from harm. And it is most likely stolen from American bases.

I work as a journalist in Saigon and across the country. I practice my profession, so I tell myself, as a foreign correspondent covering the only American war available. The Vietnamese and the American authorities list me as freelance reporter. Most of the time I work for the AP or Reuters as a stringer, not on salary and only paid when I come up with a story or photo they can use. Sometimes I get assignments and that guarantees I am paid. I usually write what we call, "home towners," stories about the troops, their exploits and adventures, which appear on page three of tabloids across America. These stories fill space but bring the war home to family and friends who normally read only reports about death and destruction. A war increasingly mystifies most Americans. I also report on the radio for the networks, using my tape recorder to send them the sounds of war or riots that I can never duplicate other than by words for the wires and newspapers. Of course, I try to get stories that no one else has but in Saigon, a competitive place for journalists, that is impossible.

Sometimes I shoot stills, hoping that one will come out to help me to pay my rent and allow me to get some food. Being a big guy, bigger than I am now, a day didn't go by without me being hungry or thirsty. But my weight fell because of the place, its lack of sanitation and my inability to completely adjust to life in the Far East. My eating habits changed the day I landed in Saigon. I had dysentery at least twice a month because my Western stomach never agreed with dirty glasses, harmful bacteria in all foods, fruit washed in river water, vegetables the same. I have to hustle to make a buck and even then, I have a hard time and never have those few extra dollars to spend how I want.

After graduating from college I worked in journalistic backwaters, like Riverhead on Long Island, Easton, Pennsylvania, and Bangor, Maine, learning my trade, developing my skills, ever searching for a breaking story that would move me though the system and to a bigger city, a better job. Mostly I wrote about local politics, rape and murder, drugs. When I could no longer take the rigidity of a newspaper and the strict guidelines that told me how to think, report, and write, I left for another, sometimes smaller place. This time when I needed change, I went to a bigger stage. Vietnam beckoned, for reasons I don't fully understand. The war had been on for years, but in this year, 1966, finally I got the courage, bought a ticket and landed in Saigon. I wanted to see the war and to report it. I wanted to be close to the action and to earn my stripes covering a war before I grew fat and lazy and reached the age of thirty.

The United States government and the Vietnamese gave out press credentials as if they were handing out candy. I got mine as a representative of the *News and Owl*, a weekly on Long Island. I visited all the bureaus looking for an assignment. I bought a used Nikon on the black market because photos sold well. The Associated Press said it would take my pieces if they had a hometown touch, you know, stories about young men from Peoria and Manchester and Queens and how they were getting along fighting an increasingly unpopular war. Soon, to find paying stories, I went to the field. Action paid far better than anything behind the lines did. Between stories, I worked for an American company from Texas. I helped repair and build runways at Tan Son Nhut, Saigon's airport. There I met the two men who would change my life, Chief Inspector Hong Phuoc of the Saigon police, and Sergeant John Castle, then with the United States Air Force.

I first met John Castle when I covered a story about a minor Viet Cong incident at the air base. He had been on duty when a small team of sappers tried to infiltrate the northern sector of the base and destroy the runway. The VC didn't succeed and the Air Force took us to view the dead enemy soldiers, to count their equipment and to chirp loudly about the good job the defenders had done. Castle, short and chubby, with thick, curly, black hair, his uniform ill fitting, his shirt wet with perspiration, served as our good-humored guide. We got our story and pictures, all after the action, we called it aftermath, and returned to Saigon in time for the next news cycle.

The next time I ran into Castle, I had been working on a construction gang for another major Texas contractor. Texas contractors were everywhere in South Vietnam and seemed to control the biggest and most costly building jobs. My journalistic activities hardly paid for my pleasure but when I had money from other work, I usually spent and wasted it in the bars on Tu Do Street. I had to turn to physical work to make ends meet and to keep me in booze and girls. An American foreman I knew from my bar hopping always helped me when I needed money. He knew I would put in a hard day's work. He understood what I did and he let me come and go as I pleased if I worked without complaint. I didn't disappoint him. My parents taught me to give my all, to all I did. At night when I ran into the construction boss, he never went without a drink. I learned quickly in Saigon that payback is fair play. Nothing else mattered.

John Castle told me he grew up in Coney Island only a few blocks the other side of Ocean Parkway, on streets as mean as anywhere. When a judge allowed him to enlist instead of going to jail for petty theft, he decided not to let the war stop him from lining his pockets. He believed you had one chance in life and he saw that in the Vietnam War. In 1965, he joined the Air Force and when I met him, he had already started his second tour. Opportunity to use his developing talent presented itself to Castle every way, each day. He had the perfect job for his illegal activities. An administrator in supply who sometimes helped with public relations, he checked goods in, and he checked goods out. John Castle started small by showing his talent for smuggling cheap Japanese watches into the country. He then extended his reach by exporting raw opium and heroin out of Vietnam.

As a supply sergeant he ran into all sorts of people, among them corrupt Vietnamese army officers, sometimes even generals, and hard men from Corsica, members of the tight-knit community in Saigon known as the Corsican mafia. Soon this disparate group bonded and devised a scheme to smuggle drugs to the States in a way never before done. Usually, jungle refineries deep in Laos processed the raw opium grown in the Golden Triangle, on the map where Thailand, Laos and Burma met. South Vietnamese generals in the Central Highlands bordering on Laos controlled the drug trade. They used their own military airplanes as if they were a private fleet. Normally, the Vietnamese air force flew the raw opium from Thailand to Pleiku. From there they shipped the tightly packed, securely woven bales to Quinhnon on the coast and then to Hong Kong where refineries purified the opium and distributed it around the world, including turning some back to Vietnam for more profit. John Castle had no problem with that, but he also made little money for himself. He did not want to be the go-between. He came up with a scheme with which he had some success through his first tour in Vietnam and greater success after he signed up for his second twelve months.

Deep into smuggling and loving every minute of it, he and a friend, another Air Force sergeant who ran the mortuary in Saigon, decided to use dead bodies to transport drugs to the States. You needed a strong stomach for the work, but Castle had that in abundance, as did his friend Sid. Dead soldiers arrived at the mortuary in black plastic body bags. There the embalmers, especially after an autopsy if there were questions how the man died, prepared them for shipment to America. But before they sewed the bodies together, and before they closed the coffins, Castle and Sid, always lighted cigar between their lips to obliterate the smell of the dead. They then placed a plastic bag filled with heroin in the chest cavity of the deceased man. If they were greedy, they went so far as to put more drugs in the linings of the coffins. Planes carrying the coffins went to Dover Air Force base in Delaware and to Fort Lewis Army base near Seattle, Washington. At both locations, Castle had accomplices who unloaded the coffins and brought them to the base mortuary. They unsealed the coffins, cut the stitches, removed the drugs, and sewed the body back as best they could. These men distributed the drugs locally, and sent them all over the country to other military bases, feeding a growing demand for high-quality narcotics. For years, no one could figure how such pure heroin entered the United States. Profits for Castle and his team were enormous and his "drug squad," as Castle laughingly called his helpers, became rich watching their Swiss bank accounts grow.

Two

Usually my only contact with the Vietnamese people takes place in the bars and restaurants on Tu Do Street, Le Loi, Cong Li and Tran Hung Dao, in villages when covering a story, or at ARVN, Vietnamese army bases. But mostly I spend my time in Saigon. Every day I nod to the street vendors who sell soup and noodles, sweet butter cream cakes and fried dough, and rarely do they nod back. The thick oily smell from deep-frying adds to the already rancid smell of the streets, gasoline, and open sewers. To these hard-working people I believe I am a ghost walking, a man with white skin, probably a soul they can't see through, transparent and with little value. Not worth dealing with, since life is so fragile anyway. I try speaking to Vietnamese in the bars I haunt, particularly when I don't want to be alone. Normally I talk to myself because rarely does anyone speak English. I find women in the bars where I go searching for companionship and ultimately, sex. Usually I end with neither. When I do succeed, no matter how much I enjoy myself, however sweet the moment for me, I always know a twinge of pity for the whore beneath me. I outweigh the average Vietnamese man by forty pounds. I can only imagine how the woman feels under my large body. When I think about that difference in size during sex, my joy flees like a jackrabbit, my orgasm takes a hike and I wonder what I, a naive, unworldly kid from Brooklyn, am doing in a place like this?

I want a real love, but I don't work very hard at it. I fault only myself for not being more successful. My lack of drive doesn't help. Should I call it fear of a willingness on my part to become one with another, a woman who would wash my socks? Nonsense. I know better. Anyway, I learned a long time ago to wash my own socks. I even know how to sew the heels and toes of my worn socks and torn underwear. And everything here wears out faster than elsewhere. Would my mother be proud if I admit I can take her place? Somehow, I doubt it. Typically, though, I, a red-blooded American male, never will stop trying. Anyway, the women I want are where the air-conditioning works better than anywhere else, in a bar, of course, and, because my apartment, really a single room up a rickety staircase above an art gallery, has only one ceiling fan, I needed cold air to survive. My hanging in bars serves as my second home.

Girls, for that is what they are, and not women to anyone, flood into the cities from the ravaged countryside looking for work, hoping to escape the indiscriminate ravages of the South Vietnamese army and the Viet Cong. They and their families learned early in the

American war, their current war in a seemingly never-ending preoccupation with war, they were never safe from harm. In the 1930s during the French occupation, old people told me they had no trouble. They left their doors open even at night because they felt safe in the countryside. That had all changed. The new war took on a different tone. These girls, many no more than fifteen years old, tried to carry their village with them during their stay in Saigon. Every bar has a Buddhist shrine combined, in a way only the Vietnamese can, with an altar to their ancestors, including photos of the dead. Incense never stops burning, its smell strong and heady. As they sit in those bars night after night sipping what I think must be gallons of Saigon tea, their concoction of light tea, lime and raw sugar over ice, they need something to remind them of home.

These girls, many of whom are small, beautiful, and delicate in appearance, but otherwise strong and determined in their spirit, never fail to surprise me with the command of the worst English they can muster. Many wear bouffant hairdos. Their pitch-black tresses are piled high on their heads, hair-sprayed to steel-like hardness. They rarely wear traditional dress, the *ao dai*, but instead are in miniskirts with falsies filling out their tight-fitting dresses. They wear high-heeled wooden platform shoes to make them taller. Their costumes, sewn by hand, are always tight along their backs. They attract Americans like me and other foreigners, more than they know. Watching Vietnamese women walking affects us erotically. It makes them irresistible when they dress that way, something I'm sure they know but they don't know, in them, a part of their spirit, for thousands of years.

I once read a writer who described a woman he knew as violently sexy, thus every man and boy's dream. The women he wrote about came from the West. If only that held true for Vietnamese women. They are different, and unlike anything in a young American's experience, especially mine. Each woman moves with an innate rhythm, probably because of the *ao dai* and its chaste but revealing cling. Maybe they are born to gently propel themselves, as if encased in an invisible liquid surrounded by a bubble. I hear Vietnamese men say women cannot help how they move. After all, for centuries they walked with bundles on their heads, and carried long poles on their shoulders, a heavy load at both ends. Strange as it may seem, women learn grace, and better for the men who watch them move. Vietnamese women never parade their sex, at least the ones I know. They have no need to sell themselves as women. Too many masters, starting with the Chinese, and then the French, over a thousand years, emphasized their ideal of what they wanted in a woman. The Vietnamese, to survive, learned to bow their heads, to be diffident, to ultimately be themselves. At least the French, in their pursuit of the ideal woman, taught them, when they could, about the kind of sex they wanted, and for good luck, threw in the art of baking bread and fine pastries.

My nights were long because I had no place to go and little to do after dinner, when it was dark before curfew. I would go to my favorite hangout, Bar California. Never the California Bar. For some reason, it would always be Bar California, the same as in Rome,

Paris, Caracas, and Beirut, cities I visited years later. Quieter than most of the joints along those streets, it had a long mahogany bar in a narrow room with low lights and real whiskey from real bottles that I never drank. Much booze in Vietnam came from Hong Kong or Japan, copied flavors in fake bottles. In Vietnam drinking hard liquor, whether Scotch, rye, vodka, and especially gin, gave me a headache in that warm climate. I preferred beer, usually safe, and learned to drink Saigon's own local beer, "33," when I couldn't get Heineken from the black market or Bud from the PX. A cassette recorder with two large speakers played Nancy Sinatra, the Mamas and the Papas and Joan Baez, until the tape wore out and the voices becoming scratchy and thin. Unfortunately for me, replacements were forever available. I preferred listening to Charlie Parker and Duke Ellington, a taste all my own.

Each night was different, yet the same. The conversation, what little I had with the resident women at the bar, never varied.

"I'm not a GI. I told you yesterday. I'm a journalist."

"What your name, GI? It make no difference. You still numbah one." She giggled and her small fist filled her tiny mouth.

"To me, it makes all the difference." I sipped my drink and watched her reflection in the mirror. She smiled shyly and leaned to me.

"Sorry about that. You very handsome. You have big nose like all Americans. You go PX for me?"

"Sorry about my nose and no, I don't go to the PX for you. Just for me. Unless you give me something in return." She ignored me because she knew I had no money and the game about the PX we played always went nowhere.

"You go PX buy me soap. Ivory soap. Smells good. I smell good. Please."

The soap did make them smell, well, like soap, sweet and clean. These girls were hard to resist. I could never tell their age, whether they were fourteen or twenty-five. They were slim and small, their long hair lustrous and clean. They were always clean. With the war on, and so much so hard to find, I don't know how they managed to stay clean, to smell fresh, and to always wear a smile. But they did and they were often irresistible. I knew running water did not exist in their homes. Many families had large, thick earthen crocks painted in brown enamel they filled with water. They used that water to wash themselves, their clothes and, when heated, for drinking.

Girls in bars rarely went home with me and most were not available for a night in the sack. The young women had an unwritten code of behavior. Get the guy at the bar to buy a drink, talk to him, flirt with him, get him to play cards when you were not playing endless games of solitaire, Vietnamese style, and make the bar owner rich. But don't go home with him because he will throw you out the next morning and ruin your reputation. A young woman should be pure when she marries, unless of course, eating came ahead of purity. They knew the war would end someday. The purer the girl, the higher is her worth. A big wedding meant much pride for the family or as the Vietnamese would say, much face. Parents raised their daughters in a host of disciplines, such as sewing and cooking, for years before that one day. They didn't want the war to deny them their just due. Most of the girls thought the same and worked hard not to disappoint their parents despite the interruption of war. Many hostesses in the bars remained chaste. They drank their Saigon tea and wept when they heard Edith Piaf sing in her mournful French about lost love, found love, and no love. The bar girls always left work well before curfew to make sure they arrived home safe.

If I wanted sex, I had to prowl the streets for the slim pickings close to curfew. I rarely did that. I didn't want to risk disease and go where too many men had gone before. But sulfur and penicillin were wonderful and always available when I thought I might be in some jeopardy. Truthfully, it wasn't often enough for me to worry. I went to bars for companionship and a few beers before bed. I listened to the sad songs and felt sorry for myself. Even when a song had hope or told a story about satisfying love, all the songs were sad for me.

Some Vietnamese women went to live with an American either in the military or in construction and sometimes with someone who worked with a government agency. You met the girl in a bar. Innocent at first, the girl often made an unexpected proposal.

"You take me home, GI. I cook. I sew. I wash clothes."

And, when done in an instant without barter or discussion, life changed for the young woman and for the lonely American.

The young women did it for money, for their mother and family, for a decent place to live and in return, they gave sex and companionship, but rarely did they give love. Most of the men didn't care, because they had regular, though unadventurous sex, clean shirts, and food, though Vietnamese, lots of seafood and rice, with French bread and canned butter from New Zealand. In my place, on the second floor over a shop selling trinkets, pottery and woodcarvings, I had barely enough room to move around without crashing into the walls. Another person, though small and slender, would never fit comfortably. Each night I went home alone where I made notes in my journal, planned my next day, and slept fitfully until morning. That is, before I met Sergeant John Castle and Detective Chief Inspector Hong Phuoc of the Saigon police murder squad, the man in charge of trying to solve civilian crime.

When I first met Castle, he and I had little to say to each other. He served as a temporary guide for the press, I as a busy reporter. More to the point, I graduated college with honors and he didn't get past the eighth grade before he quit school for good. Though we came from the same lower class, where we grew up, I moved on a different path. He had that harsh Coney Island accent, while mine, though also New York, sounded more glossed over, as if from the suburbs, probably Long Island. My roots in Brooklyn only intruded when I spoke too fast or added an extra letter or two to words that I had already finished. At home, after high school, the obvious differences in how we spoke would have set us apart. Here it didn't matter what accent we had. I wanted to leave my past behind. Castle didn't care. Probably we would never have met back home and surely we would never interact. But in war, strange things happen. At Tan Son Nhut when he escorted us to where the action took place, he said little, offered even less. We knew he could not wait until we departed.

About one month later, I saw Sergeant Castle again. I was broke, which was often and I was back to work on a construction gang for fast money. There were times I tired of going into the field to cover stories on spec that I sold for almost no money. I had become tired of rice and bean sprouts or soup from street vendors that I could never be certain where the meat came from. I had done my share of running over the last nine months and now I had to take my life a step at a time if I were to survive. Digging ditches served a purpose. It kept me from starving.

There were many days, when on the verge of deep depression, I started to believe that perhaps journalism, or at least covering a war, no longer held an attraction for me. Maybe I didn't have enough drive or enterprise to go after stories on my own. I depended on the networks and wire services to find things for me to do, instead of going out into the field to see for myself. The field, where the fighting took place, is where, unfortunately, wounded and dead American made the best stories. Could someone think me lazy? Maybe. Did I have the right instinct for the story? Maybe not. I knew I needed more seasoning. Being a foreign correspondent, especially covering a war, didn't come easy. I grew up too soft in my surroundings where near poverty only affected me when I was very young. Because of that, I worried about my lack of drive and how I used it as an excuse for drinking beer and smoking pot. Saigon had too many diversions. The women were one. The usually cheap booze and plentiful, cheap cigarettes from the

PX at eleven cents a pack, was another reason. My just-mentioned pot, and a very high grade at that, was too easily available to keep it attractive. There would be other distractions the longer I stayed in South Vietnam.

I had only myself to blame for falling under the spell of the Far East. I had a version of spiritual yellow fever, something that afflicted many French during their long, dictatorial stay in Vietnam. Days in South Vietnam had a languid feel despite the war, the dislocation and the daily horror. Life moved at its own tempo, the people treading slowly and slower, all steeped in a timeless past, trapped, perhaps forever until we and other foreigners finally left them at peace. Yet, I never felt fear walking down a Saigon street. Terror is a weapon of the war, frequently used against innocent civilians and armed soldiers. Incidents of terror were frequent and indiscriminate, but I never had any fear. Mixed with the noise of bombs, artillery and machine gun fire, a walk through Saigon's streets had its own tone. Sometimes when silence took over, rare, but real, it caused me to worry more than when noise ruled.

My hang-up centered on the women, lithe and beautiful, and the electricity they gave off as they moved in a rhythm of their own as if born to it, innate, unconscious, yet knowing. Sometimes a slight smile crossed their faces when you looked at them, or they you, a smile either from nervousness or politeness, yet rarely of introduction. I had difficulty understanding the nuance of their culture. I enjoyed most watching dozens of these young women walking in the streets or riding their bicycles wearing the traditional ao dai, the long dress with long sleeves, buttoned at the neck and tight across the body, their waists so slim I could put my hands around them, if they allowed. The everyday dress they wore was white cotton with silk black long pants, and heels two inches high. When they rode their bikes, they wore black gloves to keep their hands clean. Most women wore their hair long and straight down their backs to their waistline. They moved like rippling water, one small wave after another, yet together, all part of a piece, gently flowing to the sandy shore. Young women in their ao dais on a Saigon street brought to my mind Mozart and Schubert, romantic, joyous, sweetly sad.

At Tan Son Nhut that morning, my shirt off, my fair skin getting burned in the hot sun, a bandana circling my head, I dug into that ditch as if I needed to pay penance for my many sins, few of which I thought would permanently damage me, anyway. Out of one eye, I saw John Castle. For some reason he remembered me and made his way over to say hello, wondering what I, a journalist, was doing digging a ditch. I laughed and ignored him but he would not go away. He stood watching as the sweat poured from my face. It is not hyperbole to say my perspiration fairly cascaded over my body. But it felt good.

"Have a beer with me when you're finished," he said.

I thought for twenty seconds and agreed, why not, and said as much, my mouth echoing my mind.

"Why not? Where do I find you? I can't wander on the base without an escort."

"Don't worry. I'll tell the police to get you to my hooch. Then we'll relax and talk."

I returned to my backbreaking shoveling and strangely satisfying work and got through the afternoon thinking about a cold beer. I also wondered why Castle wanted to see me. Did he have a story? The work, the sun, and the dirt allowed me little chance of any coherent thought.

When my shift ended, as promised, a jeep with two American Air Police arrived. I did a quick wash with the hose attached to the water truck, used my shirt to dry myself and jumped aboard the idling vehicle. Five minutes later, we arrived at a one-story barrack inside the airbase.

"Here we are," said one Air Police, a corporal with yellow hair and bad skin, his accent Georgia, Alabama, or somewhere close. I got out and they left, smiles on their faces, in a cloud of dust.

His mansion or hooch, as Castle called his living quarters, had everything a man could want in a war zone. But Vietnam was unlike any war in history. Men at the front had apple pie and some wore shaving lotion into battle, until they sadly learned they could die by allowing their distinctive scent to give away their position. Anyway, Castle's domain had a queen-sized bed, two refrigerators, a record player, a shortwave radio, two air-conditioners, a washing machine, and a stockpile of food, beer, wine and cigarettes to rival the PX. The cold air inside the large room hit me hard. I shivered badly. I could feel its icy presence beating back my sweat. It woke me to the same smile I saw on my escort's faces. I thought I entered heaven, or at the very least, the American dream in Saigon.

Castle greeted me warmly, thrust a cold Miller beer at me and offered me a seat. He settled into an expensive, blond leather lounge chair with controls on the side and worked them until he lay almost prone on his back, the buttons on his shorts at his belt open, exposing his expanse of stomach, adding to his generally unkempt appearance. Each time he wanted to get up and sip his beer, he had to jiggle the controls to return to an upright position. It annoyed me to watch him struggle, but he didn't seem to mind his effort. He probably thought he had a home in the suburbs.

"I like you, kid," he said.

Kid? I would be twenty-six on my next birthday. He could be no more than thirty. Kid? His beer. He could say anything, to a point.

"Why? You hardly know me." I drank more beer.

"I think you can use some help in getting through the day."

I started to answer but he held his arm up, his palm outspread to me, with one finger pointing at me, a regular gesture of Castle's I would soon know but one I would never enjoy. An American understands when someone beckons with a finger that it's harmless. The Vietnamese think it an insult because finger pointing and calling a person by wiggling the finger is only for animals, mainly loose dogs in the street, lower than humans are. Being in Vietnam, I learned to respect their customs, when I could, when they let me, and I understood how offensive many of our signals were when we did them without thinking. It never stopped Castle. He appreciated power and he knew it came to him when he ignored what he called, "local customs."

"Fuck their customs," I heard him say. "If they can't do what we want, how we want it done, then double fuck them. It's our war and we can do with it as we want."

Though he lacked an education, he had the perfect take on Washington's war. He would have fit in well at meetings in the Pentagon. As it happened, Castle's small war had more success, and gave him more pleasure, than America's big war. And he lost almost no men on the battlefield.

We settled in, so easy despite my early misgivings, drinking beer, sharing stories of growing up free-spirited for me, wild and unfettered for him. Were they the same? I didn't know then, but I would eventually find out. His experiences were more similar to mine than I thought, especially the ones where we ripped off candy from the counters in our local luncheonette.

Later that day, both of us half in the bag, he offered me a job I decided I had to take for self-preservation and more than a little curiosity. Strange what drives us to the new. Before I agreed, I wanted to know more about the job.

"What do you mean by help?" I said.

"Help with money. I don't think you make very much as a reporter or you wouldn't be working on that construction crew."

"You're in the Air Force. What could you offer me?"

"I won't be in forever. I get out in three weeks, four days, twenty-two hours, eighteen minutes. Then I change my life for good."

"How?"

"I plan to stay in Saigon as a civilian and continue my business." He leaned in and whispered to me with his chair still in a reclining position. "I'll be rich with all I ever wanted. You can come in with me if you want. I need a front man, but it could be dangerous."

Dangerous? Surely, it had to do with drugs. I knew that much without asking. Rumors were everywhere about Americans and their involvement in the drug trade. I knew that Air Force morticians used dead bodies to send drugs to the States. Though true, the stories were impossible to prove. I smelled a story. If I could break that, I could then write my own ticket. But what did John Castle want from me?

"What are we talking about?" I said.

Castle moved his body back, fiddled with his lounge chair and lay prone before he answered me.

"I want to trust you. I have to trust you. Can I trust you?"

Yes." I nodded, sipped my beer and waited. I had a headache from the beer. I dragged deeply on my Camel.

"I run a drug ring," Castle said. He stared at me. I didn't react to his words, sitting still, holding my breath, only wishing I had my tape recorder, not thinking I should not be there. I had to remember everything he said and write it later.

"You're not surprised. You probably heard things about me." "About you? Nothing. Usually I don't bother covering drug stories. They're not for stringers. Staffers cover the stories that get the headlines."

"This is no story. What I tell you doesn't leave this room. If it does, you're done, fucked, and probably dead. Do you understand?"

I understood and that made it worse for me to sit there drinking Castle's beer, thinking whatever I did, right or wrong, I might be dead. He could really kill me without thinking twice. In Castle's eyes, I saw that he and only he decided right from wrong. He always came out the winner. What could I do to get out of there? I realized nothing. I should never have been there in the first place, but my wallet had no money. Being hungry and vulnerable tempted me to take a different path with my life. I couldn't leave then, even had Castle opened the door to let me leave. Too late. He had hooked me. The beer had taken its toll on my empty stomach. His grip tightened on my emotions, his hands seemed wrapped around my heart. I found it hard to breathe as I tried to anticipate his next move.

Now Castle sat higher in his chair from Middle America. He pulled himself up and faced me.

"Come closer," he said. "I want to watch your eyes, you fuck. I want to see your skin, hear you breathe. Come closer, man."

I did as he asked. I saw his pasty skin, the few freckles around his nose, his pale blue eyes and sandy hair, his marked face from chicken pox which he shaved probably every other day, his near floppy ears and thin lips. If I went to work for him, I would see that face every day, and I hoped not so close. *Get used to it,* I thought. *There are worse things.*

He told me again he would soon be out of the Air Force. Instead of going home like a good American anxious to rid himself of Saigon, he planned to stay and run his operation from a villa he had already rented in what we in the press called, Scag Alley, scag meaning heroin, a warren of streets off Le Loi near the William Tell Restaurant. Sometimes called the Village of No Return by American deserters, men fleeing a war they feared and hated, who managed to die on their own a little each day in the arms of their girlfriends, barely able to see and feel, their lives going up in puffs of increasingly sweet, demanding smoke. Here they smoked pot, ate hash fudge, drank hash in thick vegetable soup like minestrone, and smoked heroin. Deserters married Vietnamese women, obviously without a license, fathered children, pimped when they had to because they thought it natural. Other deserters and their women set up robbery rings, mugging merchant sailors and construction workers, and sometimes killing them when they resisted. Anyone could be lucrative prey when he wandered down those dark and swampy back streets in search of an exotic thrill. The smarter and tougher deserters organized gangs made of sailors who had jumped ship and construction workers tired of sweating all day too tired to play when they wanted. They stole from the bases around the city, taking anything not nailed down and then sold it on the black market. They regularly robbed pharmacies and hospitals and then sold medicines and bandages on the black market, beating the Viet Cong at their own game. Castle fenced their goods, and supplied new women when they tired of their current girlfriends. He helped them stay free and elude the law by giving them protection for a price. Most of the time it made no difference, because these men who could not handle the war or the officers who ran it, usually died of an overdose or from contaminated drugs or from a knife in the back, their bodies dumped in the Saigon River. When the bodies washed up on the shore, the United States conveniently blamed their deaths on the Viet Cong. They rarely were caught unless by accident or stool pigeon. Fortunately for John Castle, he had a convenient scapegoat in the Viet Cong. Rarely did anyone associate him with the ugliness he helped perpetuate.

Castle had a similar operation, vastly more important to him, in Soul Alley, not really an alley but many streets that ran one into the other near Tan Son Nhut Airport, where much of the drugs came in medium transports from Laos and the South Vietnamese hill country. There, Castle had four laundries where he processed the drugs and got them ready for distribution, wrapping them in small, carefully folded pieces of brown paper. In addition, each laundry had three rooms in the back and each room had a bed, one chair and a washbasin where his prostitutes worked day and night. Each laundry had two washing machines imported from Hong Kong. When the machines worked, and really did the wash, they paid for themselves. Still, the prostitutes did much of the washing by hand and all the ironing, also by hand. Naturally, this was all done between regular and better paying work of selling their bodies. Had Castle not been so greedy he would have made a good living from his honest business. But then he would not have been true to his upbringing, and for Castle, like the Vietnamese he employed, he had to be true to his ancestors.

In each location, one older Vietnamese woman from the neighborhood operated the machines, put in the laundry, and when washed, put it on lines in the back to dry. Afterwards, she folded the laundry and wrapped it in pink and white paper thin as tissue.

Many homes were two stories high and rarely higher unless on a main street. Made of gray cement cinder blocks, hastily built, they were open to the street and had no doors as we know them. Often the houses had a small business in front in a courtyard off the street. The living quarters were inside and behind a large front room. In that neighborhood, as with many neighborhoods near and along the Saigon River, everyone always had fresh food, including rice and fish, because every few blocks seemed to have a thriving outdoor fruit and vegetable market. More importantly, the junky, whatever nationality, could score anything in that network of streets—heroin, speed, pot, and hash. Anyone could get pot cheaply and rarely adulterated, its quality the highest money could buy. Imagine the thrill of buying an eight-inch joint for no more than five cents. At that rate, just smoking half a joint a day, anyone could stay high for thirty-five cents a week. People, mainly my British friends, smashed the leaves in a mortar bowl, made it into a paste and then mixed it with fine, dark, Belgian chocolate. Once thoroughly a part of the chocolate, they added it to already boiling water and sweet condensed milk, to make a wonderful desert of hash fudge, hot or cold, depending on what you liked best. Sometimes we didn't need the mortar and pestle. When blocks of hash were available, we added a chunk directly to the fudge or even thick vegetable soup, from its waxed paper covering. Sometimes the food had a bitter taste, but its after-effect, better than delicious.

Some homes had rooms only for smoking heroin. Drug users who were American and in the military frowned on using a needle to get high. They believed that inhaling heroin would be less addictive than mainlining. Tracks, anyway, were too visible and dangerous. So smoking H had a wider appeal than sticking a needle in your arm, applying a rubber tourniquet to staunch the blood and pulling the needle out before nodding off. Damage to one's lungs and psyche from smoking a heroin cigarette were not so apparent and far less visible during inspection. They refused to accept the danger of heroin, however one took it. Vietnamese street people injected heroin into American cigarettes or they stripped the paper, emptied the tobacco and then sprayed diluted heroin on it for the maximum high. These cigarettes were available on any street corner from any newsvendor. Even the kids who sold paper cones filled with roasted peanuts knew how to get heroin, if asked. And, unlike the States, this heroin, normally ninety-five percent pure, proved an unbelievable luxury for addicts, usually for $1.25 in any currency. At home, the same bag cost more than forty bucks. Sailors, Air Force and soldiers who wanted a quick fix and feared police catching them in their barracks, went to places like Scag Alley. They found homes where rooms were set aside for heroin smoking, pot smoking and even shooting up with amphetamines, rare because of the danger of discovery. Except the kids who adored the GIs because of their generosity, most Vietnamese ignored the rampant drug use in their neighborhood.

Middle-aged women with no possibility of other income in that society in war, helped control the flow of the drugs. They, the mama sans, used children who roamed the streets, bare legged, wearing ragged shirts and torn shorts, to serve as lookouts and run drugs to

GIs and other civilians from other countries who needed drugs. Though there were occasional raids by the Saigon police, they did nothing to hinder Castle's operation. He paid off the local cops that kept them away for another day or week, depending on the amount of money dispersed. American military police could not enter a house unless accompanied by a Vietnamese police officer or official, so they presented no problem. Though Castle found it difficult to bribe an American MP, now and then he had success.

Castle ran prostitutes in Saigon other than in his four main laundries. These women lived and worked in darkened quarters on Cong Ly Street, far from the city's center. The cribs of his whores, often shanties, shacks made of tin cans pounded flat, were masks for his growing criminal network which serviced deserters with everything from guns to fake passports to seaman's papers. Fifty dollars in American money paid for forged identification cards. Fifty dollars in American money paid for merchant seaman's papers, forged, of course, under any flag requested. Fake passports cost as much as five hundred dollars, but these were difficult to make well, with the market limited. I had heard that the Viet Cong collected ID's from dead soldiers in the field and sold them back to John Castle. I could never prove that, but I believed it. Castle then converted the battlefield identification cards into United States passports.

Some men who were AWOL hung out on Tran Hung Dao Street where there were flophouses, undesirable for even the poorest Vietnamese. These crummy shacks were off the beaten path where a man could disappear for days or months, and sometimes even years. To help run his business, Castle hired Filipino construction workers who didn't want to return home. Castle also employed hardcore American deserters who didn't care what happened to them. A few deserters wandered the streets of Saigon with impunity, defying the American MPs as they danced with fate. They knew no one cared what they did or where they went. Some even ate their meals at the USO canteen and flirted with women volunteers.

John Castle proposed that I would continue working as a reporter, getting the odd job here and there. But I really would spend my time watching John Castle's back, floating freely in the wider world of Saigon, and listening for anything that could harm his operation. I would help oversee his four laundromats, his two barber shops, which were really massage parlors, and the few more expensive apartments where some of his whores lived and entertained officers and ranking embassy officials, and from where he moved his drugs. I would have nothing to do with his street whores and those who lived along Cong Li. In exchange, he would pay me three hundred dollars a week and I would have my choice, as he put it, of the teenage girls, or older if that is what I wanted, that he had in his stable.

I knew a couple of the girls he described from the nights I spent at the Bar California. Freshly arrived from the countryside, frightened and anxious to survive, willing to try almost anything to forget they were part of a war that was out of control and well beyond their limited understanding, they were there for the taking. Some of these young women arrived in Saigon angry and hurt, after expulsion from their village because they flirted with an American soldier, or worse, fraternized with him hoping for a way out poverty and danger. At first, these girls had a more difficult time than did their innocent "sisters," the girls Castle tricked into working the streets. But an angry prostitute working full-time had the makeup that would best serve Castle and his needs with the skill for a successful business. They did well for Castle because they were angry with everyone, Vietnamese and American alike. They made him more money and, of course, they lived a better life than in their jungle or riverside village, if living that life had any quality to it at all. Under Castle, and ultimately me to a far lesser extent, their days were free but their nights had to be busy or else. That "or else" came from Castle, not me. I didn't have the character or guts to punish anyone, especially a young Vietnamese woman. He disciplined his stable as he saw fit. After I started working, I managed not to be around when he sometimes whipped the women on their buttocks and thighs with a thin strand of dried bamboo. He thought the bruises would not show but the scars, like thin strips, were on their backs and buttocks forever.

Though I enjoyed marijuana, especially when so plentiful and cheap, more than one joint made me nauseous and gave me a cough that sometimes lasted two days. I preferred hash mixed with everyday food, the sweeter the better. I remember fondly eating French pastry smothered in coffee butter cream laced with hash; nothing better with espresso. I knew I deceived myself with this conceit, but I enjoyed fooling myself for the sake of a good time. I saw no harm in it.

I never tried heroin because it scared the life out of me. Coming from New York, I had seen too many friends ravaged while too young and too many men and women, heroin's victims, and wanted no part of that life. I figured my depression would pass as I lined my wallet with Castle's cash. The mood always evaporated when I could buy what I wanted, how I wanted. I had compartments for my drinking: beer at lunch, vodka, and tonic at night. A British journalist friend told me tonic, or quinine water as he called it, did the system good in a warm climate. I didn't know about that, but it made vodka taste better. Too much alcohol, especially Scotch or rye, made me dizzy and incapable of work in that hot climate. Rum gave me fewer headaches, but I preferred drinking it mixed and not with cola. The heat, especially at midday, made me high too quickly and I hated the headaches that followed.

John Castle was everything I could never be, or want to be. He didn't seem to care about anything but his own satisfaction, no matter how vicious it appeared to an outsider, and I must say, I soon learned that satisfaction with a friendly, lonely country girl was not so bad if no one got hurt in return. I decided I wouldn't allow myself to get hurt and I would do everything I could to somehow preserve my spirituality. It would be impossible to preserve the morality of any woman I had the good fortune to share my love with, and of course, sex. Anyway, I had my hands full without worrying too much about another's soul, especially when housed in drifting women.

Sitting in Castle's room then frigid from his air conditioners, and completely divorced from reality, my mind drifted back to the time I went to a village on the Mekong River near My Tho to cover the story of a man who had his head cut off for advocating freedom. It was a common enough occurrence but I rarely had a chance to get shots of the still warm head. The villagers, all ninety of them, grew rice in the flat, wet plain of the Delta. They tried to live in peace. Between the Saigon government of Ky and Thieu and the Viet Cong, they had no chance. The government owned the land in the day, the communists at night. The night before my trip, and the reason for it, Viet Cong soldiers came in after midnight and chopped off the head of the schoolteacher. They wanted to teach the villagers a lesson, set an example, so the VC beheaded the man on his fortieth birthday and then stuck his head atop a pole, his tongue lolling out of his head, flies buzzing around for a nibble, laying their eggs for future generations.

I interviewed an old man of indeterminate age who sat passively in the shade of his hut made from wood and thatched bamboo leaves. He had no teeth, wore no shoes. His gums looked worn, his feet heavily callused. Many shacks lay destroyed in the attack, a penance of sorts because the villagers had been siding with the Saigon government. I spoke to the old man through a girl interpreter, nine years old, a student of the teacher. She told me when speaking to him, I must always say, Ong, which meant, mister, but beyond that, a sign of respect for his unknowable age. We sat in the shade of a palm tree and watched soldiers of the Ninth Division doing cleanup. They could do little but apply a bandage instead of a tourniquet.

I asked the old man a question. "Why did they cut off that man's head?

"He taught our children."

"There is nothing wrong with that. Someone has to teach the young."

Though in Vietnam for six months, I remained naive about the real world in the countryside.

"Yes, but he taught them to think for themselves. He taught them we were better off under our own control."

"That didn't work for Saigon or the VC."

"You are right. He had no friends on either side of his life." "It is a tough way to live. He must have been alone."

"Yes. Alone. He had no point to his life, only a center. When there is a center without direction, a person shows others he is confused. We like people to have their thoughts one way or another. Thoughts in the middle are too expensive. Our teacher had a destiny with no bottom. He would have not lived a long life because he took no side."

I smiled. Most Vietnamese lived in a world of black and white and no gray, especially in the villages where subtly had nothing to do with the reality of life. Unless conditioned by the French, and distant villagers rarely had a touch of anything French, the Vietnamese survived by practicality that came with years of experience. They learned to endure by doing, not by thinking too much. "How long have you lived here?"

" Many years. All my life."

Then he finally smiled, revealing in full that mouth of his missing most of his teeth, his gums battered and almost black.

"Thank you. Have a long life." I bowed awkwardly and moved out of his line of sight. I heard him say something else to the child interpreter.

"Another thing," said the child. "He wants you to take a proverb with you. He hopes it will explain why the VC killed the teacher. It says: When drinking water, remember its source."

Trying to understand what he said, I paused, and then I gave it no more thought. I had my chopper to catch back to civilization, or what passed for the strange world in which we lived. Months later, after I signed on with Castle, it occurred to me, almost too late, the old man's wisdom, his age and the then mysterious proverb would forever apply directly to me.

Nine months after I landed in Saigon full of great energy and roaring to succeed, I concluded I had accomplished hardly anything. I didn't think so, but I realized someone could persuade me to do something different. If a good offer came my way, I might jump. John Castle approached me at the right time. He found me when I was on the verge of bugging out, and quitting the job I had always wanted. Finding me broke and hungry, not really that hungry, but quickly running out of funds, he almost turned me into what he wanted, and apparently, what I needed. John Castle plucked me from near oblivion, the beginning of depression, and my descent into torturous self-pity. He gave me a fresh start. He convinced me a new life would be mine and I only had to reach out and grab it. I did. And my descent came close to touching bottom before I gathered enough strength and restraint to pull myself to safety. At the start, though, I had everything

I wanted and my hunger for food and women all but disappeared.

Before I left Castle and his air-conditioned room, as he sat there and drank his beer in big gulps, he sighed deeply and spoke to me in a whisper, as if we were in a crowded room and what he had to say was only for my ears. Castle used his whisper to good effect when he wanted to say something important that always had a threat behind it.

"Now that we're clear, there is something else you can do for me," Castle said. "You look surprised. Really, it's part of your job. You signed on and I tell you what to do." A leer crossed his face. He smiled but his teeth barely showed through his lips.

I said nothing and waited for him to continue. He took another long pull of his beer, finished it and flipped the empty into a large barrel about six feet away. He lit a Camel and Salem one after the other. Castle inhaled each deeply, and separately, and then blew volumes of smoke from his mouth and nostrils. I had seen the two cigarettes mixed before, but usually not with that much of a show. I sometimes alternated the harsh sweetness of a Camel with the cooling menthol of Salem. He then paused.

"I want you to get to know a certain Vietnamese cop who sometimes has a drink where you hangout most nights. He always sits in the same place, the farthest corner and his back against the wall."

"The Bar California? How do you know where I go at night? Have you been spying on me?"

Castle laughed.

"I've been watching you and others to see who I might hire. You fit the bill better than anyone else did. But that's in the past. Here's what I want. The cop's name is Hong Phuoc. He's a chief inspector, a high- ranking detective in the murder and major crimes squad of the Saigon police. My problem is, he doesn't give a damn about the war. He's a pain in the ass. All he cares about is solving crimes. And he's honest. He won't take a bribe. I can't reach him. Every time I approach him with a deal, he turns it away and he tells me, through my go-between, my time will come. Bullshit. There's a fucking war on and he cares about crime? Can you believe it? Here's what you do. Get to know him. Find out what he wants. Where's his weakness? Find it and we exploit it and take him down. There's real value in that."

"If you know my habits, why don't you know his?"

"My girls tell me anything about most people but not about our chief detective. They fear him. He's authority, a father figure. They kowtow to him. They smile sweetly. The girls bring him his tea and they light his cigarettes, but they won't follow him, flirt with him, or proposition him. They won't ask him about himself. Too much fear, not enough balls. That is who my girls are. I can get just so much from the chicks and no more. They are Vietnamese as is he. You are not so you have to figure a way."

"You say he drinks where I drink? How do I know him? What does he look like?"

"You'll know him when you see him. He is small and he always wears a suit. His weapon is an old German Luger, the one the Nazis carried into combat. He carries it fully loaded under his left arm. His Luger works off a magazine loaded from the bottom that holds eight bullets. He carries two extra magazines and he knows how to use his weapon. He's right-handed. His jacket stays closed, unless he's in his seat. He prefers a stiff -backed chair. Phuoc looks about fifty but with Vietnamese men it's hard to tell. His hair is black, also his eyes. His skin is sallow instead of dark like many Vietnamese. I guess he gets little sun working nights the way he does. Like I said, you'll know him when you see him."

"Then what?"

"Just get to know him. Let me know everything you find out. I'll do the rest."

I shuddered without showing it, knowing what Castle meant but refusing to face its reality. I planned to face that when it happened, not before. More denial from me, but I had to survive at least for then.

"I'll try. But what do I do next? Where do I go?"

Castle took a piece of paper, and scribbled an address on Le Loi. "Be there tomorrow morning at ten. After you tell me what you learned tonight, we'll take it from there. I'll introduce you around. You'll meet the talent, old and new, make a selection, satisfy your needs, maybe make one yours, set up something permanent, if you want. We'll go day to day, but mainly get inside Hong Phuoc's head.

Find out what makes the little prick the way he is."

That night, as usual, I made my way to Bar California. I wanted to start my new job and I figured I should get into it before I changed my mind. Hell, if it didn't work out, I could always get on the next plane to Thailand, Taiwan, or even home, to New York. New York? Not if

I could help it. I didn't think Castle's reach extended that far, and I doubted he would care if I left. I arrived early at the bar, around eight, nodded to the Chinese bartender, and settled in on a stool at the back end of the room. Nancy Sinatra singing, "These Boots Were Made For Walking," flooded the room, her song on a loop because every Vietnamese young woman wanted to be cool and sexy like Nancy. White boots were the rage. None of the girls had yet appeared, it being too early. With curfew at eleven, the place would fill by nine. Men looking for companionship, a drink or sex, often with a girl young enough to be their daughter would crowd every spot on the floor. *Dream on,* I thought. If those men got two out of three, they would be lucky, and getting laid would not be on the menu. I ordered my usual Heineken, and sipped from it while wrapping my hands around the frosty can, allowing the cold to penetrate my body. I recalled sometimes that I had seen a small middle-aged Vietnamese sitting alone at the back corner table. He drank hot tea as Castle said, and smoked endless Gitanes cigarettes, French and awful smelling, not American, like me. That had to be Hong Phuoc. I wondered if he would show on the night of my first day on the job.

I always sit with my back to the room, watching the bartender at work. In the large mirror behind the bar, its shelves stacked with bottles of booze, I view the crowd I normally ignore. This night I see Hong Phouc appear quietly and take his seat at his table. He is immaculate in a dark gray silk suit. He is wearing a white shirt with a short starched pointed collar, and his maroon colored tie in a tiny knot, fits perfectly in place.

As he crosses his legs, I see he wears highly polished plain-toed black, tightly laced shoes with Italian points and heels an extra half inch high. Everything he wears conforms to him as if molded, and the contrast between his small figure, crisp and perfect, and the seedy bar, is stark. I can see he is tiny, and that says something, even for a country like Vietnam, a land of mostly small people, anyway.

Despite their size, many Vietnamese have big souls and big hearts. Generous beyond reason is how they sometimes explain why they can't do enough for you, if they like you and you are in their spiritual line of sight. Speaking of sight, Phuoc wears rimless, tinted glasses, never taking them off whether day or night. I never saw him reading anything, including crime reports or newspapers, but I knew from Castle and others he read incessantly and voluminously, otherwise how would he know as much as he did?

After getting to know Phuoc, I learned he never drove a car and made his way around the city in cyclos, motor or pedal driven, or taxis. When necessary he used what then passed for police cruisers, sometimes an old Citroen retread or jeeps painted with the logo of the National Police. His glasses were very important to him and he treated them tenderly with care. After a rainstorm we once shared, or after a particularly dusty excursion through the city's streets, he would remove his glasses, the frame off one ear at a time. Then he would wipe them or clean them with a starched white handkerchief he kept in his inside coat pocket. When done, Phuoc then replaced the glasses carefully over his bottomless, cold black eyes.

Of course, I realized who he was, once Castle told me to keep an eye on him. But, being a good journalist, I checked his background with friends at the AP and Reuters. After going through the clips, I realized I had heard about him and the frequent problems he created with his bosses in the National Police and his counterparts, the American military police. In time of war, Phuoc had become something of a legend, a word and idea I would learn, he hated. Chief Inspector Hong Phuoc did not care about ideology, specifically communism or democracy. He cared about crime, and solving it, and hunting criminals, getting them off the streets and into jail. His superiors rarely punished him, though they frequently reprimanded him. But they could never stop him from doing his job, as I soon learned to my dismay. Phuoc was patient, resourceful and successful because of his many arrests and many convictions. I soon learned he hated the war because it intruded on his business, solving ordinary, typical crimes, many of them committed in heat and anger, crimes of passion, and all against a man or woman in an uncomplicated way. Like most Vietnamese, he believed he had no control over the war and didn't have the power to stop it. But Phuoc, a man of his country if not his time, believed in the impossible virtue of patience. If more people had it, he might have the chance to cure the ills of the world. Not quickly, of course, but slowly, gently, in time, using, he liked to say, patience.

Hong Phuoc, the token good cop, the one who cared about crime more than doctrine, sits quietly in my bar, the bar I am more at home in than any other in Saigon. Now that I know who Hong Phouc is, I go to work.

Carrying my can of beer, I walk over to him. I see that he is perhaps fifty, maybe even older, but not younger. It is hard to tell age on Vietnamese men, and women, too, because their skin, for some reason, doesn't age the same as that of an American.

"I assume you speak English," I say.

He nods. No smile crosses his face. His keeps his large eyes on my face, as if he is trying to see inside my head. I can see the pockmarks on his nose and his cheekbones, probably the result of mild small pox as a child, common in Vietnam.

"I have a question. May I?" An incline of his head this time, but nothing more. He does not invite me to sit.

"I'm a reporter looking for a story, something colorful, exotic for the folks at home. You look like you might have a story for me that will give my audience something new. You seem out of place here. Can I ask who you are, what you do? Are you my story? Who do you work for?" I poured out everything I had in me before he could signal me away.

"I see you here many nights," Phuoc says. "I know you are an American journalist. What is your name? No one here knows what it is. You are a quiet man, not boisterous."

Hong Phuoc's English is precise, almost delicate, with a touch of a London accent. He speaks quietly, so much so that I have to lean in to hear him.

"I'm Adam Berg and I'm a freelance reporter. I sometimes take pictures when I remember to take my camera. I string for whoever wants my material."

"Do many want what you write?" "Not too many," I say.

Not nearly enough, I think, *but I'm lying because whatever you decide, I'll never write this story.* At least, I believed then, I would not write anything. John Castle is paying me to be a spy and help run his operation, though I didn't yet understand what he meant by that. My pay doubled what most wire service staffers earned, so I had no complaints. Yet, after only one day on the job, and not sure of my role, I still thought about doing a story. Maybe I would survive, just maybe. Phuoc struck a match to another cigarette, inhaled deeply and blew the foul smelling smoke in my direction. *Thanks,* I thought. *A lovely gesture.* I had yet to figure his game and why he came to the Bar California. Did he go to other bars, as well?

"If you do not already know, I am a policeman. I try to solve crimes. Murder is my favorite crime. I am only partly successful, but in war, solving crime is difficult because my government has more important goals than murder. It would rather fight the war. I do not fault them for pursuing those bigger issues. I will consider your request and let you know tomorrow night at this time in this place." He rose from his chair, moved around the table, said excuse me, gave me a half smile and walked quickly from the bar.

Three

Putting up a good front would be necessary for me to succeed and for Castle to get everything he wanted from me, so we decided I would continue my rounds at the various news agencies and take jobs when offered. I visited a few bureaus early in the day to show my face, and discovered few important battles I had no interest in, thus none worth covering. No agency needed a stringer regularly. Just as well. I had other things to do.

This morning, then, would be my first in a job not as journalist. I put on my Castle hat. I showed at ten on schedule and sat in the laundromat watching the young women giggle at my presence and the older women, the mama-sans, snicker at my unease. Some really did laundry, putting the clothing in washing machines until done, and then hanging it on lines in the back. When dry, the older women ironed the men's shirts and trousers, and then folded everything on a table before placing the clothing neatly in wicker baskets. There were no dryers, but in that hot, sunny climate, despite the rains that came like clockwork every day, the clothing dried fast in the backyard. Oddly despite the noise and dirt in Saigon, everything stayed clean. On the walls were Playboy centerfolds, construction company calendars, song sheets and record album covers. Ornamental bottles of whiskey, once full, now empty, and souvenir ashtrays from local nightclubs, lined the few shelves and windowsills. Copies of Vietnamese newspapers and the English-language *Saigon Post* and *Saigon News* were on a table by a small couch near the washing machines. Scattered everywhere were many cheap looking statues of nymphs and playgirls like those that I saw when a kid visiting Coney Island.

Occasionally an American or other Westerner wandered in, yes, in the morning and often drunk or high on drugs. He would give me a look of disdain, select a girl and go off to have sex in the series of back rooms that resembled apartments in a railroad flat. Each room had a bed with fresh white sheets, an end table with a large pitcher of clean water and a large enamel basin, a cloth to wash with when done, and a small refrigerator that held ice-cold beer fresh from the PX. Heavy curtains covered the windows and a fan slowly revolved on the ceiling, helping to circulate the air and cool the room, to make it passably comfortable. By noon, with the sun at its height and directly overhead, nothing prevented the heat from ruling the room. After a few days on the job, I learned to occupy a hammock in the backyard when the sun was its hottest. The little shade from the two banyan trees gave me more comfort than the overhead fan slowly flickering inside the room.

The john handed his fee to the prostitute who then turned all the money to a mama-san who immediately gave the girl her cut to prevent disagreements later and to keep the young woman happy and in line. Not each day could be as productive as the next or the previous one. They and their families still had to eat. Parents and children, meaning siblings, needed support. There had always been prostitutes in Vietnam. Concubines, the more rarefied prostitute akin to a mistress in Victorian times in the West, are also nothing new and are praiseworthy. A concubine often played the role of a second wife with the full knowledge of the first, legal wife. Dignity is the key, an idea strangely moral, understood and appreciated by the Vietnamese people. These women in the laundry are everyday whores, far from the honorable concubines for the mostly upper class, but a step above streetwalkers. They are women, with feelings, and pride, not Castle's chattel, and as I got to know them, I felt they were more like sisters to me, except the one I told myself I loved, who never said she loved me.

Sometimes I dozed in the midday heat. I stretched my legs in front of me and slumped in the wicker chair just inside the main room. I slept and did not dream, or at least I didn't recall my dreams. On my third day, I felt a shock go through my body. I jumped, looked up and saw Castle standing over me, one of his legs poised to kick me again. He had kicked me hard on the soles of my feet to wake me from my deep reverie and he was about to do it again.

"Get up, man," he said.

I jump up and knock over the table at my side. I shake my head much like a dog. I think for a moment,

I might salute. After all, he is a sergeant, my new boss, although I not in the military.

"OK. I'm up. I've waiting for you since ten."

"Rule number one. Never sleep on the job. Never. Walk around. Have some coffee. Do anything, but be sure you never fall asleep. I only want you here in the mornings until I arrive. Then you'll get your ass out of here, play at being a reporter and come back the next morning with anything you learn. That'll be the drill. If you want a chick, take one, on the house. Tip her if you want, but it's no charge to my staff, and you are my staff." He giggled, his strange laugh winking at me. He reached for the chair I knocked over and sets it straight.

"Sit," he said.

"Rule number two," he continued. "Watch the girls. Watch the mama-sans. Make sure the money goes in the right drawer. They won't cheat because I take care of whole families. There are fifty or more people under my wing, give or take on any day, and none of them will fuck with me. That means they won't fuck with you unless you let them. You'll be like an overseer, in Vietnamese, *cai*."

On hearing Castle use their language, the women's ears perk up. I feel their tension and these women, who are slaves really, look at me in differently. I have status now, and they know they can't take me lightly.

"Do I keep records, how often men come, how much money we take in?"

"No records. No paper. No notes. Use your head but don't lose your head."

Castle giggled again. Annoying? Yes. But I do nothing, fearing he might turn on me and assault me. Does he giggle because of drugs? Or is his giggle something I didn't see when we first met?

John Castle has a look that hints he is on the verge of losing control. Don't tempt me, his look says. Look at me, his look says. Despite me being short and fat, I'm very strong, and he conveys that image through his steely eyes, eyes that remind me of B-movie villains, especially Westerns from the 1930s. I know I won't challenge his look or his authority. Somehow, I am already under his control, but I refuse to acknowledge it.

This being my first week, I want it to last long enough to collect my wages. A week's pay will keep me going two or three weeks, if careful. If he fires me after one week, I will survive three more weeks before I decide my next move. With no reporting jobs in sight, and me lying back out of laziness or indecision, I need the money. So far, though, Castle's need for me seems ordinary and without the violence I assumed might accompany my job.

"Berg, you'll have one big problem. It's something you have to keep your eyes open for and not let your guard down. No sleeping or having sex when you're here. Do that on your own time. Watch out for the Saigon Cowboys. They are my biggest headache. You'll have to deal with those bums every day, unless you rid yourself of the problem sooner than later."

I knew about Vietnam's latest phenomenon in the war, the Saigon Cowboy. I wrote a story about them for a Chicago newspaper that wanted comparisons with the biker gangs at home. There were few similarities, and the story appeared buried, on page sixteen. The

Cowboys were dangerous and they had no fear. All were young. Most were under seventeen. They were ineligible for the draft because they were not yet eighteen. Many were thirteen and fourteen. Some were members of gangs, organized and run like a military operation. Others were freelancers who did what they wanted, when they wanted, responsible to no one but themselves. They rode on stolen motor scooters, Vespas and Hondas, one in front, and one in back. In daylight, they were most daring, when they picked pockets, grabbed watches off people's wrists, pocketbooks from the shoulders and arms of women. They robbed pharmacies and sold what they stole on the black market, sometimes back to the store owner, a form of protection, and even to the Viet Cong.

These juvenile delinquents didn't have a code of ethics. Money, power and fun ruled their lives. The highest bidder for their services and those who paid more money, no matter whom, won their hearts and minds, and lined their pockets. Sometimes they rode shotgun, of a sort, for the buses and cars, many with false bottoms, that departed Long Binh and Tan Son Nhut filled with stolen goods destined for the black market. In the wide-open black market, you could buy everything from new combat boots to ponchos, to tents, to new uniforms, cans of condensed milk, cans of Planters peanuts, Lipton tea, soda crackers. Inspections were cursory at the gates of the military posts, so smugglers got away free. Anyway, there were so many goods available, no one knew how much went missing. If they did know, it usually made no difference to the Americans. They had the excuse of the war they were fighting that took too much time for them to care about the thieves in their midst.

These adolescent criminals, because that is what they were, used drugs freely but stayed away from needles. Needles would come later in the war, and most by American soldiers, when despair ruled, and hope faded. In 1967, these kids smoked heroin in their cigarettes and pot in a variety of ways. Like the American soldier, they believed, wrongly, they would not become addicted. The Saigon Cowboys collected protection money from shops and restaurants, and, of course, from brothels and any whore they saw wandering the streets alone. The all-controlling pimp, an American contribution to Vietnamese society, did not yet control prostitution in Saigon, except in John Castle's case. According to Castle, he and his operation were the victims of the Vietnamese version of the Wild Ones. Daily they stopped at his laundromats, and under threat of violence, demanded and received tribute from the girls and the mama-sans. Rampant corruption controlled life in Saigon. The Saigon Cowboy did nothing different from what they saw in the elders. Money bought freedom. For a price, you could do whatever you wanted. Without money, you were powerless, and if young, you went to war, the worst fate possible.

Suddenly, part of my job is to stop the Cowboys. Sure, I thought. *Am I supposed to beat them, kill them?* I realized I didn't like my new job one bit. I had an aversion to violence, especially if it involved me.

"Use your head," said Castle. "Reason with them, first. Then get tough. Get violent, if you must. You're an American. Show the flag. Use a club. Scare the hell out of them. Tell them, not to come back. Kick their young ass. "

I said nothing. I mean, what could I say? I was far from violent. I ran from fights in grade school. I had my share of personal combat in high school and college, but then drink and marijuana dictated. Usually I lost, and sometimes I landed in jail for the night with swollen knuckles and a head heavy with more pain than I thought possible. Now, this. I didn't need that kind of trouble for three hundred bucks a week. I didn't need trouble of any kind for any amount of money. I sensed the door on my life starting to shut with what I knew would be a resounding thud. Castle wanted me to draw down on faceless kids who didn't give a damn about tomorrow. Great. They probably would prefer fighting me, once they came to attack, to the draft. No contest. No challenge. I needed a baseball bat because I would never use a gun. I knew nothing about guns. I had seen enough weapons fired, heard and seen the resultant explosions, but guns are not for me. I found them frightening. Could I see myself, John Wayne-style, pulling two six-shooters on the count of three, then firing? No. I had to come up with an alternative. But, what?

I departed the laundry and headed back to my apartment on Cong Li. I could not see me with a gun. Out of the question. Never. Guns frighten me. In the wrong hands, they kill people. A knife makes me even more afraid. I refuse to allow anyone to cut me, especially if it is in the service of Castle. I knew I would not find a baseball bat, but a club, or an ax handle would do. I longed for a broomstick, the same as the one I used playing stickball in the streets of Brooklyn when I was growing up. Probably too thin and sure to break if I wielded it thinking their heads were pink Spaldeens. I had about twenty hours to find my weapon of choice, considering that's when my newfound enemy would probably make his appearance. When I thought about it, it struck me that Castle might be setting me up, testing me. Were these Cowboys on his payroll, too? If true, it would not surprise me. They were monsters, of a sort, creatures of the war, who threatened everyone, so it didn't strike me wrong that he might be paying them to make him look good. I would find out soon enough, and possibly, I would discover something about my own courage.

From a street vendor in front of my apartment, one of many who were selling everything from food to batteries and toothpaste, I bought a sandwich on French bread, of Vietnamese roast pork, lettuce, and bean sprouts. These hard-working vendors hunker down on the backs of their calves hours at a time, cooking their food on charcoal braziers. Sometimes it's a pot of boiling "Soupe Chinoise," or at other times boiled white rice or thin, vermicelli noodles and roast pork. Both specialties are delicious. When I have time, I indulge my taste of the exotic by eating roast sparrow, frog legs, even snake, all heavily laced with nuoc mam (fermented fish sauce) black pepper, and hot chili peppers, the slender red kind soaked in vinegar, sugar and water. This day I want something simple. I have to work in the evening and I don't want my system bogged down with too much food. After eating and drinking a beer, I'm ready to restore my strength. The siesta beckoned, and, being in the country long enough to appreciate the importance of a midday break, I strip naked and lay down.

My overhead fan silently flickered as it circulated the room's already warm air, and helped me into a fitful sleep. Despite my racing brain, and my usual restlessness, I did unwind and the short break helped me though the day.

The noise of Saigon's heavy traffic and its many different honking horns and grinding motors awakened me, as it did every afternoon when I tried the siesta. Gasoline fumes seeping through the window burned my eyes and set my nostrils tingling. Usually when I wake, I have a headache. Pollution often takes a toll on me because of my allergies, but mostly and oddly at that, my hay fever doesn't bother me the way it did in New York. My day would start again after six when I planned to make the rounds of some new agency offices looking for work. I had to maintain my charade being a journalist, the beard I would use to disguise my new real work with John Castle. If a simple assignment came to me, I would take, fill it, collect the few bucks, and move on. I didn't want anything taxing, covering a battle or going into the field. After walking from agency to agency, I planned to have a light supper, maybe won ton soup and fried noodles at Cheap Charlie's and then to the Bar California. Perhaps I would have a serious talk with Inspector Phuoc, something I wanted. I realized that would be up to him. For some reason, I knew we would talk, and he might end up controlling our relationship, much the same as Castle. It made me wonder where my sense of self had gone, to suddenly find me under the thumb of two men who, in their distinct way, each now played a major role in my life.

After dinner, with the early evening light beginning to fade, I walked past the Caravelle Hotel where the old opera house loomed behind me, and down Tu Do Street to the Bar California, a cigarette dangling from the corner of my mouth. Many Vietnamese had already returned home. Mostly the young were out, including South Vietnamese troopers, sometimes walking down the street holding hands, a sight I never appreciated, but one I understood to mean only friendship. Neon lights shone in the bar windows. Moneychangers assaulted me along my walk. I waved them off knowing to change money in public, or even in a dark hallway, meant possibly finding myself mugged and beaten. I used honest moneychangers, a pair of Indian brothers from New Delhi who lived with their wives and children in a modest apartment near the Majestic Hotel overlooking the Saigon River.

Streetwalkers were nowhere in sight, it being too early for their business. Street children, though, were everywhere and hard at work. Many were homeless, left by parents to roam the streets and alleys of Saigon in packs, working to earning a living any way they could. Some were bootblacks, shoeshine boys, hawking their skill for ten piasters a shine and anything they could find in your pocket if you did not pay attention to them as they circled you. Children were decoys for the older teenagers, some the Saigon Cowboys, who tried to lift your pack off your back, your bag off your shoulder, your watch from your wrist. Others sold freshly roasted peanuts without shells and unsalted, in long, thin cones made of newspapers. These kids tugged on your sleeves, stepped on your toes, gently punched you in your side, all to get your attention. Because they had little or no body hair, they pulled the hair on your arms to see if it is real. But they were neither mean nor bad, the way I understand bad for American children. Sadly, it became clear quickly, these children no longer knew how to play. Their games took place in the street, street games such as boys playing soccer, their ball a pillow case stuffed with paper and cardboard. Their games were not childish, like girls playing with dolls, or boys copying heroes from Vietnam's mythological past.

With so much of the country destroyed, the traditional household and family no longer existed. Normally Vietnamese children experience harsh discipline at home. When I wrote a story about schools in South Vietnam and how the war caused education to collapse, and with it obedience, a Vietnamese teacher told me, "When we love our children, we beat them. When we hate them, our children, we give them sweet words." The teacher told me that they did abuse their children but not like we did in the West. He added, never take that to mean anything but love, care and attention. I found it strange to hear that force makes a better child. He did not convince me it worked.

"When they make a mistake with their lessons I punch my children in the thigh or the buttocks, even their head. Sometimes I use a bamboo stick to strike them on their wrists and arms. They admire their black and blue marks and compare their hurt with the other children. That way, they learn respect."

"It sounds like fear," I say.

"No, respect," he says. He sighed, already tired of what he must think is my weakness.

When I am about to leave his village, the teacher asks me to step aside for a moment, out of hearing. "You Americans," he whispers, "are lax and too undisciplined. You will never succeed here unless you learn patience and learn our ways." With that, he turned and walked away. I never saw him again, not that I thought I ever would. I agreed, though, conceding wisdom from him far too late for the good of his country and his people.

After more than nine months in country, I had to agree with him about patience, but my heart went out to the children. I had no answers so I regressed the way all Americans do when faced with ugliness. I dispensed sweet words, and often bars of candy and chewing gum to the kids that followed me everywhere I went. Unable to come up with something fresh, I did only what American soldiers in Europe and Japan did in World War II. I gave away free chocolate for friendship. It worked for the time my supply held out. The ancient prescription for obedience, "King, teacher, father," no longer had a place in South Vietnam. The king, read emperor, from a long line of royal failures, now lived in exile, in France. In the countryside, the Viet Cong regularly killed teachers, and those in the city worked under the strains of crumbling classrooms, fewer students by the day and their loss of authority. Fathers? Often, dead, or disappeared, or struggling so hard to survive, they had no time for the family.

All the street kids were my friends. They knew me in my neighborhood and along the streets that led to the Caravelle Hotel, the Continental Hotel, the old Opera

House, the Rex Hotel and theater and the large indoor arcade at the Eden Building, dank, dirty and forbidding to a lone American, me. At first, the children bothered me by following me everywhere, thinking me some sort of GI without a proper uniform. After seeing me regularly, many went so far as to hold my hand, especially the girls, when we walked down the street. Consider, I stood more than six feet and they were small for their age, and consider too, that many were not sure how old they were. None were in school and all roamed the street day and night only seeking cover and shelter during curfew. Sometimes they played the role of lookout for their older and wilder brothers, all lumped together as Saigon Cowboys, but hardly organized. Soon I would face some of these unruly teenagers in the warren of streets that surrounded John Castle's brothels.

My walk ended, as it always did, at seven that evening when I arrived at the Bar California, always my destination no matter where I might wander. The old neon sign had started to run out of gas. It blinked and sputtered, having trouble staying lighted. Inside it reminded me of a black and white film noir or an Edward Hooper painting, both, depending on my mood, equally depressing. One girl sat at the bar. She nodded hello when I entered. She wore a low-cut blouse in white cotton with her small, perfectly shaped breasts pushed up as far as they would go without falling out, and a tight miniskirt. On her feet were high heels made of wood that she could hardly walk in without appearing awkward. Once I made a pass at her and offered to take her home, but she said no. I didn't fit her dream of a rich American. Now we simply nodded. I still found her provocative, but recently she had cut her hair short, and I no longer found her as attractive. So, I left her alone playing solitaire, and she left me to my can of beer.

By eight, the room started filling with construction workers, merchant sailors, and civilians of every type who had gravitated to Saigon in search of wild fun. I wanted to tell them to find their pleasure elsewhere. They would not find what they were seeking at Bar California.

At exactly eight o'clock, Chief Inspector Hong Phuoc appeared. Dapper as ever, the only way I know how to describe him, he looked fresh and clean, his hair wet as if just from a shower or bath. His shoulders were square, even for a little man, and his actions precise as he walked across the room to his table in the back. Instead of following him only with my eyes, I turn my whole body toward him hoping he will see my move and ask me to come visit. But he doesn't do anything. He takes his seat, orders his tea, and lights his cigarette. I, too, light a cigarette, turn from him and watch his reflection in the mirror behind the bar. If I didn't know better, I would think we were playing a game of cat and mouse. I order another beer, and I smoked another Camel. Hong Phuoc quietly drinks his tea. No one strays within ten feet of where he is sitting. My impatience starts to rule and I decide to take the initiative, as my father would insist, and I make my move before the night will end with nothing happening. Now nine, and curfew only a few hours away, I rise off my stool, push away from the bar, and walk slowly through the crowded room to the back corner.

"Good evening. My name is Adam Berg," I say. "Do you remember me?"

"Good evening. If you were French I would say bon jour."

"But I'm American and I know almost no French and less Vietnamese."

"You must try to learn our language. If you did, you would understand our people."

"May I sit?" He nods.

"Your language is very difficult. Maybe my nose is wrong for all the tones I need to imitate. Anyway, trouble is, there are too many Vietnamese who speak English. An interpreter makes a good living here. It is a way of life and a needed skill," I say.

"Perhaps, if we get to know each other, I will teach you some words you will need every day."

"Perhaps. But what you just said, if we get to know each other, does that mean you will allow me to do a story about you?"

"I thought it over and my answer is yes. You can follow me on my appointed rounds." Phuoc laughs. "I know that is what your mail carriers say. But I am a police officer, a cop. You can still follow me."

Mission accomplished, I think. I will follow him day and night, if I can, and report each of his activities to Castle. Castle will pay me. I will have enough to eat and drink, and maybe find some love. Life will be good for me, and I might even get a story now and then to keep my hand in as a journalist.

"How did you decide to let me write a story about you?"

'I checked you out. I asked some people I know at *The Saigon Post*.

They told me you were reliable and did good work."

"I don't know how they would know. I turned in some pieces on American attitudes toward Vietnamese and they printed them without editing or changes."

"Then you should be proud they considered your work highly." "Journalism doesn't work that way. There's always someone to ask questions. They didn't have anyone. They didn't ask any questions. I think they needed to fill space, considering the crap they publish. Worse, they paid me ten bucks a story and in piasters, hardly worth the effort."

Phuoc opened his eyes in recognition. "I also spoke to Dinh at the AP. He said he liked you but he didn't think, from what he heard, that you worked hard enough."

"Dinh is a good man, but you should know he doesn't make decisions about coverage. He gathers information we use in stories. Mainly he passes along everything he hears without editing what he learns. Even when I'm not doing anything for the AP, I call on him for confirmation or an address."

The noises in the bar reached that steady pitch heard in bars everywhere in Saigon. The mix of languages, Vietnamese, Korean, Chinese, Japanese, English, German, French, Filipino and Spanish, added to the din in the room. I drank my beer. Phuoc drank his tea. We both smoked. I switched to Salem, mentholated and cooling, to soothe my raw throat. Curfew time approached and I still didn't I have anything I could pass along to Castle. I told Phuoc I had a few simple questions. He had no problem with me asking him anything.

"First, where did you learn English?"

"I learned it from the BBC World Service. I listened every night of my childhood through the time I went to the university and beyond, even to this day, and that is where I learned English. I know it is not perfect, and at times I speak like a textbook, but I understand everything said to me and know that I make myself understood to everyone else."

"Absolutely. You speak more clearly than I do. What kind of cop are you?"

"I am the chief detective, or chief inspector as we would say here, in the murder and robbery section of the Saigon Police. It keeps me very busy. Do you ever report on local crime in Saigon, or anything local, like City Hall, as they do in America?"

"I don't report crime or on crimes. None of us really does. There is too much war to have time for crime. Occasionally one American soldier robs or kills another American soldier, or a construction worker gets into a bar fight. We report those stories, but my editors, and they are many, have no interest, unless more than a few people die, or the American harms innocent Vietnamese. Do you cooperate with the military police or they with you?"

"Rarely, because you Americans have little interest in showing yourselves in a bad light, I never bring an American or other foreign criminal to justice. The expression, I think, is to sweep it under the rug. That is where foreign criminal acts go, under the rug. Your military police are friendly and helpful, but they don't care about crime, even bad crime like murder and theft or robbery."

"I want to hear more about how you go about your business. It seems to me that with the war, most people worry more about surviving than solving crime."

"I have only one purpose—to solve crime, the crime of murder to be specific. People report crimes all the time, but they do it anonymously. We solve very few. Of those we do, even fewer go to trial. People refuse to come to police headquarters because they fear authority. They are deeply afraid. Yet, they love reading about crime and criminals. Sometimes the Vietnamese language papers give bigger headlines to crime than to battles. It takes their minds off the war. Keep in mind, many believe the VC commits most of the robberies and exposing the Viet Cong might mean death. They don't trust public officials and for good reason. Since joining the force after World War II when the Japanese departed, crime took second place to national security. War is more important than crime. I understand that. My country is always at war. No day goes by in peace. Despite the war, we must solve crime. There must be solutions to criminal acts. If we can do that, solve crime with the war on, it will help the peace, if it ever comes."

I scribbled furiously taking notes, working hard to keep up. I needed more stuff to develop Phuoc's personality.

"That's good general material. What about you? I need to know more why you continue trying to solve crime when your government takes no interest?"

"Ahh. I think you might call me a black sheep, an outsider. I like to go my own way. As I moved up the ladder, and received many promotions, it became harder for my superiors to do anything about me. Years ago they made a decision to leave me alone. Better that than wasting time in getting in my way. They pay me next to nothing and I have no investigative staff, though in an emergency, I call on as many men as I need from the National Police. You see I have no false ideals, except one. As I said, my wish is to solve crime, specifically the crime of murder. I have no interest in stopping drugs or stopping smuggling. Marijuana. Heroin. They are the same to me. Your troops can use as much as they want. I do not want my people touching your drugs."

"But your people, I mean the Vietnamese people, provide the drugs and manufacture them."

"It is war. We have to do with what little we have. These things are your army's problems, your people's problems. If you cannot clean your own house, you have to suffer for it. I am not about to help the United States in its headlong fall to the bottom of the well. Believe me, though I get no enjoyment when I see the rapid demoralization of the American soldier fighting for something he doesn't believe in so far from home. "

"What do you know about demoralized troops?"

"Why use those debilitating drugs if morale is good? Why?" "That's a good question I can't answer. But here's one you can answer. Does anyone in Vietnam really care if you solve crime?" "Neighborhood people care. Crime affects their lives. Everyone in a neighborhood knows the criminals, but no one turns them in. They are too busy surviving. No one revolts. If the people were to revolt, change would happen. However, we are not anywhere near change and our oppression is still small and not enough for revolt to happen. It is wartime and restrictions are necessary. When the people in Saigon are subjected to crime, when they get hurt because someone exploits them for personal gain, I am like a fighting fish, furious in my desire and my hunger for revenge."

"That's complicated, maybe too complicated for my readers. Can you simplify?"

"Yes. We must first solve crimes against people. Common crimes like robbery, assault, domestic violence, go unpunished because we do not have room in our prisons or the stomach to prosecute. My people see these crimes as a natural part of life. Too many youngsters have only known war. We threw out the French in 1955 and the North and South have been at war ever since. It makes it more difficult to save our children from the streets. Life is, as you say, always on the hustle. Why be honest when the war intrudes on domestic tranquility? Our youth say life is too short. The draft hangs over their heads. The university system is in collapse. There are no jobs. They can make fast money by being criminals, and some do."

"Does it make the young, many probably not much younger than me, more liable to join the Viet Cong?"

"Not really in the city. There is still too much to do here, too much excitement. It is easier to get the young out in the country, than it is here in the city."

"I sense futility and possible despair."

"Yes and no. I am for tranquility. I savor tranquility. For instance, I know the associations that control the neighborhoods. I know its officers, its generals and sergeants. If crime is getting out of hand, I go see the top people. I tell them to end the trouble if they want tranquility. I go to the top, not the ring below. I want results. Results keep me going. I have little support inside the National Police, but it is enough to make the transgressors think twice."

"Sounds like an uphill battle."

"Please," Phuoc said. "Understand that I am not looking for reform. I'm looking for change, for order. And I believe it must be done within the limits of my country's laws and customs."

"Let's go back to something else. What did you do under the French? I mean, how did the French affect your life?"

"I watched the Japanese and Vichy French rule my country until the war ended in 1945. Then, still as a young man without direction I flirted with the Viet Minh. From 1940 when I was seventeen until 1953, I did intelligence work for them and carried messages. After the Japanese and Vichy French departed the country in 1945, I entered the police academy. I graduated as a patrol officer two years later in 1947. I was twenty-three. By the time I was twenty-nine in 1953, I had become a detective, but I did not confine my work to catching criminals. Vietnam had to be free. We had to get the French out of our country. They were racist, vicious toward our women and true dictators. French overseers beat men and women in the rice paddies using green sticks to cut through the skin. They whipped workers on the rubber plantations. The rubber plantations are a beautiful sight even today. The trees run in perfect rows, evenly spaced for high production. French businessmen still run some plantations but they pay very high taxes, tribute, really, to the Viet Cong who allow them to stay in business. In the north, the French overseers kept miners underground digging coal long after fresh air ran out, and only the stale air remained. Many deaths resulted. The imperious French bled our country dry by looting all our physical resources, such as rubber, timber and the fish from our fertile waters.

"In the countryside, French soldiers raped our women, stole our chickens, duck and pigs and paid nothing. The French government and its people never replaced anything they took from my country. The human toll worsened each year. The French did not attempt to give us medical care for our children or provide proper diets. We had a very high mortality rate for our young children. The French government provided selective schooling in Vietnam, as they did with all their colonies. The schools run by the French, a way they controlled all their colonies, were very good and an outlet for elite Vietnamese, but the average person could neither afford those schools, nor was eligible for them. The Viet Minh became stronger, enlisting the aid of villagers and city folk alike. You must understand, though the Viet Minh was not much better when it came to taking what they needed from the villages, they at least held out a sign for hope. Nationalism is a great incentive for freedom. In my early police years, I continued to help the Viet Minh by discovering French troop strength, the size of their units, and sometimes where they intended to strike where they believed they would find the rebels.

"Then, in 1954 when only thirty, I became careless and made several mistakes in how I did my spying. My partner discovered what I had been doing and turned me into the French. I did not blame him. He had a family. He had fear. They offered him money and protection. He was a fool but I understood his motives. After we threw out the French in 1955, he remained in the police but then he became a captain in the army. In 1965, he died in combat after acquitting himself well under fire. I believe he absolved himself of his sins and maybe he now resides in heaven. But no one can know that with certainty.

"I, however, had a different experience. Because what my partner did to me, I went to prison without a trial. I thought they would shoot me. They did not. But my French jailors did interrogate me for many days. I remained in prison for twelve months and suffered torture four times, each session lasting over many weeks. Their favorite torture was to pour soapy water down my throat and then to keep my mouth tightly closed, all the time asking me questions I could not answer because they would not let me speak. When they wanted me to speak, they kicked me in the stomach and forced the water from my mouth and nose, making me gag and throw up before I could say anything. To this day I believe they never wanted answers. They only wanted to harm me, to show they were in charge. They had me in a weak state, and in my weakness, they knew I could not defend myself. My French torturers thought they were superior, but they were not, though they were smug, and self-satisfied, hateful beyond words. No sooner had I recovered did they start again with new punishments, many of which they later used in Algeria when the French would not let go of that colony."

Phuoc paused, poured some tea but saw the pot was empty. He signaled a girl at the bar and told her, I assumed, he wanted a fresh pot of tea. Within minutes, it appeared on the table. He ordered Jasmine tea, and it had a light, amber color, and a faint, yet delicate scent. He did not wait long for it to simmer before pouring a fresh cup. Phuoc asked me to join him and I did, inhaling the steam, and savoring the light, flowery flavor when I brought the liquid to my lips. I drank. Phuoc drank. We said nothing, as with the tea, enjoying the moment. I wondered if he saw through me, if he took me seriously or knew something about my life that pushed him forward in our budding relationship? I had my suspicions about anyone who let me get too close, anyway. Could this Vietnamese cop who joined the force at twenty-three and saw his country through oppression and freedom and oppression again, really befriend me? I had an ulterior motive and I'm sure he did too, except his, as we shared tea, remained a mystery. However, as I learned, the mystery would not last long.

"There were other abuses they inflicted on me and other prisoners. Yes, I was not unique. I rarely knew any of my fellow prisoners. I heard them, though, and I felt their pain when their screams penetrated the thick walls of the prison. The French kept us in solitary and fed us rice crawling with weevils. We never had fish sauce or any other protein. I remember vividly the water they gave us to drink, putrid, always warm, never cool or refreshing. In prison I lived for the day when I could drink cool water without being afraid it would ruin my stomach."

Phuoc held his left hand out to me, palm down, fingers pointed out. "Notice that I have no nails on three of my fingers on this hand. My captors pulled them out during one grueling session and they never grew back. The fingers bled for days, and when I started to recover, one guard stepped on that hand and made it bleed again. It took months before the fingers healed, but my nails never grew again." "Why are you telling me this?"

"You said you wanted to write about me. Writing about me is not easy. There are many facets to my life and the path I traveled, the path I now travel. Without knowing where I came from and now, where I am, you cannot write a complete article."

I thought and shuddered to myself, knowing that if I would ever write the article as he called it, he would be right.

A beginning made, we finished for the night. I stood. Phuoc started to rise from his corner seat. Just then a bottle went flying past our table and smashed into the wall behind Phuoc's head. He ducked. I jumped back, upsetting the table and knocking over my chair. Shouting and screams, all incomprehensible, filled the air. A fight had started, over what I did not know, but I could guess. Usually two men wanted the same woman without realizing neither would be successful. Drunk, a touch of pot, perhaps a cigarette dipped in heroin had more than a little to do with their inability to think straight, to reason. So these men in the bar fought, but within minutes of the fight's outbreak no one knew who started it. As usual, there would be no winners.

And this time, the fight would end for another reason. It annoyed Phuoc, especially that his evening was nearly ruined when the bottle flew past his head. He stepped gingerly around the fallen tables, maneuvered past two men pummeling each other, reached the bar and pulled his weapon, a World War II-issues German Luger with a pearl handle, its magazine which held eight shots, already in place, his finger on the trigger. The black metal of the legendary combat weapon, burnished to a rich black finish fit perfectly in his small hand. Phuoc handled the gun like the professional he was. I hardly believed my eyes when I saw him holding it, aiming it at the crowd, daring them to make him use it. Then he pointed the gun toward the ceiling and fired two shots in rapid succession. The thundering noise reverberated in the room. Plaster fell from the ceiling. First, everything moved in slow motion, then, abruptly, the fight and the shouting stopped. If I doubted it before, I now knew that Hong Phuoc was a serious man, not someone to playfully tease.

Chief Inspector Hong Phuoc climbed from a still standing stool to the top of the bar. Once there, he stood, all five-foot-three of him, the Italian silk suit he wore, still immaculate, and, holding the Luger in one hand, waved it slowly around the room.

"I am Chief Inspector Hong Phuoc of the Saigon Police. You have made me very angry and you ruined my cup of tea. It is enough for one night. Clean the bar. Straighten the bar. Then leave before I call my police officers and make them arrest you. A night in a Saigon jail will not be pleasant."

At first, no one moved, being unsure who and what directed them. They watched Phuoc in disbelief. Then Phuoc again waved his weapon around the room. That told the drinkers, the bar girls and the proprietor, that Phuoc was serious. I took notes and wished I had my camera. It would have been a terrific picture, a sight for my American audience—a small Vietnamese cop in plainclothes standing atop the bar in a joint on Tu Do Street, stopping a fight with his German Luger and a big pair of balls. The patrons started cleaning up and without another word, Phuoc jumped down from the bar and departed, soon lost in the crowded street. I didn't know when I would see him again. I hoped it would be the next night, same time, same place. If not, I believed he would find me. I had much to tell John Castle. Phuoc might be his opponent, perhaps his nemesis, and if so, Castle should know as much about him as possible. I wandered home, copied my hastily scratched notes on a clean page and went to sleep, knowing that I faced a possible confrontation of my own, tomorrow at the laundry.

Four

Morning arrived sooner than I expected. Though I had spent more than eight hours in bed, sleep had been difficult. Despite my fitful night, I managed some rest, but not much. The dark night had disappeared, replaced by sun and noises from the street. Restless, and apparently dreamless, I had too much on my mind to awake feeling refreshed. I woke hungry, but first I showered and shaved before heading to Givral, for fresh papaya sprinkled with lemon, crusty and chewy French bread, and several cups of strong, black espresso. Fortified, ready to meet the day, and hoping I would not have to confront the Cowboys coming to visit the laundromat, I jumped into a cyclo and headed to work. I should add, I had my club with me, in case I needed it' It was a handle from a shovel three feet in length that I used to dig my ditches when working construction. It being Saigon, no one noticed me carrying it, and if they did, they didn't care. Each person had a choice of weapons to defend himself, if needed. Some carried a weapon while others did not. Mine was a thick, cedar club. If I wielded it properly, it would do much damage to the recipient when I swung the club. I didn't know if I had the guts to use it, but I knew I had the strength, if needed.

I arrived at the laundromat early. Still closed after a long night of activity, only some old men and skinny, undernourished, stray dogs were sitting in the courtyard. I entered the front door cautiously, not knowing how anyone inside might greet me. The large front room was empty, as I expected. No men ever stayed the night because there was too much danger if you moved around near or worse, after the curfew. Raids from the local police, and the National Police were possibilities. Constant pressure from the Saigon Cowboys for protection money and free sex didn't make life in a whore house pleasant. And American military police, though not allowed to enter a Vietnamese home alone, sometimes made raids to round up American strays, drunks or catch anyone who had gone AWOL, absent without leave, sometimes by mistake and not on purpose.

A foul, dry, stale smell of crushed cigarettes filled the room. The ashtrays were still full. Half empty plastic drinking cups, some with dried wine or liquor at their bottoms, littered the end tables and the floors covered with rattan throw rugs. The whores were deep asleep after a night of hard work. The maids or amahs, as we called them— the word from the Chinese—had not yet arrived to clean. Usually they were here by eleven. My watch said 10:30. I found the wall switch and tuned on the overhead fan, a wonderful invention in the

Far East to cool a room or a body with little effort and expenditure of energy. Clutching my club I circled the room, and went out the front door. I left the door open in case I had to return quickly. The open door and the fan helped cleanse the air, though the damp weather and heat never allowed any room to lose its odors, unless someone willed the smells away. Obviously that was impossible.

I dragged a white plastic chair from the main room and sat outside, leaning against the outer wall of the house. I had one of several small boys in the neighborhood bring me a cup of strong Vietnamese coffee—taught them by the French—laced with chicory and thick, sweetened, condensed milk. When I finished the one cup, I sent a boy running for another. For them, they were playing a game. For me, I enjoyed the convenience of having someone do my work for me. The cost, always for me would be almost nothing in piasters or dollars. We had a good time because the boys lined up and each had a chance to get a tip for their effort. In line, I controlled them and they didn't make me nuts pushing and shoving for the few cents I gave them for their run to the restaurant. I smoked several cigarettes and waited for the people to wake inside Castle's place of business and, of course, for the Saigon Cowboys to show their faces. Soon my watch showed eleven thirty. The neighborhood had come alive. People were awake, active and struggling to survive despite the war. A barber cut hair down the street, the bicycle mechanic repaired broken wheels on another corner, cyclo drivers congregated outside a small restaurant and waited for a fare, and women carrying baskets on long bamboo poles rushed everywhere. As the day got hotter, the smells increased proportionately.

The women inside the house were soon awake. I heard them chattering. Their singsong, bird-like sounds filled my ears. I heard a motor bike and then saw a man, clearly a Westerner, and as he came closer, an American, moving up the road toward the laundromat. To my surprise he carried on his back a load of soiled laundry. He stopped his machine at the entrance, nodded to me as if he knew me, and entered the house. More voices, this time, American and Vietnamese mixed with broken English. Within minutes the young man, probably my age, and probably working for an American company, emerged, hopped on his motor bike, kicked the starter, turned and departed. Over his shoulder, he said, "They told me it'll be ready tomorrow. I hope so because I need it back by then."

"Good luck," I said and returned to my lonely vigil.

Because of all the noise on the small street, I found it hard to tell the difference in sounds that came from the wider avenue one block over. I tried to stay awake, but the sun's warmth forced me into a satisfying sleep, something I found impossible at night. I wished for shade, but I couldn't find any outside. Despite the heat, I had to stay in place at my post waiting for the juvenile delinquents to make their appearance. I needed more coffee, but that would keep me up through the night and I needed all the sleep I could get once I got to bed. I had to depend on my jangled and frayed nerves to help me stay alert. I dozed until the distinct putt-putt sound of Lambretta motor scooters, made in Italy and a great favorite in Saigon, got louder by the minute as they approached the laundromat. Finally my wait was over. It was my time to shine, to succeed or fail. I had to be successful for myself, and, also to satisfy John Castle, or my job would end. I might find myself headed for Bangkok or Hong Kong to try my luck in one of those still exotic cities.

To my relief and surprised delight, they had come at last, those young men who called themselves Saigon Cowboys, and as I suspected, each teen had his own Lambretta, not the Vespa, more common to young women and old men. They pulled up short and skidded on purpose some fifteen feet away from where I sat, creating a cloud of dust like they had seen motorcycle riders do in a B movie. I eyed them as they got off their motors and watched them as they ambled slowly toward me. I didn't move an inch. I held the three and half foot shovel handle firmly in my right hand. They stopped and sneered at me, only their sneers didn't work very well. I wanted to laugh but I knew that would make matters worse. Openly laughing at a Vietnamese male under normal circumstances would insult their manhood.

I knew I would have to defend myself and angering them would weaken my defense by making them believe they were stronger. I had to stay calm, usually difficult for me, but unusually so then. I paused for an instance wondering what I was doing. I, a journalist, though not very successful, who had not been in a fight in years, might be on the verge of spilling blood, including mine, for three hundred a week and the promise of my pick of any woman I wanted. *Take a second look at your position,* I said to myself. At least take a second look at me. I did, but nothing important came to the surface. This wouldn't be the last time in the next three weeks that I would search inside myself, but later when I did, there would be unexpected revelations.

I faced three angry kids, none over sixteen, wearing bright, Hawaiian shirts with big flowers, tight khaki pants and white headbands. The headbands probably originated with the Japanese antiwar demonstrators who snake-danced their way through the streets of Tokyo. I stood over six feet and 190 pounds and they were at most five-five, and maybe 110 pounds each, if that. They were skinny compared to me. Though out of shape, I was bigger and stronger than they were, but not for years tested in a fight. I hoped to survive in one piece, if a fight developed.

They stopped. I didn't move. I smiled. They smiled back. I started to rise slowly, then when I did, I moved too fast, the plastic chair fell, rattled against the side of the house and fell to the ground. My three antagonists leaped back a few steps as if shot. From the corner of my eye I could see that all activity on the street had stopped. The one who looked older than the other two spoke, and when he did, and what he said, almost made me laugh. I did everything I could to keep a straight face.

"Shit you, American GI," he said. He didn't seem to understand that I was not a soldier, not a GI, but a civilian, a journalist thrust, because of what I thought was bad luck, but really perhaps bad judgment, into a situation that might get worse before it got better. Could I extricate myself sooner than later and avoid damage to myself? That thought nibbled at my mind, but I knew it would raise its ugly head later. Later, then.

Not now. My work here demanded my full attention. I had to concentrate.

"What did you say?" I needed time to get my composure. Surely I thought he could come up with something better than that. But, no. Shit you, American GI! There would be more.

"You don't come here and shit the Vietnamese people. You numbah ten, GI." He screamed that last line. He turned to his friends as if to say, *See I told him, I told that American. I'm a big man, see.*

"Is that all you have to say?" I said. He looked at me puzzled. I realized he spoke little English, having only a few words and phrases he could utter and liked to hear. Maybe he'd practiced in front of a mirror the way actors did. I knew that not to be true. But I found the conceit amusing.

"You go. You go now!" He gestured wildly with his arms as if to dismiss me from his life.

Unable to restrain myself, I finally laughed, and did a terrible thing. I mimicked his voice, a bad insult because I took something from his soul, the soul that he owned.

"You go. You go now," I said, trying to sound like him, but I had the wrong accent and the wrong intonation so it didn't really work, I thought. Despite my failure to capture him, whatever I had done, worked. His fury burst and he rushed me, but for once in my life, I moved faster than an attacker and as I sidestepped him, I cracked him on his back with my shovel handle and sent him sprawling into the dusty street. He looked like a crab out of water, scuttling to right itself after a strong wave had washed it ashore.

I moved back from him, but I kept myself between him, his two friends and the open door of the laundromat. I heard a scream from the women inside. They were talking fast or crying or both. If I lost, their lives would be worth very little. Mine would be worth, in the words if the now nearly defunct Cowboy, shit. I couldn't have that, so, breathing heavily, my heart beating excitedly at what my mother would say, a mile a minute, I prodded the fallen boy with the end of my club.

"Get up. Get out of here. Don't come back," I shouted. "You may not understand what I'm saying, but we're the new management here, and we don't tolerate your kind." I thought I sounded like a school teacher. But if it worked, I didn't care.

His two friends ran to help their fallen leader. He had taken a bad hit, but he was not badly hurt. Dirty from the street, his dignity had suffered. I knew he would get over it and survive to ride another day, harassing worse than before anyone in his path until the draft finally got him, if it did. If he lived through the few ineffectual weeks of basic training and then the battlefield, whether jungle, paddy or mountains, where he would eventually find himself, he might become a man in spite of himself. Until then, at fifteen or sixteen going on thirty with the mind and spirit of a spoiled child, he would have nothing in his mind or heart to keep his life together.

The three boys departed not as they had come. They drifted away, dragging their scooters with them, quieter and less defiant, their clothing rumpled and dirty. The street was normal again. Inside the laundromat, the women, young and old, were whispering, their crying ended, their lives back to normal, the way they were every day. They would dress and wait for the men to arrive.

Winded from the physical exertion and tired from my adrenaline rush, though no more than a few minutes had passed, I had trouble catching my breath. My heavy breathing seemed endless. My heart beat in my chest as if it were too large for its assigned space. I still held the shovel handle in my right hand. Different shaped floaters danced in front of my eyes. My plain white cotton shirt had soaked through with my sweat. I needed a cigarette and a drink and a piece of ass. It didn't matter in what order. I realized how lucky I had been because there were no real blows exchanged. I outlasted my enemy on my wits and I did almost nothing physical. I assumed those three mobsters in waiting had enough and would not return. *Done with that, what next?* I wondered.

In the coolness of the front room of the laundromat, it took me another thirty minutes to settle down, to get my heart beating normally, and my mind thinking straight. Outside the laundry, I ate a street-side lunch of roast pork on freshly baked and buttered French bread with lettuce, bean sprouts and heavily sweetened ice tea. I gobbled my food. I stayed another two hours waiting for Castle to show but he never did. In the middle of the siesta, I hopped on a local cyclo and, angry because I interrupted his sleep during the sacred siesta, the driver pedaled me faster than usual through the nearly empty streets and back to my apartment.

At home I took a late nap before I started my nightly round of bar hopping. In the past, before Castle came into my life, and, along with my salary, gave me a bonus of women on demand, I would search for a whore in many bars lining the street. I had little luck in finding a woman, but a good time moving in and out of the air conditioning. Even before Castle, I refused to prowl the streets fearing disease or worse, a beating. Usually I sought a young woman, preferably pretty and pleasant to talk to, but this night and the ones that followed, I went looking for Hong Phuoc. After dropping in on several different bars, I ended my evening, as usual, at Bar California. At closing, I wandered home alone and unsatisfied.

My next three days were uneventful. Mornings I worked at the laundry serving as a guard and counting receipts, but never joining a girl in bed. That would come later and it never satisfied me. John Castle never appeared once. After I demanded she speak to me, Mama-san told me, Castle appeared late at night before curfew and picked a different girl each time for his pleasure. And, Mama-san said, "He, Mistush Castle, he very drunk. Falling down. Maybe him high? Don't know." A sad shake of her head concluded the one-sided conversation.

I didn't surprise me that Castle, drunk or high, had become a steady user. He acted like a kid in a candy store. With so much at his disposal he must have found it impossible to keep his hands out of the till. Those times I saw him with nothing more than a beer in his hand convinced me of the possibility he could go overboard and that he would enjoy his descent. I knew, because he told me, he had been a recreational drug user in the past, but everything in his life pointed to the susceptibility of his falling deeper into the pit of heavy drugs. Only a few weeks free of the military for good and now as an American running prostitutes and drugs, I expected, as he surely did, to see his power begin its rise to new heights.

My next three nights at Bar California proved to be worthless in my lonely, but truthfully, halfhearted pursuit of Inspector Hong Phuoc. I couldn't find him anywhere and I did little to dig him out. The girls who knew Phuoc the same as they knew their own names, pretended he didn't exist. "Phuoc who?" they would say when asked. I didn't give up easily and asked until I saw no benefit in asking again. Had he enough of me? Did he think my idea of a story about him no longer worthwhile? He could have been busy solving crimes or tending to his life in the wider world. Was he on to me because he had heard of my connection to John Castle? Meanwhile, the owner of Bar California had repaired the damaged ceiling. The plaster had dried slowly leaving two circles of gray against the white around the two holes made by Phuoc's lethal Luger.

When I least expected it, Phuoc appeared but not at his usual table. On the fourth night of my vigil, he stood behind me, having arrived quietly, or should I say soundlessly, before the bar filled with its usual customers and the regular bar girls. He tapped me gently on my shoulder so as not to frighten me. I looked up from my beer into the mirror and saw his face staring at me. I tried to play down his arrival, pretending to take for granted his appearance, seemingly out of nowhere.

"Good evening," he said, ever polite in a voice barely audible.

I turned and nodded hello. I had no idea how to greet him or what to say.

"I am back," he said. "I was busy with other matters that could not wait and because our business is personal, I did not want to involve another member of my department."

Bless his English. Perfect. Precise. There was only a hint of his sounding like a Vietnamese. Sprinkled with a patina of the BBC World Service, I found myself doing a double take whenever he opened his mouth to speak. What he said, and how he said it, could not possibly come from that man's mouth. But it did. I watched that mouth of his filled with yellowing teeth, worn by age, bad food and water. Saigon's lousy dentists had tried to get inside his head to make repairs on his mouth. They had failed. I wanted to tour his brain to see what made it function before I committed myself further. I knew, however, with all I could be involved in, it would be impossible.

I turned to face Phuoc.

"Shall we sit?" I said.

"Not tonight," he said. "Meet me for lunch tomorrow at noon. I have business at the National Assembly in the morning. I'll be in front of the Caravelle."

"Will I know you in daylight?" I asked. A smile on my face, as I teased him in a way he did not expect.

Before he could answer, I saw his puzzled expression. His English, not as perfect as I thought, made me quickly say, "Will you wear a flower in your lapel?"

He paused, as if confused with my attempt at humor, but then he relaxed and he understood my teasing enough to parry, "But how will I know you? There are so many Americans in my city, you all look alike. Give me a hint." He gave a slender laugh and a crooked grin. I, too, grinned.

"See you then," I said.

Hong Phuoc dipped his head and walked out through the thickening crowd, many of whom were in the bar the night he fired into the ceiling, but now, none of them recognized him. Talk about looking alike. For the moment I gave up trying to figure anything out, but I did know how different our two cultures were. I smoked another cigarette, this time a Salem, instead of a Camel, to cool my raw throat. I drank my beer and made ready to go home. Alone, us usual, unsatisfied in my loneliness, and prepared to accept my lot, so I thought. But this night I sat as if waiting for the unknown and when it arrived, nothing for me would ever be the same again.

My life changed when Thoa Trang walked into the bar and into my life. At first I didn't notice her. Later I wondered how I could ignore her. Many Vietnamese women had the same look. Long hair, small bodies, large, wide eyes and small nearly flat noses. I hardly glanced at one woman over another, especially in a bar. Either they would wear the traditional *ao dai*, flattering in its simplicity, or a miniskirt, slut-like in its appearance. I didn't know Trang existed until she sat next to me, almost as if she planned it because fate left the stool next to me empty. She wore a plain dress, with no fancy embroidery on it, and a white tunic and black trousers, much the same as young women wore at work or in school. I saw immediately she was a Vietnamese beauty with deep-set black eyes set against a dusky skin, as if she had spent too much time in the sun. Trang seemed nervous, fluttery, almost birdlike. Was this young woman a regular? I wondered. Did she have a name? I now had two reasons to be in the Bar California, Phuoc and a wisp of an enchanting young woman.

It was eight at night. Tu Do Street was percolating early. Food vendors were everywhere. Their makeshift stalls covered half the sidewalk to the roadway. Many South Vietnamese Rangers were in town. I wondered, had a military operation ended or were there plans to begin another? They wore camouflage uniforms striped yellow and khaki, like a tiger's coat. Supposedly it gives them a feeling of great power. These young men, reputed to be serious warriors, were wiry, thin and angular, their uniforms, form fitting, their faces deeply burned from the sun. They were hard and gaunt. Though not bad fighters, they are not as good as they thought. When they walked down the street, they did so two or three abreast challenging everyone to defy them. No one does. They ignore me when I step aside to let them pass. I have no need to annoy anyone. I was not looking for a fight.

It was a night of odd accents and strange languages not usually heard in such profusion. Though I heard those sounds regularly, usually I knew them to be quieter, less raucous. I knew there were many merchant ships in port. I heard Scandinavian, but I couldn't tell if it was Danish, Norwegian, or Swedish. But the men were blond to the core, their eyes blue, their skin, beyond fair. Other men spoke German, Japanese, Korean, and English only heard in the British midlands.

I knew the Bar California would have bigger crowds than normal. Money will flow. The young bar girls will sip endless glasses of Saigon tea, thin Jasmine tea, heavily laced with coarse brown sugar and fresh lime juice. They will sit on their bar stools and entice these men, many of whom are sailors on the town for a night, to freely spend their hard earned money on cheap champagne that will cost twenty-five dollars a bottle. The promise of a good time will flow from the lips of the bar girls in broken English and poor French. They will rarely deliver, because most are not prostitutes like the ones who live and work in Castle's laundries. Some are whores, though, and sometimes men wander off with them to a back room or a room above the bar where they work. But all these young women have one goal, to make their guests drink as much of the sweet, junk wine as they can handle. The more booze a sailor guzzles, the less able he is for anything, especially having sex. When that happens, the woman earns more money, and, in the end, it's always only about money.

When curfew arrives and everyone must be off the street, these unwitting men face the hazard of navigating their way back to their ship. Often too drunk to walk, they wander aimlessly down one street or another and slide to the ground peaceably in on the street or, if lucky, in a doorway before they pass out. Then enterprising street thugs roll them, often in alliance with the cops who share in the loot. They will have their money removed from their pockets and wallets. Their rings and watches will deftly disappear, only to appear the next day on the black market. After midnight, a South Vietnamese police wagon rolls through the streets picking up drunks and strays who have wandered off their course. The police deposit these men, left over from their frolic, in some vermin-infested jail for the night. The next morning, if they have any money left, they pay a small fine, and return to the ship in time for their departure. Once back on board ship, another boisterous port beckons until they return to Saigon on their return journey.

All the activity in the street made me apprehensive. My thoughts were on a young woman, very pretty and doll-like, whose name I did not yet know. I wanted to see her again, to talk, to know her. I hoped she would return to the Bar California but I couldn't be sure she would. She might be a freelance, a wanderer, who went from bar to bar, picking up business where she found it, rather than a regular at one place. Finding her at the bar did not guarantee she would spend her time with me. I didn't spend much money. Usually two beers were my limit and I rarely bought a drink for any girl who decided to try her luck and sit next to me. I think they used me as a decoy or to have someone to talk to when it was quiet and they were lonely. I didn't care. When the girl I sat with had charm and beauty, she could get away with almost anything, but she never had access to my wallet.

This night I felt would be different. Too many sailors roamed the streets, their pockets flush with cash, their libidos cooking, for me to have a chance with someone like that unknown woman to amble back into my life. These bar girls worked for a living. They smelled a good pay day and they deserved to get what they could because it didn't come along often. It happened once a week, if that. When it did, no one had immunity to its heady bite. I hoped I would get my chance, but as a permanent resident of Saigon whose life partly revolved around that street, if not that night, I knew there would be other opportunities.

Neon lights in the windows of the bars and restaurants started to flash and flicker when evening turned to dusk and then to night. Young women started arriving for work. Some came in cyclos, their hair heavily sprayed, lacquered and hard, their *ao dai's* in bright colors, some even richly embroidered with flowers and dragons. Other women arrived on the backs of motor scooters, sitting sidesaddle, the skirts of their *ao dai's* flapping behind them. Then there were the young women who discarded traditional dress for garish miniskirts and tight fitting, low cut cotton sweaters. When they exited from their transportation, they had flair and showmanship. How they moved said to the onlookers, "We've arrived. We are ready to do battle for our own good, and not yours," they showed, despite the war.

Excitement built along the street. The bars grew crowded. Sounds of laughter from inside the bars, and shouts and rock music flowed out to the street. It didn't affect me because my wallet stayed full, and, because I helped run Castle's laundromats, I had all the free sex and booze I wanted, if I wanted. Though truthfully, I had not yet moved much in that direction. Management had its privileges, and I took advantage of the few perks I could not do without, though I never drank during the day. Drinking at high noon made me want to sleep. Alcohol went to my head quickly in that hot climate and I did not place it high on my list of pleasures. The occasional joint worked because pot made me dreamy, and didn't stay long in my system. Neither drink nor marijuana did me any good during sex. Free sex is every American boy's dream and I dreamed about it as much as anyone. I felt for the soldiers in the field and their frustration. I at least had freedom of movement, freedom of mind and a draft deferment for a bad, often-operated-on knee. I could do what I wanted and only had to worry about my conscience. The GI had many higher authorities to placate. Did the sex I had when I wanted it and at will satisfy me? Hardly. Realistically, it served as a release for pent-up frustrations and allowed me to have a gentle time, a relaxed moment in a bar at night, rather than always hustling after the unattainable. Sure, I had a good time. It happened quickly, was neat and often sweet, though never memorable. More to the point, I had no intention or desire to bring one of those girls home to my mother.

There were too many revelers filling the small Bar California for me to make my own space. I peeked inside and didn't see her. But I needed a name when I did see her. I pushed my way to the bar. The bartender nodded hello. I leaned into him and asked him as best as I could, in a voice higher than normal, but not yet yelling, if he knew the name of the beautiful girl from the other night. I knew he never forgot who sat with whom. He grinned.

"Very busy night. No time for talk," he said. "Help me," I said. "Take a minute."

He rubbed his thumb and finger together, the ageless symbol that said, pay and I will talk. I placed fifty piasters on the bar. He wolfed it into his hand.

"Her name Trang. She not here tonight. Too busy. Back tomorrow.

I tell her you came looking?"

I smiled and told him to tell Trang I will be in to see her. Trang. It had a good ring to it as I rolled it around my tongue and savored her spirit in my heart.

Five

Every night for a week, I went to the Bar California in search of Trang. I sat on my usual stool waiting for the mystery woman who enchanted me. The bar was not that big. Should she arrive she would see me sitting and waiting. I spoke to no one. Each night the bartender, hardly my friend, gave me a sly smile, popped open a cold can of Heineken, and left my beer and me to my own thoughts. Everyone was friendly, yet all were wary of my presence. Many did not know what I was doing in the bar or why I spent time there. After nine months I still had no girlfriend and never spent money on any of the bar girls. They were not hostile to me and they waited to see how my vigil would turn out. I guessed they wondered when I would finally find someone to my liking. I did have that someone, at least in my head, but so far all it was, was a dream. I was sure they had already figured out it was Trang. The bartender knew. I asked only about her and I did it every night. Each night I wondered when I would finally meet her.

Phuoc appeared early one of those nights and we shared our usual pot of Jasmine tea. Until the past week, we had been seeing each other regularly. With no developments about the dead girls, we said little, beyond a nod and smile, between sips of tea and drags on our cigarettes.

On the eighth night of my vigil, at the start of my second week, Trang appeared. She walked to where I sat and gave me a small bow. She asked if she could sit. I told her, yes.

"You Adam?" she asked.

"I'm Adam. Adam Berg," I answered, my heart beating faster than I thought possible.

Trang giggled. "And you are?"

"I Thoa Trang. I come from near My Tho. My home."

My Tho in the Mekong Delta is rice country, heavy with Viet Cong, a difficult place for Vietnamese to live, and worse for American troops to work. A part of the land with unpleasant weather, where heat prevailed, where whether it rained or not, it was always wet. Soldiers had no place to hide in the mostly flat country, and there were frequent enemy ambushes from irrigation ditches in the rice paddies. The region did not have a large population. Those who lived there resisted change. When I covered stories in the Delta, most of the day we stayed soaked to the skin, slogging through the deep mud of the rice paddies, crawling over earthen dikes to keep the flood waters down, where leeches sucked as much blood as they could from us. The Mekong Delta was not my favorite part of the country to cover stories. I preferred the mountains and hills of the Central Highlands and the beaches of the coastal plain. At least in those places, especially the mountains, I had a hint of seasons that changed, even if only a small amount, instead of hot and hotter and where the nights were often oddly cool. In the right circumstances, with the enemy hopefully far from your perimeter, you could get a few hours of sleep at night. I wondered how this flower, Trang, survived the muck of a thousand years of growing rice. Maybe all beauty rose from muck, especially one like Trang.

I found it easier to look at her and think about her, than to talk. She had poor English, a limited vocabulary, and I spoke hardly any Vietnamese. We seemed to go together perfectly, as unrealistic as that may appear. So, we said nothing to each other. From the time I started reading adventure novels set in the 1930s, I believed I needed a relationship with a woman where, as two lovers, we could talk and say whatever we wanted. I wanted a woman in my life that would tell me she loved me and could say, why. I wanted a woman in my life that would be honest with me and tell me about her unhappiness with me. I wanted honesty. I didn't see that in my parents, and perhaps it is romantic, but I needed romance and its sometime unreality in my life as I lived with the horror of war.

Trang knew bar talk, knew its few words well, otherwise we could not carry on any conversation. I could live with that because I had in front me a young woman with large, generous eyes, a marvelous smile and so much charm that it might have surpassed her natural beauty. Whoever said beauty is only skin deep never met Trang. And if Trang only gave me her beauty to gaze on, I could be happy. At least I thought that, then.

'Drink?" I asked.

"Yes, please. You drink champagne?"

"No, just beer."

"You no drink, I no money."

"I'll give you the money instead of the bar. I refuse to drink the swill they accuse of being champagne."

"Swill? What mean swill?"

"A very bad drink. Maybe poison. Not fit for people. Like drinking piss or what pigs drink. No thanks."

Trang had a puzzled look. Then she rose from her seat and started to move away from me.

"No drink. No money. No sit," she said with a smile.

"Try to understand. I'll give you and the bar money. Both. Stay so I can look at you."

She didn't understand what I meant. My dream of an exotic romance was dying in front of me. I thought it had no chance of growing into something more than a romance between a bar girl, Trang, and a hanger-on, a lovesick adolescent, me.

Maybe I could teach her English. Then we could reach inside each other and we could speak in unexpected ways. Perhaps I could tease from her an intellectual side she never knew existed. My mind raced with the possibilities. When I stopped to think, I realized I didn't really believe that anything did exist inside her except, as with so many Vietnamese, the need to survive. She counted her survival in money, whether dollars, piasters, franks, marks, lira.

I threw ten dollars on the bar. Trang stopped moving away. She saw the green bill fall onto the wet surface. I told the bartender I wanted thirty minutes. He let the ten sit there, watching it, as it got wet.

"Thirty minutes, thirty dollah," he said.

My patience already thin, my frustration high, I growled back, "Fuck you. Twenty bucks are all you'll get and make sure Trang gets her cut. No champagne. No whiskey. Maybe a beer. But Trang sits and she and I talk." *It could become a habit,* I thought.

We smiled at each other in the way only enemies can. I knew he understood nothing of what I said. I didn't care. *Fuck you,* I thought. He belonged in the army not pimping in a sleazy bar.

"Why don't you do something for your country? Join up. Get a gun. Fight. Kill some VC. Earn the right to exist."

He started waving his arms, frantically like a windmill.

"No. I not VC. No. No. Not VC." An indignant look crossed his youthful face. Acne pocked his sallow skin.

"I know that. Take my word for it. You're not VC. They wouldn't have you. But go kill a few and leave me alone to look at Trang for the next half hour."

I waved my twenty. His hand flashed out and grabbed it. I picked the wet ten off the bar and pocketed it.

"Don't forget to give Trang her cut." "She get cut."

"Make sure you do it."

He nodded yes and went to serve another customer, a sucker from the West, probably an American, sitting with a bar girl in a tight fitting sweater. I went back to looking at Trang. How would I reconcile her beauty with her inability to speak English when I knew her only understanding of the language was Saigon bar talk? How would I put her in perspective with my infatuation starting to border on madness? I wanted to touch her, to feel her creamy skin, to caress her, if only for a moment. We were in a bar where they allowed no touching. I would wait to do everything I could to know her texture so I could inhabit her soul. Yes, I dreamed while awake and I had no shame. It sounds out of hand, I know, but I felt as if I were sixteen and I had to let my feelings run their course before I could move on to what might be a normal life.

After that night, I started to see Trang outside the bar in ways limited by who we were—I, an American, she a Vietnamese. Gradually we became closer, though we rarely touched. When we did touch, hand on hand, fingers across a forearm, my rapid move of fingers on her cheek, only in the darkened bar, we were furtive and guarded, unsure what we were doing or where it would lead. At least I had no confidence in our relationship to do more.

When we walked in the street, we never walked side by side. She always moved slyly behind me, careful that we never touched or gave the appearance we were together. When we ate in restaurants, usually we sat in the back or in a corner, never where other Vietnamese, especially men in uniform, could see us. That would have been like lighting a fire in a dry forest. South Vietnamese soldiers hated the sight of a Vietnamese woman with a white man, especially an American. They felt threatened, their manhood pushed aside by a free-spending pale face. Those soldiers thought it bad enough that they had to accept foreign aid from the United States. Worse, we were reminders of how the French desecrated their landscape and took advantage of their women. Rape had been commonplace during French rule. Rape of teenage girls brought smiles to the faces of the French colonialist. The French taught what they called their women, how to bake bread and much more, including the finer arts of sex. The French wanted their women subservient and pliant. As plantation overseers, they got exactly what they wanted when they ruled. The average Vietnamese, and the young men in uniform, didn't want to see that happen again, if they could help it.

Despite spending more and more time together, Trang never said she loved me. I wanted to hear her say it, but I expected too much. I could do nothing to change how she expressed herself or why. What could I do about her? We could hardly speak to each other beyond the worst of pidgin English. We spoke in monosyllables. We used gestures, not words. Hand gestures were often the only way we showed affection. Sometimes sitting there in the murky room, I ran my fingers across the supple skin on her arm. Once I tried touching her cheek in public. She jumped back in astonishment, angry for me being forward. Her eyes narrowed and her nostrils flared. Possibly, she feared recrimination from people who saw what I did. I'm sure my sudden move where people could see what I did, was too much for her to process.

Early on in our relationship, I welcomed that she stayed away from commitment. I tried teaching her English and some of my words rubbed off, but the language never took hold. Yet, she made herself understood, especially about the life she led and the land she came from, through words, gestures and pictures. Over many days, and many hours of talk, I discovered where Trang came from, how she grew up and her way of life.

Trang told me in her village she knew everyone. Everyone worked together in the fields to plant rice, she said, and then they harvested it and husked it on flat ground. After the rice dried, they raked it and swept it into piles. When ready, she told me, they put the rice in sacks and stored what we needed and sold anything extra. Her father, a strict man, ruled the house, she said. He had hardly any education and could not read but he understood politics. Her father was a real peasant. Tho, so small, was too big for him and even when he traveled there, he couldn't wait to get back home, only ten miles away. He hated the Viet Minh even when a boy. As an adult, he hated the Viet Cong and the government more. He wanted his freedom and for everyone to leave him and his family alone. Trang told me her father loved her. He rarely showed he loved them, she said. But he protected her, she said, and provided food and clothing for her and her sisters. He would not hesitate to hit Trang with a bamboo switch when she did something wrong, she said. She knew he loved her because he hit her, Trang said.

Trang said her mother made her happy. She sang, she said. She taught poems, and when they were older, she helped Trang learn to cook and to sew. Trang needed to know all that to get married, she said. Trang said her fondest memory of her mother was the way she did her hair. Her mother never cut her hair and wore it long down her back past her waist. When working, she rolled it behind her head in a large bun to keep it from interfering with her task. Trang fingered her short hair and told me she wished she could wear it long like her mother but the bartender would not allow it.

"Too old," he said. "You are not a ba, a grandmother, he said. I want no old people in my bar. Americans want young girls, not old women."

"So, I have to keep my hair short," Trang said. She smiled. "I don't like short hair. It is not the way of a country girl."

During the day Trang told me she went to school, did her homework, swam in the ponds near her village. All the children had fishing poles that they used to catch fish that swam in the ponds. In the rainy season, there were more fish because the ponds were fat with water. "When we had many fish, my father would sell the catch and we would have extra money for the times when we needed it. My father, like all the villagers, wore simple clothing of black cotton trousers and a black shirt. You Americans think we are wearing pajamas. We do not. They are not, but I won't argue with you," Trang told me, this time with a wide smile.

I learned from Trang that she had three brothers and two sisters. Two brothers and one sister were older than she was. "To protect the first-born from evil spirits, we never give a child the rank of number one. The first child in a Vietnamese family is always number two. It puts too much pressure on that first child to succeed and it protects the child from the devil who normally goes after the firstborn to kill the child." Trang's rank in the family is nam, meaning number five but she is really number four. When they refer to her, they call her chi nam, meaning sister five.

"Tell me about your brothers," I said.

She stopped talking, became silent and then she cried. I could not stop her. I knew she could be emotional, but her lengthy crying and ample flow of tears surprised me.

"No more talk today," Trang said. She turned from me and bowed her head down to her chest. She reminded me that when some Vietnamese are upset, they lower their heads, turn away and speak very quietly, if at all. They withdraw to depths I found impossible to penetrate. It is as if they were putting themselves in a sealed container, to be open only in some future time when the hurt, insult, or memory passed. When it does pass, it does not mean the person forgets what made him or her withdraw.

Trang told me her memories stay with her forever. None ever disappear. I learned to understand that nothing ever fades from her heart, her word for memory. Her recollections lived inside her for all time. It may not have been how she said it, but it is what she meant.

Six

Not being a company man, despite having a regular pay envelope, I decided one morning to play hooky from my daily stint at Castle's main laundry and not go on my regular visits to the other three he owned. John Castle would be upset, and rightly so, that I had other interests, though he said I could go after a story now and then when I wanted. He paid me more money than the film cameramen who did jobs for the networks. I couldn't complain. I felt like a whore, doing a senseless job, counting chits and chatting with girls who barely understood a word of what I said. Most of the time when I spoke to the women who worked for Castle, I did it to hear myself talk. Before Trang was in my life and, other than the times I worked with my photographer friend, Lee, I had hardly any real friends in the press. Either they were too busy, or they ignored me. Some staff people thought I was a pain in the ass and a not very productive one at that. In retaliation, I ignored them. It didn't do me much good for my standing among my so-called peers. Let them come to me, I reasoned foolishly. They rarely did and I spent much of my time alone. Lately there were too many days when I was ambivalent about who I was, where I was going, what I was doing. There weren't enough of those days yet to make me quit Castle and face the consequences if I did. I decided to worry about Castle and his reaction another time. He could dock my pay for one day if he didn't appreciate my absence.

Instead of showing at ten in the morning as usual, I made the rounds to those news bureaus most likely to hire me to cover a story, however minor it might be. Going to the bureaus late in the day, limited my chances of getting an assignment. Then the editors rarely had anything for me. But I wanted to get out to report and use my skill as a journalist. I didn't like the thought of getting rusty. I walked into the AP and saw Lee loading his cameras and equipment, getting ready to cover a story.

"What's up?" I said to Lee, and anyone else who might have been listening.

"Buddhist demo right down the street in front of the old opera house," said Lee.

"Yeah, the damn mothers are looking for the sympathy vote," said Joe, the day editor, sitting across the room, his typewriter groaning beneath his heavy fingers every time he typed a new sentence. Along with everything he did, the assigning reporters and photographers, he usually wrote the big wrap-up lead story of the day that had everything in it but the time and temperature in downtown Cleveland. "You want to cover it, Adam? I could use a few hundred words to go with Lee's pictures. You know how the police love to crack those bald headed monsters."

I told him I would go for the hell of it. Joe cackled at his words, and returned to his writing.

"Good. Get your ass out of here. I got a deadline," he said. At the AP, they always had deadlines.

"We got to take a few extra handkerchiefs," Lee said. "They'll probably use gas to break the monks."

We soaked the handkerchiefs in water and put them into a small plastic bag in Lee's camera case. I kept one in my back pocket in case we separated and I had need of it. The National Police used a caustic strain of CS gas to stop demonstrations. When the Buddhist monks marched against the government, the police derived sardonic glee using the gas in large quantities against the marchers. When that happened, we tied the handkerchiefs around our nose and mouth to protect against the acrid fumes. But the handkerchiefs never really worked. I could never get the cotton square around my face fast enough to prevent gas getting through to my nose and mouth, then to my lungs. My eyes would burn for days after exposure to the CS gas. The police and the Buddhists assembled when they said they would. That was rare for both sides. Both groups appeared near the American embassy, a location where the demonstrators knew they would get attention from the press. At least two dozen cops in starched white shirts and dark gray pants lined up across from some fifty monks in saffron robes whose bare, shaved scalps were wet from their sweat in the hot sun. Monks carried burning sticks of incense and chanted anti government slogans. Police linked arms, and carried hand-held grenade launchers with canisters of CS gas. The two sides taunted each other, daring the other to make the first move. We were close enough to the contestants to see the spittle flying from their mouths. Lee took pictures. I made notes. Other still cameras and reporters were present along with American network TV news crews. We were waiting for something to happen. Action would come enough. It always did. The story had possibilities for TV because you only had to point your camera and shoot as the event enfolded before your eyes. While we waited, I smelled burned charcoal and fermented fish rising from the many food vendors in the streets.

Bystanders lined the sidewalks waiting for their daily dose of street theater. Regulars at the Continental Hotel outdoor bar watched from prime seats. They were far enough away not to get hurt but close enough to feel the effects of the gas should the police release it. I looked around and saw John Castle all in white, seated at a table with two Vietnamese women wearing tight dresses and laughing at everything he said. He wore aviator sunglasses with mirrors on the outside of the lenses. I looked too long in his direction and that gave him enough time to see me. Since I was tall, made it easy for him to see me in the growing crowd of reporters in the street. He smiled my way and touched his hand to his forehead in a salute that said hello. I acknowledged him in the same way and went back to watching the police and Buddhists jockey for position. I had never seen Castle at the Continental, my part of town, and I wondered if he went there for a purpose. Was he spying on me? It made me nervous to think about him, knowing he never did anything without a reason. I hated being paranoid, but my paranoia would wait. I had an assignment, so first things first.

The bluffing between the two sides continued and I wondered who would crack first. Most of the time the police became bored and started to break up the demonstration before the monks could start marching. The police hated the monks because they thought them unpatriotic. I once saw a monk accidentally step on a cop's toe. That frightened cop swung his baton to force the line of monks back. The monk he hit fell backwards and crumpled to the ground. An officer then ordered the other police to fire tear gas. They did and a melee resulted. Monks fled down side streets as the police wielded their clubs and rifle stocks against any available body and they aimed at heads. Onlookers also ran. White clouds of tear gas filled the air. A riot followed with no one the victor.

This day was no exception. Something happened to make the cops angry. The two lines fell apart as everyone pushed and shoved. Next thing I knew, tear gas canisters exploded. People ran in different directions. I couldn't find Lee so I had no chance to cover my face with an extra wet cloth. It was good that I had some protection from the wet handkerchief in my pocket. I hastily held it to my mouth and nose. It didn't help much. The tear gas burned my nose and mouth. My eyes were tearing uncontrollably. I had a story but I had no idea what happened, except a peaceful demonstration turned into a small riot. Tear gas hit the street. Men and women ran and some people hid from the cops. A cop smiled when he hit me. He seemed to enjoy kicking and punching me. I was an American and obviously, a reporter whom he wished would leave him alone to do his job. I rubbed my thigh where the cop struck me. There would be a black and blue mark for days. I didn't much care.

I looked for Lee, but he had disappeared. I assumed he went back to the AP. But I expected that from Lee. He appeared and disappeared seemingly out of nowhere and we didn't depend on each other to get the story. Sometimes when we were only sitting having a drink, I would turn and the chair next to me would be empty. I would turn back to watch traffic or a beautiful woman, and I felt a soft tap on my shoulder. Lee would be sitting next to me, a smile on his a face, a cigarette hanging from his lips. I never saw him enter or leave. He always surprised me, yet he never surprised me. He never missed an assignment and always knew when he had his next job. For some reason he enjoyed working with me despite my inability at times to focus. The men on the desk at the Associated Press knew Lee liked working with me and they rarely sent him out alone or with a staff reporter. No one, including the Vietnamese staff, who wanted you to know they knew everything, seemed to know where he lived or, for that matter, much of anything about his life. Did he have a wife? Was he the father of children? Did he have a girlfriend? I never found out. Did Lee have a home and what I called, a life? Once I asked Lee where he slept at night.

"Here and there," he said. He gave me a wide smile, winked and circled his fingers in a gesture of confidence, but he told me nothing. I never pushed him for an answer but to this day, my curiosity remains unsatisfied.

In the middle of the street, with the tear gas still lingering on the asphalt, I stood by myself, nervous, my eyes stinging from the gas, and my throat, raw from inhaling its fumes, hoping I could find my way back without any difficulty. I knew where to go, and turned my back on the remnants of the demonstration. I went back down the street to Nguyen Hue and the Associated Press bureau where I would file my story. Maybe by then Joe, the night editor, would have some word as to its meaning from the American officials who watched the demonstration in hopes of discovering its reason. Something, by the way, they or any of us, rarely understood. Ultimately we were witnessing a struggle for power, a battle for constituencies that neither side could control.

After filing a story with fewer words than usual and almost no analysis, that would probably be added later, Lee's pictures being better than my words, my words mostly serving as captions, around two o'clock I made my way to the street and stumbled into the Bar California. It was very early. Hardly anyone sat at the long bar or at the tables. When the bartender saw my red, swollen eyes, he surprised me with his sympathy. He gave me a clean, wet towel and warm Jasmine tea that instead of drinking, I used to gently cleanse my eyes. By four that afternoon, the swelling down in my eyes and the taste of gas almost gone from my mouth and throat, I sat at the bar drinking cold beer, a smile on my face. I felt good because I could still get out there, have some fun, file a story and make a few bucks. Despite seeing Castle at the Continental, I had a good day after all.

Seven

After lunch one day, I asked Trang to come to my apartment. The midday siesta had started and the streets were nearly empty. Trang surprised me and said she would come with me. Demurely she walked three paces behind me, her head down, her motions contained, her eyes seeing everything, yet showing nothing. She feared the police and the cyclo drivers because they insulted her for being with an American. When walking with me, she behaved like a blind person, and like many blind, she acted as if she had acute hearing whose ears missed nothing.

We looked around carefully before we entered the building where I lived.

I didn't care who saw me but Trang did. I assumed she cared about her reputation. As a young Vietnamese woman, she feared all Vietnamese men mocking her and verbally abusing her. I understood her anxiety and I sympathized with her so I didn't rush her. That would have been fatal for our relationship.

I went in first to a dark and quiet vestibule. I waited for Trang at the foot of the stairs. She appeared in a few minutes and followed me up the one flight of stairs to my apartment. The early afternoon heat had already penetrated the thin walls of the building. Inside I turned on the large ceiling fan, a staple in Saigon, to start making the room cooler. Though not perfect, it did help. I double locked the door. We stood in the room not knowing what to do next, or, more accurately, wondering where do we go from here. I stepped back from her and admired the beautiful silk *ao dai* she wore. The silk was from Japan and Thailand. It was cheap and plentiful even in wartime. Flying dragons in red flowed over the yellow dress in the back and in the front that ended with flowers that looked like peonies in full bloom, all from the head of a talented dressmaker. I marveled at the beautiful and often-inspired embroidery that covered the sensual dresses worn by Vietnamese women.

I approached Trang as a lover. For the first time, I wrapped my long arms around her small body. I thought she would feel fragile like a skinny rabbit, but she fooled me. Her body was firm, not brittle. Her small breasts pressed against my chest. I knew she could feel me in my state of arousal. She made no move to release herself from my loving grip. She did not try to free herself from my arms. Trang pressed even closer to me as we stood as close as two people could without making love. Then we moved toward the bed, almost falling as we did, as if we were Siamese twins. Without tipping it, we managed to sit on the edge of the bed, more like a wide cot with enough room comfortably for one, usually me. I kissed her face. I kissed the nape of her neck. I ran my hands across her body. She didn't kiss me on the lips like a woman from the West. Vietnamese women never kiss a man fully on the lips. Instead, Trang, as with all Vietnamese women, laid her nostrils against my skin and sniffed deeply, inhaling my scent, probably Old Spice, my favorite at the time, and then pecking me playfully with her lips on my forehead and mouth. Only prostitutes in Vietnam kissed a man fully on the lips, not because they liked it, but because Western men enjoyed it. I didn't push it with Trang. *One thing at a time,* I thought. And what is a kiss anyway with so much else going on? With all that I felt, her soft hands touching my face, the small kisses, her hand in mine, the style of kissing I grew up with meant nothing.

She unbuttoned my shirt and moved her hands over my chest. She smiled sweetly, shyly. I wanted her to remove her *ao dai,* but I couldn't handle all the snaps, buttons, and loops. They were too confusing and too daunting to a neophyte. Trang stood and motioned to me to wait. I started to turn my head, thinking she might not want me to watch, but she smiled and said, please, you can see. Trang started slowly to undress. Silk rustled as the dress dropped from her shoulders. I watched her move with elegance, as if in a dream. When almost undressed, with a circular motion of her hands, Trang, signaled me to turn and face the wall. Now standing, and holding my breath, I wondered what I would do next, hoping for perfection, praying, in my way, that I would be up to my expectations and not disappoint the woman I had been waiting patiently for what seemed forever.

Her wooden sandals fell to the floor with a light sound, wood on wood. I could hear her slipping her black trousers from her waist, then down her legs, and finally off her feet. It took only seconds. The rustling of silk against her body had become too much to bear. I wanted to look, but I told Trang I would wait to see, so I did not watch her. I wanted to say I love you. But I did not. I never would, then nor in the future. I couldn't handle that kind of commitment. Was it immaturity, or my fear of the unknown? Would I discover Trang as a woman only in the moment of making love? Would my feeling for her be timeless and true? Would I find myself? I knew I had good luck on my side with Trang as a modest woman, especially after those whores in Castle's laundries.

I took off my shirt and removed my trousers. My rubber and leather sandals slipped from my feet. I swung myself easily onto the bed and waited for Trang to get in next to me. I kept my face to the wall. Seconds passed before the bed moved and her hands touched my back. I asked her if I could turn and see her. She said yes, please. I turned and our bodies touched. A chill went through me. Trang shuddered. We said nothing. I kissed her gently and ran my hands across her naked body. I wanted to enter her quickly, but I also wanted to prolong the moment. We had nothing but time. The moment did not end, not then, at least, but I knew it would, as I was sure Trang also knew.

Despite the fan moving overhead, trying to cool the room, Trang's body stayed warm, as did mine. I touched her where I believed I could never dare to go. Being there, the tips of my fingers gently caressed her once hidden self. A chill went through me. I kissed the moisture from her upper lip and with my index finger, I wiped the tiny beads of water from the bridge of her nose. She now allowed me to stroke her at will. My hands slowly grazed the skin on her body, exciting me as my fingers started to know her intimately. I heard no sounds from the outside. We were in a silent shell, divorced from reality. I didn't hear the overhead fan. I only heard Trang's even breathing as she and I were about to join a world separate from anything we had ever known. After a few minutes of silence only broken by our breathing in unison, I entered her with such ease it made me want to weep with joy. Trang sighed deeply as she started to move her body with mine. I didn't want the feeling to end. Trang held me tightly inside her as if to keep me there forever. I did not argue. I felt empowered as never before. Her cheeks turned red and everywhere her skin became flushed. Beads of her sweat again appeared on the bridge of her nose. I licked her nose, drinking in the sweet salt of her self. Her breathing intensified. She smiled, her body relaxed and giving, and about to give more than I realized she had. I thrust deeply inside her. Then it ended when I could no longer control myself. A surge of joy coursed through me body like a prolonged electric charge. I tensed, then came and then yelped and with that release, I felt as if my body became unglued. My mind, what was left of it, felt cleansed beyond reason. Only emotional and physical pleasure in all its purity, ruled. I held myself inside her before finally moving from her. I settled on my half of the bed with one arm touching Trang's now damp and smooth body. I saw tears in Trang's eyes, yet she smiled delicately and then fully, showing her evident happiness. She searched for my hand until she found it and clasped it firmly in hers. Though I said her name repeatedly, she never used mine when we were intimate or after when we rested.

Later we sponged each other with damp towels, kissed and made love again. We drank cold water, ate fresh pineapple and held hands. Then Trang dressed and departed. I didn't think of it then, but later, on reflection, I realized she had lost her virginity long before me, but it didn't matter. I wondered when I would see her again. Realistically, I asked myself how I would see her again. Would our love-making become regular? Would she accept me as her lover and let me care for her or would she continue working the bars? I knew I felt love for Trang. I didn't know what she thought of me. I couldn't abide knowing she would sleep with anyone else. It was dilemma for me that would take a great deal of thought to know how I would act with her in the future, even how I would be the next day. I hoped I could pull it off without making a fool of myself.

Eight

The next morning, I awoke to Saigon at its best. Bright sun, cloudless sky, endless heat rising from the street, some people rushing about as if on a mission, others dawdling, figuring a way to get through the day, street vendors hoping for a sale, the traffic snarling rather than growling. It seemed a good day, rare in that city. After my day with Trang, my world was in good shape. In that torn city I called home, even if it was temporary, I hardly sensed the signs of war. The city, never at peace, appeared refreshed. It was the start of a new day, putting on a play, as if life were normal. I hoped for something clean, new. I lumbered slowly up my street and headed to that part of the city where I felt most alive. In several square blocks near the old opera house and now the National Assembly, ABC, CBS, the AP and NBC had their bureaus. There were several movie theaters, quarters for American officers at the Rex Hotel, the headquarters for the American propaganda effort, the Saigon City Hall, shopping arcades, the Caravelle Hotel and the Continental Hotel, a major bookstore, with bicycles parked neatly in rows on almost every corner. Those two major streets, Nguyen Hue and Le Loi crossed at their center, giving space to a park between the two hotels, and Tu Do, its brassy bars and cheap shops filled with trinkets, and fake antiques, a block away, made those avenues very busy. People moved around by foot more than they did by bike, motor scooter, car, or cyclo. I wondered where they rushed to, and why, what with the war and uncertainty that life held for the average Vietnamese. The simple answer that life went on, though true, cried for something profound, surely not from me when I, too, looked for answers. For some reason I never discovered what kept the Vietnamese going. Perhaps I should have tried harder. Perhaps. But then, I never figured out what kept me going.

I had never seen Inspector Phuoc anywhere but in the in the Bar California, in the dark, and always through a heavy fog of cigarette smoke. I would soon see him for the first time in daylight. I knew I would recognize him, but what if I did not. If he looked different in the sun's hot glare at midday, would I still recognize him? That was hard to imagine but it was one of those unusual thoughts I had on occasion in Saigon. However, it did not mean anything. I saw him standing halfway between the old French Opera House, its white washed facade peeling from the sun and rain, and the modern ugliness of the Caravelle Hotel, far from an architect's dream, and in stark contrast to the fake 1930s French style of the buildings that dominated those streets. When I looked across at Inspector Phuoc, the senators and representatives in the newly elected national assembly, formerly a proud building of past colonial glory, were rubber stamping a bill for President Nguyen Van Thieu to further suppress the already weakened freedom of his oppressed people.

Diminutive is how I can best describe Inspector Hong Phuoc as I observed him for the first time in daylight. I have to call him diminutive, rather than simply small, or smaller than small, tiny in every way. I stood in front of Givral's, the coffee and pastry house and an important meeting place in the heart of the city. Even from a quarter block away, I could see him standing still, as if in a vacuum, the dust from the dry streets swirling gently around him without making him dirty. Walking toward him and getting closer, I saw flies buzzing around his head, never settling on him. He still wore his tinted glasses and I watched him remove them carefully, from one ear at a time, wipe them clean with a white handkerchief he kept inside his coat pocket, and replace them as he had taken them off, from one ear at a time. He wore glasses to see objects close and to read, but never to drive or for looking at anything distant. I soon got to know his eyes, sometimes bottomless and coal black, other times, warm, and strangely, sweet, as if mimicking a small animal. Most of the time, even on official business, he walked. Only when on a raid, did he ride in an official car. Then he had a driver, fearless, dangerous to pedestrians and other vehicles, but never to his inspector, for whom he had great loyalty.

People gave him space when they walked past him as if they knew he possessed some hidden power they feared could hurt them. There were sidewalks in many parts of the city, but they were always dusty, and rarely clean. Public sanitation had a low government priority. Private sanitation barely existed. Surviving the daily rigors of life played a more important role than clean streets. People's footsteps gently kicked up a smattering of dust in the stifling heat. We were still in the dry season. The heavy rains had not yet started. But each year of the war was like the previous for most things except the dead, of which there were more. When the rains came, they arrived like the setting on an alarm clock. The dust would settle, but only for a moment. Despite the rain, and the washed, healthy smell, it momentarily brought, Saigon ever dirty, never managed to be clean. The sidewalks and unpaved streets remained dusty, and polluted, filled with the detritus of war and the displacement of people.

Though I knew I would soon eat lunch, before I met with Phuoc, I couldn't help myself and I indulged in two pieces of remarkably tasty French pastry dotted with chunks of dried fruit and a very strong cup of French-style coffee while waiting for Phuoc to appear across the square. After seeing him, and happily fortified with rich food, I looked both ways and started through Saigon's midtown traffic, cursing loudly, and dreaming of the comparative orderliness of Times Square at rush hour. The traffic light at Nguyen Hue and Le Loi was useless and I marveled at how easily the Vietnamese navigated the midday rush. *It's their country,* I thought and with so much else other than traffic to occupy their lives, the Vietnamese had figured a way to survive.

I made it to the corner of the Continental Hotel, skipping, I thought, like a lumbering elephant. I waited patiently at that corner, but probably too patiently before dodging again across the black tar street between the traffic to get to the other side. Chief Inspector Hong Phuoc stood, immaculate in his dark gray silk suit, a white shirt with a short, starched pointed collar, his maroon Dacron necktie with its tiny knot fitted perfectly in place, wearing his highly polished, yet plain black-laced shoes with their Italian points and an extra half inch on his heels to make him taller. Everything he wore fitted him perfectly, as if molded onto to his small body, including that extra few inches of cloth in his jacket to compensate for the weapon he carried in a heavy cloth holster under his left arm. As I got closer to him, I thought I could tell the obvious distaste he had for me, or hopefully only how I looked, thus his dislike for me, as I approached. After his seemingly outward unhappiness, he looked at me in a more friendly way. He put his hand out for French style rapid fire, series of pumping handshakes. Nothing friendly, mind, only a series of well- modulated movements of our hands to show we had met.

After we touched, he looked up at me, sweating in the heat, my shirt outside my trousers for convenience and comfort, my hair askew and he motioned me with an imperceptible nod of his head to follow him. He moved fast for a small man and I had trouble keeping up. I followed him down the street that ran alongside the Caravelle Hotel past the side of the Opera House.

"Come, we will have something to eat and something to drink," he said.

Though apprehensive about what would come next, I shuffled after him like the dutiful wife I could never be.

I did not look forward to the food, having earlier stuffed myself with the French pastries, but a cool beer would be perfect. At least I could get back some precious water wasting out of my body. We walked two blocks past a heavily guarded American officer quarters, and a small bar filled with overanxious prostitutes working the early shift. Then we turned into a small, clean, Vietnamese-French restaurant, called quaintly, Rue Pigalle. Red candles in ceramic holders stood on each table. And each table had a red-and-white checkered cloth and napkins in teak holders to match. The Vietnamese owner greeted Phuoc with respect and warmth but he made sure he ignored me. We sat in a corner, Phuoc facing front, while I sat with my back to the door, my chair tipped back, the way I did as a teenager in a pizza joint.

"We shall order first. Relax. Then we will talk. But you must cool off. To do that, remain perfectly still and savor the air-conditioning, America's marvelous contribution to our society, in our time of war. Savor it, for the moment because you never know when it will shut down, not in a blackout, but forever."

I looked around the small restaurant, empty, though still lunchtime. I ordered an American beer, whatever brand they had. I told the limping waiter, probably exempt from the draft because of his disability, it didn't matter what kind as long he brought me an American beer or, in a pinch, German and ice cold. Fool that I could be, I told him to include it with a glass of ice. I would take my chances with bacteria for the sake of drinking something cold. Dysentery, always a problem for foreigners, plagued everyone I knew as well as me. But better a cold beer than warm beer or no beer at all. I attempted a feeble joke about only drinking beer stolen from the PX. The waiter looked puzzled but Phuoc understood and made a sour face. There was no laughter, only a cold, empty stare. Phuoc ordered red wine. Soon both drinks arrived. His came in a plain bottle from Algeria with what looked like a just-printed label. Mine was Miller from Wisconsin, in a can, with beads of water running down its sides. I drank deeply from my ice-filled glass. Phuoc drank carefully. His wine was very dry, new, and puckering as if bottled yesterday. Only we knew that could not be. It had to be at least a week old, having arrived by air probably that morning.

Phuoc ordered what would become a familiar meal, small steak, well done, probably buffalo, French fried potatoes and a lettuce salad with oil and vinegar, and, of course, nuoc mam on the side laced with slivers of red pepper, hot to the touch and the tongue. I had a large plate of broiled river shrimp, French bread, New Zealand butter from a can, and a lettuce salad with oil and vinegar, but I did not have nuoc mam. Though I didn't mind the ubiquitous nuoc mam, the fermented fish sauce Vietnamese served with everything, I didn't enjoy it universally unless cooked in food. Simply dipping food into nuoc mam left a sour taste in my mouth.

Lunch finished, we sipped our coffee and smoked. Phuoc bent to get the leather portfolio he carried everywhere. He usually held it securely by a leather strap around his wrist. He brought it to the tabletop, pushed the dishes and cups to one side, and pulled from it a handful of newspapers. Phuoc handed these to me with a nod.

"Read these," he said. "They are part of a case I'm working on and I want your opinion. Maybe there is a story for you."

I took out my notebook and lit a Camel. I offered one to Phouc who gently declined, offering me a Gitanes instead. I declined. Phuoc sat back, smoked, and waited for me to read. I riffled through the pages quickly and noticed that each newspaper had an official stamp in the upper corner in red ink. Seeing the stories were from the two dreadful English language dailies, *The Saigon Post* and *The Saigon Daily News*, I didn't expect good writing, and more importantly, accurate reporting. The two papers relied heavily on news wire roundup reports on the war including official United States and Saigon government handouts. They also used American gossip columns, American and English sports scores, movie reviews, the weather in Southeast Asia, and other filler they could find that cost no money or that they could steal without having to pay for the rights.

"Where do I start?"

"I turned down the corner of the page you should read and I underlined each story in red."

The Saigon Post, February 7, 1967 (Page 4)

Police this morning discovered the body of a young woman dead. She was floating in the Cong Li Canal. Clad like a school girl in a simple ao dai of white tunic and black trousers, she was thought to be about sixteen. Because she had many bruises on her face and body, foul play is suspected. The young woman had no papers on her person. They found no jewelry or other personal effects. Police would not rule out the possibility of suicide and say they will investigate, but they said she had been raped.

The Saigon Daily News, March 8, 1967 (Page 2)

The naked body of a teenage girl was found yesterday stuffed behind a large pile of garbage and discarded tires on the road to Long Binh. Police said the girl had been raped and strangled. She had serious bruises on her face and body. Police do not have an identity. No clothes were discovered in the area. Police also said, these things happen during war and if anyone knows of a missing woman, perhaps aged twenty, they should step forward.

The Saigon Daily News, April 9, 1967 (Page 7)

A young, unidentified woman was found dead last night, her throat crudely cut and her clothing torn to shreds. There were recent bruises on her face and her body and she had been raped. She had been wearing a Western miniskirt and a blouse, sheer white, and see-through, with a French style brassiere. Her high-heel shoes were at the side of her body. Chief Inspector Hong Phuoc said she had to be a prostitute because a proper Vietnamese woman would not dress in that fashion. The search for her killer will continue, police said, but the war will make it difficult to find him.

The stories appeared almost word-for-word in each newspaper, as if someone dictated it to the reporter or what passed for rewrite. Phuoc made an appearance only in the last story. I handed the sheaf of papers back to him, lit another Camel, and took a long drink of my now-warm Jasmine tea. I sat and waited for Phuoc to say something. These stories were not different from the one I covered and wrote about, and put out of my mind since I witnessed the funeral back in January. But these were different. They were terse, had no color, nor did they have heart. He continued to stare at me and still said nothing. I wondered if Phuoc know about my story. It played in *The Saigon Post* but the newspaper's style did not allow for bylines. Phuoc had to know something. Perhaps he saw the story reprinted in the daily digest put out in English and Vietnamese by the Vietnam Press Agency. I wanted to hear from him first before I divulged what I knew, and told him of my experience.

Sitting and watching Phuoc watch me I tried to recall where else I had been in those months. Time had a way of compressing itself, making one day or week seem the same. Except the monsoon season, sometimes called seasonal winds, little about the weather, and the war, the food and the people, changed from moment to moment. The dry monsoon extended from mid-October to mid-May, a time of little rain in the south. Then, the northeast monsoon brought dry and cooler wind from the Asian mainland, south down from China. The rainy season, or the wet monsoon, ran from mid-May to mid-October. It connected one end of the year to the other. Called the southwest monsoon, it covered most of the country with low lying clouds that never dissipated and drenched, like clockwork, the country with rain, especially in the south and the coastal regions below the DMZ. Outside Saigon, the heavy rain turned roads, military bases and airstrips into muddy fields. In Saigon, the rain flooded the streets, clogged drains and sewers, those that existed, but oddly, within hours, all the water brought by the heavy downpour disappeared. No wind ever blew for long or with sustained intensity in Saigon.

Paper and debris usually didn't twirl in the streets. Instead, trash, the waste of the neighborhoods, floated and fell on gentle currents of air, waves at noon much like at Brooklyn's Coney Island or New Jersey's Asbury Park. Here, every bit of garbage stuck to something else, as if matted, like papier-mache, if you could believe once alive, once a jumble, but now limited and numbered. For the people living in Saigon, many now refugees, the daily process of moving from street to street, alley to alley, within one neighborhood or to another neighborhood, had its own peculiar rhythm, one mostly off key. Living in any manner, that is, surviving, really, had only one reward, that was to reach tomorrow. And as brief as that may have been, it was the only dream many held.

During the wet monsoon, the North Vietnamese and Viet Cong on one side and the allies, South Vietnamese, American, South Korean and Australian on the other, built up their forces before they went on the offensive. Usually the allies in their attempt to disrupt the enemy counterpunched. The dry monsoon meant good weather for offensive operations for both sides, so there was more work for me in the field with the troops. February 1967 saw me with the 25th Infantry Division in War Zone C, near the Cambodian border in the province of Tay Ninh. The operation, called Gadsden, designed to stop enemy troop movement through Cambodia and down the Ho Chi Minh Trail, gave me too few stories and so I had little success. We thrashed around heavy jungle, slept poorly while wrapped in ponchos, ate boring C-rations and found no Viet Cong. I stayed three says, saw no combat and filed one story for the AP that paid me little for my time and energy. That was the life of a freelance reporter.

In March, Reuters assigned me to cover a major operation involving thousands of American troops. I went with the First Infantry Division on Operation Junction City, also in War Zone C. A major assault in search of enemy troops, this one had everything, including a parachute jump, the first of the war, which gave us great pictures but little else. But the well-entrenched enemy had other ideas, including several successful ambushes against the American forces. Troops from the First Division and from the 173rd Airborne, suffered heavy casualties and I didn't have an easy time, either.

I was on the edge of an ambush with the 173rd Airborne. The squad I had been moving with found itself under heavy fire at night. The jungle was dark anyway. At night, seeing anything clearly was worse. As I fell to the ground, the last thing I saw were streaks of sunlight peeking through the heavy foliage. I hugged the jungle floor as closely as I could. My body suffered bruises from protruding tree roots. I pushed my face into mud that a rotten stench all its own from decaying leaves and dead tree trunks. I could barely breathe. I shut my eyes tightly, only allowing myself the luxury of sneaking them open when I thought I might be safe. My heart pounded in my chest. My palms were wet with my sweat. My fatigues were filthy from clinging to the jungle floor during the firefight. The men in the squad I traveled with reacted as I. They had weapons, though, automatic rifles, hand grenades, grenade launchers, mortars, a sharp knife if needed. I did not. I had a pad and a pencil, and my old Nikon camera. I never carried a weapon. The troops' uniforms were filthy, encrusted with mud, torn from flailing around in the bush. They knew to be silent, not to wear cologne, a dead giveaway to the VC that Americans were in their midst. The vacant stares and sweat-streaked faces of the young men belied the fear I believed they felt, but could not show. As Americans, they couldn't show fear anywhere, whether in the jungle, a street corner in New York, a farm in Iowa. They had to go out almost every day to search for an elusive enemy. Most of the young American soldiers had no sense of why they were fighting, but they knew they wanted to survive. Every GI I met had a simple explanation, their rule of the jungle. He had to stay alive, and he did as best he could by helping his buddy stay alive. He watched your back. You watched his back. Nobody watched my back, though they made sure I didn't get hurt, or worse, killed when I patrolled with them.

When I traveled with Lee, he looked out for me because he had greater experience. I tried to learn from him, but he taught by example, not by note. I tried to keep my eye on him in combat but I found that impossible. He moved like the wind, silent, and swift, the way I supposed American Indians moved in the French and Indian War. I learned I couldn't keep up with him, so I stayed with the sergeant, the squad leader, somewhere in the middle of the squad, and when he ducked, I ducked. Lee and I were not always a team. There were no guarantees he and I would cover stories in the field together. I didn't want to take the chance of going out alone, but I did, sometimes for the hell of it, other times to prove I could do it. Worse, on this last mission, leeches infiltrated my combat boots, and clung tenaciously to my calves and ankles. When we stopped and could smoke, I rolled up my pants, applied the red-hot tip of my cigarette onto however many leeches there were, and watched their blood bloated bodies shrivel and fall off my leg to the ground. That capped my decision about the field. I had enough of proving my manhood to myself.

When I returned to Saigon after Junction City, I filed my story for Reuters. As expected, they paid me on the spot. I asked for piasters that I needed to live. A check in dollars would take too long to clear. I went to my apartment, had a drink, showered and went to sleep. But I made a decision not to cover combat again soon, if I could. I had enough of the firefights and endless treks through the jungle. There was too much danger around me and too much fear, my own and from the soldiers on both sides. I wondered why I put myself through that mental and physical pain. I had nothing more to prove to neither myself nor anyone else who might care, though I doubted anyone existed who might care what I did. I had begun to realize that sleepless nights in the jungle or on the side of a mountain were not worth a byline in an unknown newspaper halfway around the world. Forcing me through yet another passage into manhood under fire had lost its charm. Screw it. I preferred sleep, sex, good strong coffee, and a flaky hot croissant, rather than another senseless march through the jungle. In April and May, I stayed close to home in Saigon, not venturing into the field, meeting with Phuoc, as when he showed me the clippings about the dead prostitutes, and spending as much time as I could with Trang.

I wondered if being in Southeast Asia had anything to do with the difficulty I had in keeping my life on track. I knew that without journalism, I would be lost. Most of the time, I trudged around Saigon, either looking for work, or in the last few months working for Castle, doing very little of anything, I have to add, but getting a steady income and staying out of his way as much as I could. I checked his books, made sure the girls got their fair share, saw that the sheets were clean, and smiled when I visited his four locations, each a laundry, each a whorehouse. Lately Trang had become a significant part of my life and another good reason and strong excuse for not leaving Saigon.

After another meeting with Phuoc, I asked him again, what he wanted me to do or say about the dead women.

"We should play at being detectives. I will enjoy that," he said. "I will start you with a simple question. Do you notice similarities in the deaths?"

"Yes, I see some. I also see that you are involved. Was that you in the early stories? I see where they quoted you by name in the last one?"

"I gave the information for all the stories but allowed them to quote me only in the last. The investigation, because there is one, is on my desk. I took it because I wanted it. After the first few murders, I saw a pattern emerging."

"OK. Here I go. I'll play detective for you. There is a pattern. They were all raped. They were young. Several might have been prostitutes. Maybe all were prostitutes.

Each woman had been badly beaten with bruises on her face and body. None had identification."

"Go on, but look for more. Think of more." "I can't find anything else."

"Look at the dates on each killing."

"February seventh. March eighth. April ninth. They are one month apart but for one day later in each month."

Phuoc smiled broadly. "Yes, I think you see the pattern." I thought he might applaud my effort, but he didn't.

"Do we have a serial killer?" Though apprehensive, my question, conjured visions of a major story.

"Today's date is May third. We may know what we have on May eleventh."

"Meaning?"

"Perhaps the killer will strike again. The deaths all occur one month apart by one day. I don't know why there is a day's difference each month but there is. When we find the killer, I will ask him." Phuoc sucked hard on his Gitanes and blew the smoke off to one side. "I see you have some evidence, obviously circumstantial, but not much. You'll need more than a sequence of dates to convince me." "Don't be hasty."

"Why not. It seems it's all guesses. Nothing more. A few dead girls. Perhaps all whores. Why should we care?"

"Prostitutes," Phuoc corrected, trying for refinement and to give the job of whore a bit of class.

"OK, prostitutes. But, explain," I said.

I got my notebook from my back pocket where it mostly had been for the past week. Its edges disheveled from my sweat, and when I opened it, the blue lines on the first few pages were hardly readable from the book sitting too long in the heat and mainly sat on by me. Playing at being a journalist again made me feel useful. I started taking notes. I titled the first page, "Mystery of the Dead Women," knowing that if anything came of the story, the title would probably change.

Phuoc sat up straighter than usual. He spoke an octave higher than a whisper, just enough for me to hear him but making sure that no one else could.

"Something bothers me. There is bruising on each woman and the bruising has the same pattern. Each woman had a round bruise under her left eye, as if someone used a club with a round knob at its end to hit her repeatedly. Despite that, I believe the killer used only his fists. The most recent dead woman had what you call a black eye. I found another black and blue mark on her upper left forehead but in each case, the mark looked like it came from a heavy ring, one with a pattern in the gold and from stones, maybe diamonds, along the edges. All the women also had heavy bruises on their left rib cage. Each woman had her ribs broken. The killer also cruelly crushed the left breast, only the left breast, of each woman, destroying her natural form and beauty, her sacred self." He sighed.

"You have a way with words," I murmured as I scribbled furiously. Phuoc kept smoking and uncharacteristically lit one cigarette from another. I had never seen him do that before that afternoon.

"It is important to note that the man used his right hand only, as if the man who did it, had no left hand. He had to be swinging from his right side and he used his fist, not a club. That means, to me, he wanted to be closer to his victim when he hurt her. Using a weapon separates the person from his victim. Using fists or feet, tells me he is sadistic. We have one clue. The last dead woman put up a fight. We found bits of skin under her long fingernails. We can't trace the skin because we do not have the equipment but her fingernails were broken, though recently manicured. Now we know we are looking for a man with scratches on some part of his body, but where on his skin we do not know."

"Can you pinpoint the time of their deaths?"

"We found each woman, we think, within two days of her death. Bodies decompose fast in our climate. We have poor tools and an ancient laboratory but we know our climate and what it does to the dead. We must bury the dead quickly or they generate disease. Bodies bloat what seems immediately, sometimes in hours. The flies then begin to lay their eggs. Maggots hatch and get to work eating their way through the once live person. The result is terrible; the smell, awful. Our technicians are often medical students with little training to do an autopsy or help learn the cause of death. Consider, too, that our medical school is barely in operation because of the war. We are turning out no doctors, and those we do, go to the front. The country has very few doctors in the military, anyway, and those too old to fight have their hands full at home caring for the sick and the wounded and those who normally fill our few hospital beds. Any possible medical help the police may get does not exist."

"I know your hospitals are a mess. I recently visited the Grall Hospital, one of Saigon's largest and busiest. Seeing the nuns trying to care for people sleeping in hallways, seeing open wounds and dirty bandages, made my stomach turn. I wrote a story that Reuters picked up but the American news companies wanted no part of it." "They want stories about their own. I can understand that. I would do the same."

"So, how do you do your work?"

"Because we have poor tools and no training, we go by smell, touch and instinct. We couldn't do any autopsies because our best guess is that the women died by ruthless violence to their person, by a ruthless, violent man."

I nodded. "You said that. Any fingerprints?" I asked.

Phuoc looked at me as if I were dumb, or stupid, and probably both.

"You see too many Hollywood movies. Consider, please, that we are the lowest division of the National Police. The government wants to kill communists and to stay in power. We want to fight crime, solve robbery and murder. I, at least, have a free hand. I have been doing this work for many years. My counterparts in smaller cities and towns have no freedom. When their bosses catch them looking into normal, everyday crime, they get into big trouble. I know detectives who end up fighting in the jungle because they disobeyed orders to ignore robbery and murder. Never mind. That is not your concern. We are not the FBI. We have no equipment to do simple things like gathering fingerprints. If we wanted, we could not lift, as you say, prints. But truthfully, we do not look for prints. We also rarely look for clues other than the obvious ones. Meaning, I do not look for clues. At every murder scene, with so much debris, dirt and garbage, it becomes impossible to tell what is a clue and what is not a clue. Also, sadly, I have no staff. I have one desk and no assistants unless I have to visit a crime scene. I am the only one in my department." He smiled sweetly letting his truth sink in what I found hard to understand, though easy to accept.

"I have told you much. Now it is your turn to tell me what you know."

He put his hand out like a traffic cop to stop me from answering. "I know you covered a similar story in January for the AP. I know it had wide distribution. I also know the AP sent it out with photos shot by cameraman Lee, your friend. I want you tell me where Lee lives so I can get copies of all his photos in case the killer appeared at the funeral. I know he moves from house to house, one family member to another family member. It's his way and the way of many Vietnamese because of the war. His photos may show something that will help, though I think I know the man behind the killings."

"Truthfully, until you showed me those clippings I had forgotten all about that story. I was paid fifty bucks, sold the dollars on the black market and lived off the story for a few weeks. I told the story of a terribly sad funeral. Hardly anyone attended. I could have wept because no one else did. That's all I recall. I saw nothing suspicious that day and I doubt that Lee's photos will help. I'll find him and send him to you. I'm sure knowing who you are, he'll be willing help."

"You see, your story took place early in January. I believe that girl may have been the first. Because of that, the pattern makes even more sense."

"If there is a pattern, and, yes, everything points to one, the killings could have started earlier, last year in the fall of 1966."

"Of course. But your story is the first in print. In retrospect, I believe your funeral, was also the first. I found your story after the others appeared. I checked the newspapers and found no other references. *The Saigon Post* butchered your original piece. So I think the murders started January third and the dates got advanced a few days because the killer got busy with something else, or his planning for the other murders had not advanced in his warped mind."

"You said you thought you knew the killer. Can you name him?" I leaned forward, dragging deeply on my cigarette, my pen poised and ready.

"I am not willing to say at this time who he is. I think I know who might be the killer, and what kind of man did the killings. I will not give you a name, but soon I think I can give you my theory about what kind of man is doing the murders. I need your help before I give you a name, though. Will you help me?"

Hong Phuoc paused long enough to let his request work its way through my brain.

"Yes." I answered quickly, probably too quickly, without thinking, understanding almost nothing of where it would lead, nevertheless, willing to battle with the unknown whatever the result.

At first, I did nothing. I enjoyed the money Castle gave me. I had the freedom to hang out and to do as little as I wanted about anything else. I didn't have to face selling myself to one or another bureau chief and to write stories cheaply for the sake of appearing in print.

Sure, getting the occasional byline sweetened my life and made my parents happy. It didn't happen often enough to make up for all the times I filed one hundred fifty words that ended on the back page of some local paper that no one read. Before Trang and I were intimate, I started to enjoy sex with Castle's prostitutes. The best part, there were never any attachments. A few knew about Trang and knew Trang. They understood why I had no interest in them, and were always courteous, kind and generous of spirit. Despite any moral misgivings I might have had, life could not have been better, until Phuoc started dancing inside my head as he tried hard to tease me back to reality, his local reality, despite the war.

I had done my share of running my first nine months in South Vietnam. Castle's offer gave me the chance to enjoy my life a step at a time without looking forward or back. I moved horizontally through my days in Saigon. Easy enough. Now Phuoc laid out another plan for my survival, realistic and tougher because it took old-fashioned hard work. I knew his path would give me a better life in the end. I had to find the strength to move onto another plain, almost like a Buddhist, instead of sinking into the depths of depravity. Under Castle's rules and guidance I could keep having a good time without thinking. Yet I knew tomorrow would always be in doubt. Tomorrow had no clarity. That is where Phuoc started to reach me. I had no plan. Phuoc knew that. He saw that he could take advantage of me. He had a simple dream. He told me if he were rich or even a thief, he would not be happy. His humble beginnings and the ethic of his deeply ingrained Buddhism did not allow him to seek hard after money or material gain. He had only his badge. Phuoc had earned it the hard way and it kept him honest in his unquenchable pursuit of crime. It helped sustain Phuoc, to keep him going in time of war when no one else seemed to care about civilians, and the young women whom he knew died senselessly. For Inspector Hong Phuoc, finding the man who murdered those women had become his passion and his obsession.

Nine

Phuoc and I started meeting for lunch several times a week. We exchanged little more than pleasantries, but we brought each other up to date on our lives, mine far more than his did. He stayed guarded about his home, wife, children if any, how he lived. I filled him in on any stories I had in the works, most of which were figments of my imagination. But I danced around my affair with Trang, telling him only so much and no more than I thought he needed to know. I did not want criticism about my cross-cultural romance, especially when he might instruct me how to handle a Vietnamese woman, something I had hints about from my Vietnamese acquaintances. Be strong, they said. Let her know her place is to make you happy and do your bidding. Make sure she knows how to sew and cook, they told me, because when sex fails, something should be there to take its place. I listened, took mental notes, and told anyone who had the time to hear me, we were having an affair with no thought of marriage, and, if nothing else because it felt good and right, her being with me, I with her.

One day after a good lunch in a small Korean restaurant behind the Caravelle Hotel, Phuoc approached me about something that surprised and frightened me in equal parts.

"We know enough about each other now, don't you think? Mutual trust and all that." He sound like one of those BBC announcers on the World Service Phuoc had been listening to and revering for years.

"Yes." I answered yes, because I could not say otherwise. He had become my valued friend. I had no idea where we were heading.

"I have a secret vice, my only vice. Without it, I cannot get through the day. Can I trust you to accept it for what it is and for you not to be critical of me or condemn it?"

"I've gone this far with you. Yes and yes. You can trust me." "Come then. Walk with me. We will visit the Prince Hotel off Tu

Do and I'll explain."

Curious, but also oddly resistant, and allowing myself no choice because I had to understand what he meant, I agreed and we started walking. People were still enjoying the siesta. The streets were quiet and almost deserted. I knew the Prince Hotel, a seedy place with cheap rates and of dubious reputation where many British and Australian journalists stayed. The bar had a dart board and served Guinness, the real brew that everyone wondered where it had come from.

Drugs were a burgeoning problem not only for the troops but also for civilians and especially for some journalists. I had heard that the owners of the hotel, including their Cambodian manager, did not allow hard drugs in the building, but allowed an opium den to flourish in the basement. Intrigued, I walked with Phuoc and listened. Did I have another story in the making? I would know soon enough.

"You see," Phuoc said as we crossed the street, "I am what the British in their infinite wisdom call, an opium eater. Opium is my addiction, my pacifier, and my soul catcher. Thomas DeQuincy is my guru. Samuel Coleridge, a hero."

I gasped, sucked in my breath, but said nothing. Surprised, I couldn't do anything but to stare, my eyes wide. I found the information startling. Phuoc looked up at me and caught the expression on my face. I lighted another Camel from the one I had already smoked to its butt. I inhaled as deeply as I could without making a fool of myself.

"After the French released me from prison in 1954, I had terrible pains in the backs of my thighs and along the shoulders, mainly behind my neck, the two places they frequently beat me. I needed relief. I sought solace in Buddhism, and in the worship of my family, but those did not work. I tried aspirin, which did not work. We did not have medicinal morphine in large supply and if we did, no physician I knew would help me for fear of someone catching me. We had something else that was part of an underground culture developed over many years. We had opium and no one condemned its use, though a doctor would rarely recommend it as a painkiller. Most people frowned on using it without understanding its virtues. But, they winked at it as a vestige of how we once lived. It is better to have some using opium, than to publicize its so-called danger. Few used it those days as even fewer use it today. To recuperate, I returned to my village some thirty miles north of Saigon. There, an elder suggested opium. One day we traveled to a larger village than mine was, and he introduced me to its sweet joy. After one pipe, the pain subsided. I remained in my village for six weeks learning its health-giving joy and its transporting effect on my soul. Since then, I make sure I smoke at least once a day. Over the years, one session with the pipe is never enough. Sometimes I smoke four, five, six times a day, each time with ten pipes, with each pipe having a hand-rolled ball of opium. That is why you don't see me some days for many hours. It is therapeutic for my pain and enlightening for my mind. Even the dreams I have about each case can reveal more than I get from grappling with the evidence when awake."

We stopped when we had arrived at the dilapidated entrance to the Prince Hotel. I took a deep breath and tossed my still burning cigarette into the street.

"We are here. It is time to enter. Come," he said.

Before we stepped inside the lobby, I noted the shabby entrance, the battered sign announcing the Prince Hotel, and the dirt-encrusted glass doors. Phuoc paused, as if a bird in flight. He told me he remembered the previous night and his yellow-stained ivory pipe, the one he always used that the owner stored in a special cabinet in the basement. I waited for him to guide me further to the opium den inside the Prince Hotel. In the tiny foyer, he paused before we went through a beaded curtain that served as the next set of doors.

"It is impossible for me," he continued so quietly that I had to bend to hear him, "not to think about the finely rolled ball of dark brown opium, tightly-packed that the manager here specializes in. When smoked, it is so sweet. Believe me, once you inhale, and do it quickly as you must, and suck it in deeply, as you must, you will never be the same again. It seems slow when you inhale, but it is fast. You must be gentle when you do it or you lose its beauty."

Phuoc told me the opium ball to an outsider might look like dark brown, sometimes bitter tasting fudge, much like I and my friends would mix, the fudge that is, with pure hash. But once inhaled, Phuoc told me, the opium brings the loveliest of remarkable dreams.

"Opium lifts me far above all those who do not indulge because they lack the experience to understand the wondrous beauty of where it leads. It unlocks doors and allows me the chance to share in universal secrets. I know this, and I tell you this because I consider you my friend. Because of the war, it is more important than ever for me to smoke. It is more important for me than to eat or drink or make love, especially to make love. When I am tense or under pressure, sex is a chore and requires great physical energy, of which I have little to spare."

He paused, and placed one hand gently on my forearm, as if to say, "Wait. More is coming." I recoiled a bit, not used to a man's touch before I realized that Vietnamese men touched each other and even held hands. It took me time, but I got used to seeing two South Vietnamese soldiers dressed in camouflage uniforms walking in the street holding hands or with their arms entwined like lovers. Only here it meant friendship, and did not have the stigma it had back home. I knew Phuoc had more to say, so I said nothing, being his guest, a tourist about to enter an exotic land.

After entering the dank lobby of the hotel, we walked through a beaded curtain and to the front desk. Phuoc struck a bell with the palm of his hand and waited for someone to appear.

"Stay with me. The patron, as we would call him in French, manager to you, and as he wants us to call him, should appear soon. Then, if you let me, and you have come this far, I'll take you on a new journey. I'll be your spiritual escort to a new country. Many nights I come to the Bar California after my pipes. I feel mellow, gentle, wondering why people harm each other and why they kill each other. I come here to get calm from the rigors of the war. Opium is my corrective to war and its daily horror."

In a few minutes, the manager made his appearance, and like many elderly Vietnamese, his body had no density, what my father would call only skin and bones. I thought if he were against the light, I would see right through him. His yellowish skin, pulled tightly across his head, looked opaque. Surely malnourished like most opium addicts, whom I assumed he was, I wondered how he moved through life without the slightest wind blowing him away. If I didn't know better, I would have called him an esthete, perhaps even an intellectual, at least in how he seemed, not necessarily in how he thought about life and love and philosophy. I had no idea what went on inside his head. Without question, he lived and breathed opium in a way that put Phuoc to shame, at least in the narrow life he led running the opium den, the main reason for the hotel's existence.

I found it hard to look at the patron without gazing intently at him. He had one very long pinkie nail on his left hand. I estimated it at three inches. I thought it fragile and wondered how he managed not to break it when he used his hand. How did he maneuver through life with what I thought an incredible impediment? His thin face with its high cheekbones and large protruding eyes had one long black hair easily four inches growing from a mole to the right of his chin. I wanted to pluck the hair from his face but I knew that would be the worst show of respect and one I could ill afford. Instead, I stared, smiled weakly and uneasily and waited for Phuoc to take me to the next plateau. I couldn't tell if the patron noticed my uneasiness, but I decided the hell with it. It didn't matter how he felt. Not really. It only mattered how I felt and how I would act when I got to where I was going.

"This way, please," said the patron in English with a heavy French accent. His dark blue suit had a sheen from too much wear. His shirt, once white, now dirty and worn thin from age, fell loosely over his body. His black tie had lost its shape long ago and now hung loosely around his neck. About that nail and the hair on his chin, rarely did I find two Vietnamese who could agree on their meaning. Some thought each meant long life. Others assumed that alone and together, they were fashion statements, a stylish revolt against the mundane and the modern. Then there were those who told me, the nail in particular and perhaps even the hair, represented the past, a life once dominated by the Mandarin class that bureaucratic culture imported to Vietnam from China more than one thousand years ago. Whatever the long nail and the long hair meant, I had to accept what I saw as something culturally different, a way of life I could not explain, rare and unusual, but harmless.

The patron bowed his head in acknowledgment we were there. With his long pinkie nail, he beckoned us to follow. He took us behind the front desk and through another beaded curtain. Past the beaded curtain, we followed him through a heavy wood door he closed softly behind him and gestured for us to go down a steep flight of steps. At the bottom of the steps, we went through yet another door and entered a room half filled with Vietnamese men in their underwear reclining on the rosewood platforms used as beds by many Vietnamese. A sickly sweet smell assaulted my nose. I inhaled quickly and tried to show it did not affect me. I saw Phuoc take notice of my reaction, but he said nothing. Of course, he had been here often. It was his opium den, where he went to escape and he could be a better guide because he knew it well.

Each wood bed had a porcelain pillow shaped like a shoebox with an indented section for the head, much like a yoke. The idea being that once you lay down your head, you didn't move it until you awoke. The four platforms took up most of the space. There were blankets in need of a heavy wash. Each man had a long pillow that he wrapped his legs around, to help him sleep without moving around much, another Vietnamese cultural difference that said too much movement in bed when sleeping, or here, while drugged, meant the person would rest poorly. I thought the hotel could be a good customer for Castle's laundromats, his legitimate business and front. None of the addicts noticed we had entered the only world many of them knew to be real. Each had a pack of cigarettes at his side and a few had small transistor radios tuned low to Vietnamese music. Some men lay with their legs entwined, their arms touching, their eyes glazed in a trance. In one corner, I saw a shrine with burning incense and old fruit around a statue of the happy Buddha surrounded by many small, laughing children, a sign of posterity. Several men, because they did not have space on the beds, lay on the floor of highly polished hard wood. Each man had his own wood pipe next to him or cradled in his arm, the smoking done, the dreams already at work. Some men whispered to each other, their faces close, and their lips hardly moving. Amiable talk among friends, and I wondered how much they understood but I understood the social aspect of opium, the congenial atmosphere. I was nervous. My time would soon arrive when I would smoke my first pipe. I wanted to run. I had mixed feelings about staying, but I knew I could not back out.

Phuoc led me by my elbow to his platform bed. It was where he smoked. He told me to undress to my underwear. Like many Americans, I wore jockey shorts while the Vietnamese men were wearing basketball style underpants. Within minutes, we were ready. I sat in awe and perhaps horror because I had no idea the effect the opium would have on me. To honor my presence as a first-timer, the patron elected to prepare my first smoke in a borrowed pipe. He took an apparent delight in rolling the ball of opium for me, tightly, he told me, to make the smoke I would inhale more effective. He pushed his handiwork deep into the bowl at the end of the pipe. He wanted me to relax, and warned that should I show fear, the opium would work against whatever it might reveal. He told me that he understood my caution, and appreciated my anxiety, but after I had one pipe, the others would come more easily. That is, he emphasized, if I allowed the drug's magical power to work itself around and through my mind. The patron told me to lie back, to get comfortable and copy the men around me. He told me to hold the pipe with two hands and put the mouthpiece between my lips. He then struck a wood match and lit the ball of opium. It flared as if covered with alcohol, and he told me to suck in deeply and then hold the smoke and its essence long in my lungs until I could not hold it any longer. I did as told, drawing the powerful, sweet drug into my lungs. I closed my eyes and thought of nothing. I brought the smoke into my chest and held it for what I thought a long time before exhaling. It took about a minute to smoke my first pipe. After exhaling, I felt light-headed, distant, and divorced from reality. I couldn't feel my legs or arms. I thought my head floated in another dimension. The dirt and smell didn't matter. The other men in the crowded room didn't matter. I lost track of Phuoc. I started to dream.

In my dream, first I walked down a long flight of steps and found myself in a dark room with one small light in a corner. The walls and floors were of some soft material, the color forest brown, and the air clean and sweet. I had the room to myself. That is the way I wanted it. I searched the room and found it empty. Then at the height of my eyes, I saw a window without glass or bars. I walked to the window and looked out. Dazzling whites and blues of all shades filled the cloudless sky. Birds sang. I saw no people. I wept either for joy or for sorrow. It made no difference to me, because as I wept, I also smiled. I had never done that, either awake or when sleeping.

As quickly as that dream fled my mind, another took its place. This time I went up a flight of steps, not down. I was in a narrow room, instead of the wider room from my first dream. Here, too, I found a window without bars or glass. Narrow at the top, wide at the bottom. Though difficult, I struggled to climb the wall so I could see out. Soon I reached my goal. Looking out over the land, I had a remarkable view of an endless world of green meadows, colorful flowers, blue skies, health, happy dogs and horses. Again, I saw no people, except one fleeting wisp of a woman in the distance. I didn't want either of my dreams to end, but they did, and I woke, dazed, perspiring, one leg wrapped around a large, crushed, round down pillow, the other leg touching Phuoc. Fifteen minutes had passed but I thought it had been hours. I moved quickly away from Phuoc's leg, not used to the Vietnamese manner of touching another man without it being sexual even when drugged.

Drying myself of my sweat with an end of the dirty blanket, I patted myself down and dressed. I lit a Camel, and an attendant scurried to me and handed me a hot cup of strong black tea. He smiled faintly, and backed away from me without turning. I waited ten minutes, sometimes nodding off but pulling myself back before going into a deep sleep. I had one pipe, my first, but

Phuoc probably had his daily ten in one sitting, the norm for a confirmed addict. I wondered how he could keep hitting on the pipe without falling apart, but then I didn't understand the full effect of opium. I mean one pipe and I went to another world. Practice must really mean perfect. He would be out for at least an hour or more and then he would need, he had told me, an hour beyond that to properly recover. I decided not to wait for him. I threw some piasters on the blanket near where I slept, and left, sure that I would see Phuoc sooner than later. Finding Phuoc's mind or penetrating his person would be a major task, tougher even than find the physical man. Perhaps, it was something I did not want to pursue.

Back in my apartment twenty minutes later, I became woozy. With the dizziness, a peaceful feeling settled over me. I remembered the patron telling me that the effect of the opium would reappear an hour later and my dreams would be sweeter, the sensation more delicate. I tried my best to ignore the heat, turned on my overhead fan, dropped my shoes from my feet, threw off my clothing, and returned to my dreams. Or the same dream. It never varied. The dreams had a pleasant air to them, including the one where I went down those steps to the wide, empty room. I never dreamed of violence or saw violent colors. And the dreams never had people, but one, the image of that woman in the distance, a wisp, floating.

I never slept better.

Ten

I gave Trang a key to my apartment so she could visit me when she wanted. And she did, often and, best, when I least expected to see her. I didn't demand when she should come because I wanted her to be free of any pressure from me. Coming and going as she pleased, I knew, gave her the independence she needed. I wanted to interfere in her life but I could not without creating a bad situation for myself. Sometimes she appeared late in the afternoon, other times, early in the morning, or often during the siesta. We always made love and each time as we became more familiar with the other, the intensity of our passion increased. We still had no language in common despite my attempts to teach her simple English. She and I rarely said anything more than a broken sentence or two but we bridged that gap when we made love. We let passion dominate our brief time together. One day I came back from my tour of the laundries and found a shrine in the corner of my one room apartment. Not very big, it stood in one corner of the room. Three pictures rested on a small table, one an older man in the middle and on each side of him, a picture of a young man, probably his two sons, in uniform. Surrounding the pictures was a bowl of fresh fruit, and slow burning sticks of incense. A statue of the Buddha sat in the middle of the altar, and behind the photos. Everyone called this Buddha the happy Buddha because he had a big smile on his face and many children sitting on him everywhere. I had not seen Trang for many days. I knew she had put the shrine in place and I guessed the photos were of her dead father and her two brothers. She had hinted vaguely to me once that she had lost her father and two brothers in the war. But why did she put a shrine in my apartment, in my bedroom?

I found out the answer when she showed at my apartment the next morning. She had a big smile on her face, as if to say, *See I did something special but I'm not sure you appreciate its meaning.*

"Tell me," I said to her. "Tell me what this means and why you put it here. Don't you have a place for it where you live?"

"Yes," she said. "I do have a place. It is where I live with three other girls. We all have shrines. We all lost brothers in the war. I want to have an altar here, too, so they are with me when I am with you, she told me."

"Your brothers are in uniform. Were they killed in the war?" "Yes. Killed in fighting," she said.

"Where?"

"One near Can Tho. One near Quang Tri City." "When?"

"Brother on left dead two years. In 1965. VC ambush. Younger brother on right, dead last year in big battle."

"The man in the middle? Your father?"

"Yes." Her face screwed in anger. "VC kill my father because he no give extra rice. He say family and village need rice. VC very angry. Beat him. Cut his head. Mother cries every day. We hate VC. VC no good."

Her shoulders shook and she started crying. Then she wiped her eyes and turned away from me out of shame or pride. I did not know which. I had never seen her cry or show any sign of weakness. Normally she was stoic. She never showed pain, anger or sorrow. Normally. This day I saw something different in her and I didn't know how to handle it. I decided it would be best to let her weep and then recover her control.

I knew from Phuoc that most Vietnamese worshiped their ancestors, whenever or however they died. At the death day ceremony, relatives gathered in the home of the deceased. Each person would bring one dish of food specially prepared to please the dead ancestor. They would offer the food to honor the dead, holding the dish in front of them and bowing as they did before placing it on the table at the altar. A few days later, a relative would replace the old food with new, in a never-ending cycle. Perhaps without saying it, Trang started to introduce me into her family circle. If so, she did it with typical Vietnamese indirection, a method that worked well, especially on the American mind. I knew if nothing else, I would keep the food and fruit fresh at the altar for her father and two brothers. But incense created a problem. It made me sneeze so I hoped that Trang and her ancestors would excuse me for not lighting the joss sticks when they burned down.

She continued weeping after telling her story. Despite my decision to allow the space she needed, I went to comfort her anyway, but she shook me off and knelt in front of the shrine. Her two hands together not clasped, but touching and moving in an up and down motion as she prayed. She finished her prayers and sat at my feet, her head on my knee, her hands clutching my legs. I wanted to make love but I knew that would be a mistake. Her mood didn't call for passion. She wanted comfort and sometimes our love making with its fervor worked against solace. I tried to find out the reason for putting the shrine in my place then but she could not put into words why then. I guessed it might be an anniversary. I wondered if she were thinking of moving in permanently and wanted the place to have a Vietnamese touch to it. I would welcome her living with me, but I didn't believe she would move in and, so, threw the idea out.

We held each other close, warmly, and affectionately. Then, unexpectedly, we touched and touched some more until we were making love as if time were our enemy, it being all we had to conquer to survive, and we had no choice but to be as intimate as possible. When done, after time had stopped, and feeling complete, we basked in the aftermath of our deeply felt sex. We slept and I did not dream for the first time since I started smoking opium. I thought sex might be the antidote to the sometime mess of my newly drug-filled dreams. Then she rose to her feet and made us a pot of tea. We sat on the floor, our backs against the bed, sipping the tea and still saying nothing. Usually I babbled on about something that had been inside me and Trang would look at me, not understanding a word, saying nothing, as if the sound of my voice comforted her. Toward late afternoon, she washed her face, gave me her usual Vietnamese kiss, her nose against my cheek, and made ready to leave. At the door, she turned and gave me a wistful smile.

"I not be back few days," she said slowly, struggling with the language. "Keep eye on altar." She pointed her index finger to her eye and smiled.

I shrugged, and said, "I'll take care of your altar." I had become used to not seeing her regularly, so I could live a few days without her.

"You take care," I said. I held her hand a few seconds longer than usual. Then she took her hand from mine, and she dipped her head to one side. Then she opened the door just wide enough for her to slip out silently.

I did not know then, I would never see her again.

Eleven

On the day when I emerged from the Prince Hotel basement after my first session of two pipes that I had by myself, I saw, to my surprise, Phuoc sitting in the dingy lobby of the hotel smoking his usual Gitanes and sipping a small cup of tea. A clay pot of tea sat in front of him, and steam rose from its spout. Two pipes may have been two pipes too much for me. My feet felt like lead. My head was like an airy balloon. I smiled when I saw him and I pointed to me, as if to say, waiting for me.

"Yes," he answered. "Come with me," he said as he rose from his chair. "We can have more tea in another place."

Still, in a comfortable daze, I followed him into the street. *Lead on,* I thought. In my hazy state, I would follow Phuoc anywhere. We walked slowly down a depressing alley behind the Prince Hotel. Small children ran free, the back flap of the pants for boys and girls lay open allowing access when needed. These kids used the street as their bathroom, the same as the mangy dogs who also defecated and urinated in the street when the urge demanded. Older children ran and played after school. The small houses, more like shacks, were close together, almost on top of each other with little room between them except a narrow path. The neighborhood was poor like so many in Saigon, out of sight away from the main drag, and a mystery for the uninitiated. No Westerners ever went into such a neighborhood. Old men sat and smoked in the narrow front yards of their homes. Old women did the cooking and washing inside. The old survived because they were aged and useless in the war. Their sons, in some ways equally useless, and definitely wasted in a war they would never win, were away at combat, or at least in the army trying to stay out of combat. Daughters were at work or if lucky, in school.

The walk seemed to take forever. My mind slowly came back to reality as the opium wore off. We stopped by a large two-story home, out of place in this neighborhood of mostly shacks. In the front courtyard, behind a low wall, there were three tables and eight chairs made of plastic.

"This is a good place," remarked Phuoc.

We were in a restaurant run by the family who lived in the house. He motioned to me and we sat. A girl of perhaps fifteen came out and spoke to Phuoc in Vietnamese. Phuoc answered her and then he told me he ordered hot tea, Jasmine for him, harsher black tea for me, and warm French bread with butter, probably made in New Zealand from a can, and strawberry jam from Hong Kong the girl told him she had from the black market.

I lit a Camel, pulled up a second chair and stretched my legs across it. The hot sun felt good on my face but the pollution, always a problem in Saigon, made my eyes tear. I suffered from allergies when I lived in New York but many had disappeared after I came to Saigon. Some were still active but less so, despite the heavy vegetation, and only when I went into the field. Luckily, I never sneezed when on patrol. That would have been disastrous and dangerous for me and the other men.

We didn't talk, preferring to luxuriate in the sun until the tea and bread arrived a few minutes after we sat. Phuoc placed his package of Gitanes on the table, tapped out another cigarette and lit it. His harsh tobacco made my nose twitch. Phuoc poured the tea, mine, the stronger drink, from my pot. Our waitress sat on her haunches by the inside door of the house watching us, but never moving a muscle. She exhibited the patience of the Vietnamese, a virtue beyond my understanding. The opium hangover allowed me to think I saw a projector inside the young woman's head that played a slide with the words, "This too, shall pass." It also said, "You Americans, as with all the other invaders, will vanish in time." I knew I could see that, but I couldn't guarantee what I saw inside her to be anything other than a figment of my imagination.

Phuoc and I drank, ate and smoked. "Maybe you can help me," he said. "How?"

"Tell me what you know about John Castle and his operations." Phuoc dragged deeply on his cigarette.

The opium almost gone from my system, I paused and took a deep breath. We had discussed Castle, but never in detail. How much did Phuoc know and how much could I reveal without compromising and endangering myself?

I know very little," I offered.

"Please, Mr. Adam," he said. When he used "mister" before my first name, not my last, I knew Phuoc to be serious. I could sense the disdain in his voice. A frown crossed his face. "You know much. I know that. Do not take me for a fool." Anger, something I had never known, crept into his voice.

I fumbled my way in starting to talk, finding myself hemming and hawing, but he stopped me before I said anything. He told me he knew about Castle and the drugs he peddled, but it didn't bother him. "I am after bigger fish," he said. "You have more information. It is that information I want. I want to know about the brothels he runs that he thinly disguises as laundries. I want to know the number of women in each laundry.

"More importantly," he continued, "I want to get an understanding about Castle and women. How does he treat those women? Do they suffer? Are they happy, though I do not believe any prostitute is happy."

Phuoc told me he knew that Castle had four laundries. His spies found it fascinating that some women, usually the older whores, really washed and ironed clothing between turning tricks, my word, not his. Phuoc thought it unbelievable.

"They do my laundry and they do a really good job, especially with my shirts. It took a while but they now understand when I tell them, no starch in the collars." I smiled.

My guilt probably too strong to resist Phuoc's plea, I told him what I knew, first about the drugs.

I said that Castle had runners, many only thirteen and fourteen, who distributed packages of cigarettes soaked in heroin. First, his people would cut the bottom paper and cellophane of the pack with a sharp razor. Without removing the individual cigarettes, they use a hypodermic needle to carefully inject each cigarette with a shot of heroin. After the cigarettes dried, the worker resealed the bottom of the pack. The runners then sent the packages to newsstands and stores that sell books, yes, books, throughout the city. Rarely did any buyer take a whole pack. Too expensive. Users bought cigarettes one at a time. Sometimes a merchant sailor would buy a whole pack before shipping out. Most buyers were American soldiers, construction workers and other civilians. Whole packs made their way to military bases like Long Binh, An Khe and Cu Chi where users could pick then up at the real laundries that ringed those locations. Rarely did a Vietnamese buy drug injected smokes. Surviving each day was hard enough for the South Vietnamese without developing a drug habit. Anyway, and Phuoc knew this, most Vietnamese preferred opium if they could afford it. Opium had an upper-class tone to it that heroin did not. They would rather use hashish flakes or hashish oil they could mix with food or put in a pipe combined with tobacco. Before the war ended, though, using hard drugs would be a problem in South Vietnam.

Phuoc told me stop talking about drugs. "Enough, please," he said.

Though important, his interest centered on the deaths of the prostitutes, and not on drugs and their distribution. He wanted to jail the man who had been killing the young women. He called them girls. They were girls in a dangerous trade and they were dying. He hated that they lost their lives so young. Phuoc had a simple mission to solve those crimes. His life would then be complete. Solve the murders and save the girls. Phuoc told me he believed Castle had something to do with the killings. Despite his lack of interest in how Castle distributed his drugs, Phuoc knew that drugs drove the killer. Phuoc did not believe a sane man, a man in his right mind, would kill that many women indiscriminately. He wanted the information from me before the killer struck again.

Phuoc said this to me gently. He made no threats, yet I knew he had the power to make my life miserable if I didn't cooperate. He could have the foreign ministry pull my press credentials and yank my visa. He could put me in jail. He could have me thrown out of the country. I didn't want to leave. I had too much unfinished business with Trang. I had to sort out my life and the trap I found myself in with Castle, in which I had willingly put myself. Now caught between the drug-addled madness of John Castle and the deep Buddhist ethic of Inspector Hong Phuoc, I had to find a way to free myself and live. Castle frightened me more than Phuoc. Castle, because he followed no laws, had a longer and more menacing reach than Phuoc. Yet, it made sense for me to throw in with Phuoc. He, at least, represented the honest and true, the real me, where I wanted to be, not the man I had become in a moment of desperation. Only time would tell if I had made the right decision.

When I started talking again, Phuoc didn't shut me down. I told him he understood Castle's operation better than he admitted. Castle had me as the only American working for him for reasons I didn't understand. He had a South Vietnamese army deserter and several Filipinos whose visas had run out. There were a couple of ethnic Chinese from Cholon who specifically worked with drugs, a deserter from the Thai army and one Korean, a former band leader sent from Seoul to entertain the troops who fell in love with a prostitute and stayed.

Phuoc grunted. "I know about those men. Why did he hire you if he had them?"

I hesitated and then blurted out, "To keep tabs on you."

Phuoc smiled gently, almost proudly. "Did you? Did you keep those tabs on me, as you say?"

"To a degree, yes I did. But I never said anything to Castle. I told him about the opium after he had me followed. He didn't care that you used opium. He knew about it. Spies, again. He had many spies. His money bought information from everywhere. Castle thought opium an interesting touch. Back home, it would make you vulnerable. Not here. Here it made you special. He got angry with me because I had started to use opium and refused heroin. He hated that I thought heroin crude and life-threatening, but that I treated opium as unique and not habit forming. I know it could become a habit. But man, it is good, especially in those few hours after I use."

"Tell me more about his prostitutes."

"Usually they are young women who come from villages all over the south. Brought up decently and well, they are obedient to their family, especially their father. Selling themselves is furthest from their minds.

War makes life in the villages precarious. It's easier for the younger women to wander from tradition, and take a dangerous bus ride to a big town or even a city. There, work as a prostitute beckons, but for a Vietnamese woman it isn't honorable. For that matter, it isn't honorable in any society. Few remain in one place for more than several weeks before they move on to a bigger city with more opportunity. Each step along the way gets them in deeper to a life they can't escape. They are perfect for Castle and others like him. He isn't the only pimp. A few women stay longer with Castle and help run his laundries. When possible a woman goes to live with an American who is a construction worker, an army deserter, or sometimes an officer. That's the best deal they can find. But that doesn't happen to many. Occasionally a girl gets pregnant and leaves to have her baby elsewhere out of sight from her friends. She rarely returns to her village where she would be an outcast. Most of Castle's prostitutes are illiterate, though a few can read and write about the same as a child. That's my view of them. They are all pleasant young women, many pretty, caught beyond saving in the war. But you know all this, so why ask?"

"I am checking my knowledge against yours, a stranger to our culture and country. Everything you say is accurate. That is pleasing. It means you understand more than you realize. That, too, is pleasing. Based on what you told me, I now have to formulate a plan."

Phuoc nodded his head vigorously to show me he was deep in thought. He ran his fingers across his forehead and dragged deeply on his Gitanes, held tightly in his other hand. By then my head had cleared of the opium. The bright sun burned my eyes and I wished I had my sunglasses. I poured us more tea and picked the breadcrumbs off the plate, nibbling at them as I waited for him to say something. "Your assessment is quite good," he said, his BBC-accented English, as usual, perfect. With his use of assessment, and the inflection he gave to his sentence, I sometimes thought I might be listening to the World Service from London. I smiled and waited for him to continue.

"We have to have a plan," he said. "And the plan revolves around you keeping a close eye on Castle. You could be in deep trouble for breaking the law. Morally you made one big mistake. You were foolish to join with Castle. I do not know what you were thinking."

"Easy money? I thought I wanted a change of direction. I don't know. I was tired of selling myself for the right to cover stories that were often dangerous and not very satisfying." I shrugged, a child again, my wrist slapped by Hong Phuoc.

"I will help you solve your problem, but you must help me. I want you to tell me everything about Castle. No. Not what you just told me. I want to know what he does every day. I want to know where he goes. You have to observe him carefully. Does he have scratches on his arms? We have discovered skin under the nails of the last dead girl, as I told you. Perhaps she struggled and scratched him when she tried to defend herself. Are his fingernails broken? A strong man using his bare hands strangled each woman. Perhaps he broke a nail when he killed. Are his knuckles bruised? All the girls were brutally beaten. No man can walk away from beating someone that badly without broken skin on his fists."

I knew I would soon see Castle. Normally I tried not looking at him when we met. When I looked too closely at him, he squirmed in his seat and managed to turn away. He was not a handsome man, probably a reason he hated scrutiny. Once he asked me why I stared at him so long. I tried telling him I was looking past him or through him, and not at him. He didn't buy my explanation, but I tried being careful in the future. I saw no need to anger him, especially when he smoked as much heroin as he did. I thought of the clichés to describe him: short fuse, a loose cannon. Then I thought how unpredictable he might be. No longer in the Air Force, being responsible only to himself, he could and did whatever he wanted. Danger and Castle were synonymous. Not a brave man, I didn't want to give Castle the opportunity to test my courage when I thought I would surely lose to a man who seemingly cared little about his own life and nothing about the life of his opponent.

"You are young. Your life has many years left for you to do much. When I succeed in ridding the world of John Castle, I will free you from your lethargy. Then you will leave Saigon and start over somewhere else. Perhaps you will write this story. When you do, please treat me kindly. Until then, we have work to do. I am depending on you, Mr. Adam Berg."

I looked at my hands, their fingers picked to the cuticles, unhappy and caught in a web of greed and deceit. I felt sorry for myself, but I knew it to be temporary, and that there were possibilities for redemption. I repeated that to myself: redemption had possibilities and I looked forward to them. In biblical times, it might have required a conversion, but in Saigon in 1967, I had to concentrate on rescuing myself from a hole with slippery walls that I had difficulty climbing to freedom. I needed handholds and Phuoc just might be the answer. We walked out of the alley, with me following just a pace behind Phuoc. It made me feel safe. When we reached the street, we parted, I to my apartment, Phuoc to who knew where.

Twelve

Deep asleep, on the morning following the opium experience I had alone without Phuoc, my first intense opium experience by myself, yes, two pipes for the first time, followed by my long tea and talk session, I heard heavy knocking at my apartment door, insistent, impatient, hands banged on the wood, imploring me to get up. Hands that were small, but very strong. I did get up, and stumbled to the door, shouting from my interrupted sleep, wanting to know who had the nerve to wake me and enter my dreams, half-formed, yet more distant than usual.

"Who's there?" I said.

"It is me, sir, Nam, from the laundry." "What the fuck do you want?"

"Mister Castle, he said you come with me now. He not see you for many days. He want see you now."

"Balls," I mumbled to myself, but knowing I had no choice, I opened the door and saw standing there, Nam, at twelve years old, already a towel boy in Castle's whorehouse, the one I called the main laundry, where I went every morning for coffee and a freshly baked baguette. Without even shuffling his feet, he entered my one room apartment on a hop and a skip. Then he stood there, unsure what to do to next, his bravado dissolved once inside my room and looking at me in my underwear. He saw naked and nearly naked American men all the time because the brothels were busy places. As one of his bosses, he didn't think he would ever see me undressed. After all, I stopped using any of the women for pleasure and he knew as they, I never would use them again, because I did not need them.

"You come now. Mister Castle want you now." He started pulling on my arm but I shook him off as if he were a flea.

"Not until I'm ready. First I have to shower, and then get dressed.

Then I'll go. Now, get out before I lose my temper."
"I wait for you."

"Not here. Go back downstairs and when I'm ready I'll be there." Nam understood what I said, but his eyes revealed that he would rather stay inside and wait. He had never been inside an American apartment and he suspected we lived differently from the Vietnamese. Well, I did live differently, but not that much. Except for my bathroom with its Western toilet, I sometimes slept on reed mats that I covered with a sheet. I had a small, bed, a cot, really, which Trang and I shared for making love, but many nights the floor did just as well for me. I had stick wood chests for my clothing and personal effects. I had a small desk I picked up from a neighborhood school for my gray Royal portable typewriter. I had no telephone—personal phones were rare in Saigon—and never used the kitchen to cook. I stocked my refrigerator only with cans of Budweiser, Heineken, and bottles of juice I bought in the PX. I also kept in the fridge about a dozen rolls of Kodak Tri-X black-and-white film in case I had an assignment to take photos. I had two windows that faced an alley and at night, I covered them with blinds made of the same reed that covered my floor.

"No, Nam," I said. "You can't stay here. Wait downstairs and I'll join you soon." I gave him fifty piasters. "Get me a double espresso and a loaf of French bread with butter and get something for yourself."

Disappointed he could not bring me with him as instructed, Nam left. I locked the door, showered, dressed and met him in front of the apartment fifteen minutes later. My breakfast waited, as did the cyclo. I joined Nam in the basket seat and we were on our way. I sipped my coffee and chewed on my bread during the ride. I had not seen Castle in many days and wondered why the sudden summons as we rolled through the crush of Saigon traffic in the still cool morning. I opened *The Saigon Post* I had picked up at the corner newsstand.

The Saigon Post, May 10, 1967 (Page 2)

Police said a young woman thought to be in her twenties was found dead yesterday morning near Tan Son Nhut Airport. Her body had been hidden in the weeds behind poorly built shacks in a back alley near an American bachelor's quarters. Police said the woman had been raped and strangled. There were severe bruises on her face and body. Police are continuing their investigation but do not expect to be successful. Chief Inspector Hong Phuoc said, "Unfortunately in war with so many foreigners in Saigon, it will be difficult to apprehend her killer."

Another morning. Another killing. They would either end soon or go on forever. I believed they were a result of the war. I didn't know how many other killings like these occurred when the country wasn't at war, but war had been part of life since the late 1930s and in 1967, I saw nothing changing in the future.

Castle. Castle. Castle. His name rolled around inside my head as the cyclo plowed its way through Saigon's traffic. I wondered what I had gotten myself into and where it would lead. I knew what he did was illegal, thus, I, too, had become a criminal, of sorts. He paid me. I willingly took his money. I could not accept that I had become a serious criminal, or a dangerous criminal. But I functioned as a criminal, none-the-less. I knew I had also become a voyeur of sorts. At least, that's how I thought of myself. Castle told me he provided a service to lonely and unhappy men by running prostitutes in his laundries. A doctor visited them once every week to give them a shot of penicillin whether they needed it or not. He said they were as clean as the clothing they washed. When some girls weren't working at washing, drying and ironing clothes, they earned their keep on their backs, or whatever position a person preferred. Castle joked about his women doing backbreaking labor. I didn't think him funny, but I smiled anyway, afraid not to because he could lash out at me physically and possibly verbally, always willing to hurt first and reason second.

I hardly did any real work for him. When I started the job, I collected receipts for services, but not money. I never touched money. Then after two weeks, he told me to stop handling any paper at all. He wanted me to continue visiting his four laundry brothels as his representative, he said. But he didn't want me involved in their administration. The ladies, as he called his whores, had to be aware that someone is watching them. He told me he could not be everywhere. They need someone to keep on an eye on them, he said. They didn't know I had no power but my size would be enough to keep them in line. Castle reminded me to take whatever I wanted. Taste the girls, he said. It will do you good, he suggested. Take what you want, when you want, but don't spoil the goods. These women are weak, yet they appeared to enjoy their work. At the beginning, when I took advantage of Castle's largess, I never demanded more than any women could deliver. I managed to be gentle and never cruel. Because they would take no money from me, I often tipped those I spent an hour or two with by giving them the perfumes they loved, all available cheaply on the black market—Dior, Channel No. 5, Ma Griffe, Soire de Paris.

Most of the girls were prostitutes by necessity. Like Trang, they had to earn a living in a society disrupted by war and traditionally closed to and hostile to women. Only Trang chose another path. Uneducated women might find menial work like washing floors or sweeping streets. Educated women, those who had a smattering of another language, sometimes found work in tourist shops and American or other foreign-run businesses. Castle's women were different. Despite being whores,

I never understood their justification of doing laundry between tricks. I thought it might be a fallback position in case the sex business failed. My inability to speak Vietnamese and their reluctance to divulge their feelings, didn't allow me to understand the reasoning behind their dual role.

Lee, my Vietnamese photographer friend, tried to explain that a thousand years of subservience made women what they were—and he would not have it any other way. Lee, who was part Chinese, spoke some French, and enough English to get along well with the Americans whom he depended on for his living. He told me to back away from Trang. He insisted, she and I could never be a couple, my term, not his, because there were too many cultural differences for us to be successful. Before Trang and I had become intimate, Lee reminded me to stop being a hopeless romantic. He told me plainly to start sleeping with her soon or someone else will, and then, in Lee's words, I would be up the creek, fucked by my own goodness.

Lee had high moral standards about life, particularly about good and evil. Raised as a Buddhist, by a Chinese father and a Vietnamese mother, most of his philosophy would confuse a Westerner, but he didn't care. After covering the war for five years, he lived in a world of black and white, literally and figuratively. Though so much around him was lush and green in all shapes and forms, Lee preferred to shoot in black and white. He believed it told a better story than color. He loved to see the violent contrasts that evolved in low-level light under the dense jungle. The color gray had no place in Lee's view of the world. When the AP started shooting color, Lee resisted, despite the roll of color, his photo chief gave him when he went into the field. He insisted that his reality happened in black and white. He told me color is not real, and suggested I look at life and Trang the same way. Sure, he said, Trang is sweet, just as are red and green and orange, but colors fade. Lee reminded me to enjoy Trang before her color faded. I agreed with Lee's thinking on still photography. Color took heart from a scene and sometimes made me turn away in disbelief that something I knew as ugly could be so beautiful. But his reflections on Trang were troubling. Lee did not know I had already made love to Trang. Like Lee, I believed, if I had not done so, I might lose her to someone else and to the war. We had made love several times a week since our first time and each time we were more comfortable. It didn't surprise me she had already lost her virginity. I could understand that she had once been sexually active. I didn't care. Many girls grew up fast in Vietnam because of the war, though most didn't become prostitutes. It felt right that I didn't take her virginity. I would not have gotten any excitement from that because I didn't collect pelts.

Castle believed otherwise. He told me taking virgins had to count among his greatest accomplishments. After, he said, the girl thanked him, and begged him not to tell anyone what happened. Some girls, he told me, thanked him for the joy he gave them and a few, after mild coaxing, agreed to work in one of his laundries.

After I arrived at his number one laundry in Skag Alley, we shook hands and then we sat outside sipping dark coffee. For the first few minutes we smoked. We said nothing. Once chubby when he was in the Air Force, but now a free man, he trimmed down to where he was skinny. Thin as a pencil sharpened to almost nothing, Castle looked like the nub of a man, a wraith where once he resembled a fatted calf. He ate on the economy, meaning almost no starch, some rice and noodles, little meat of what was available, and vegetables. He had whittled down his size and increased his intake of drugs, but I didn't think he had started mainlining. That would have been the end. Castle's face reflected his drug use, being lean now, with deep shadows under his eyes, an ugly man with no handsome features. He shaved every other day because razors irritated his skin in Saigon's heat.

"Tell me about Trang," he said to me, his voice sounded like a file against iron, a permanent scratch from inside his throat.

I said nothing, a catch in my throat preventing me from answering. "Don't be surprised I know her name."

"She's just a very pretty girl I met in Bar California." I recovered enough to respond, but not enough to mask my emotions.

"Watch out for the pretty ones. They will get you and hold you and make your life difficult," he warned with a grunt and his usual self- satisfied giggle.

I wanted to know how he knew about Trang. I thought I kept it a secret, especially from him. He laughed.

"I know all the girls in Saigon, professional and part-timers. But I know the ones who work Tu Do Street best, especially those who work at the Bar California."

"Spies?" I wanted to know.

"No," he said. "Ownership. I own a piece of the Bar California, your home away from home. I get a cut of everything. That means that I know everything that goes on there every night. Do you think I first met you when I escorted you and the other hacks around Tan Son Nhut? Don't be stupid. True, we met by accident out there. Call that coincidence, but I spotted you at the bar weeks before. Call our meeting at the base nothing less than good luck."

John Castle smirked, the muscles in his face hardened, and his eyes glittered strangely.

The situation infuriated me but I said nothing. There I was, keeping watch on Phuoc for him. Then I became Phuoc's friend at Castle's insistence. Phuoc trusted me at the beginning, even to sharing an occasional pipe and teaching me about opium. Now learning that Castle had his hands in more things than I realized, including Castle having Trang watch me and report to him made me very nervous. Worse, it irritated me to find myself in this maze of distrust. Trang. Castle. Most likely the bartender. Surely, some other girls at the bar also watched my moves. I believed that Phuoc must also have been watching me, looking at me as an object and not a person. Thinking about it, I realized he and I had nothing in common. There were about twenty years between us, and we were from two worlds that could never get together. I thought about Phuoc and his motives for our friendship, and I became wary of its reality. Did we have a real friendship, did Phuoc only use me as a sounding board for his theory about the five or six brutally murdered young women? I had no doubt that Phuoc wanted me to help get enough evidence against Castle. When he had what he needed from me, would he discard me like rubbish? I knew I would know in time and I didn't want to consider how I might suffer.

Another ugly thought had to do with opium. I had no discipline. Opium reached into me quickly. It was all-consuming. Did Phuoc see that? Did he know I would try the pipe and when I did, that I would enjoy it and maybe start on the road to being hooked? Did Phuoc as a guru from the mysterious East look at me and say to himself, there goes a man made for addiction? And once he discovered how easily I had become friends with the pipe, did he have me where he wanted? Sadly, I knew there would always be opium for me in Asia. Was that a sign of my growing addiction? I had heard that opium makes one addicted only after a long time, but for each person, time means something different. Just as I couldn't judge how long it would take me, that is, how many pipes it would take before I sunk to the lowest depths, I found it hard to guess where I would be in the future when the struggle ended between John Castle and Hong Phuoc.

I decided never to underestimate Mr. Castle again. His knowledge of Trang and our then budding, now consummated relationship troubled me. But he didn't know we were full-time lovers. It meant that his spying didn't always pay off. Did he send her to me? I didn't think so. If so, I didn't want to know. Did our meeting happen by pure chance, enabling Castle to take advantage of Trang and me? I believed that to be possible. Castle worked best when he could take advantage of opportunity. I had no doubt she reported my movements to him or to one of his Vietnamese minions. How did I reconcile her spying with what I detected as the start of affection, if not love, from Trang? I might be wrong about her but I wondered about her talent as an actor and her ability to fool me. Could I be wrong about everything?

I decided to find out more about Trang before Castle had his chance to further embarrass me. Sitting across from him, I alone knew that Trang had been going to bed with me, love or not. He didn't know how far we had gone in our relationship. At least, that part of my life remained private. As infatuated as I had become, sex still ruled. I had no thoughts of marriage. I wanted to justify my existence as a man. I would give Trang an opportunity to prove herself to me as a friend and lover. I knew Trang had already given as much as she got. I felt that every time I touched Trang. I found it hard to understand why she wanted so little from me. She never took money from me. When I went to the PX, her needs, the things she ordered, were far from greedy. When I smoked opium, I dreamed that someday our story might fit into the book I hoped to write. Despite Castle's reach, I felt safe from his prying eyes. His spies may have seen Trang enter my apartment, but they never knew what really went on behind the closed doors and the drawn bamboo shades.

"Do you get money from Trang for working the bars?" I asked Castle, knowing that some girls paid the manager of the bar where they worked for the right to use their charm on unsuspecting Westerners with big bankrolls.

"It's the other way around. I pay her and the others. She gets a cut from me."

"Is she your informant for everything?" Castle laughed.

"Yes and no. All the girls pass me information, but only when I ask. They never volunteer. When I threaten them with losing their job, they speak freely. Most speak hardly any English so what they tell me is worthless. Sometimes they tell me more than I want to know. I find much of what they say hard to believe. About you, Trang says very little. She says you rarely touch her. Occasionally you stroke the skin on her arm. You go to lunch. You're very proper. You've never seen her after curfew. She thinks you're very strange not to demand more for feeding her and dropping twenty or thirty bucks a night at the bar just to talk."

Castle knew too much, but he didn't know everything. He made me feel small because he had invaded my life. I signed on with him for a change and to put a charge in my life, not to let him dominate me. My trust and faith in Trang as a person of integrity nearly died, but my love for her became stronger. In some ways, she didn't control her life. I resented that Castle had a hand in how she lived, and I hated him for it. I also knew I could do almost nothing to change the system. Of course, I knew she worked men for a living. I assumed she didn't sell her body but Castle, ever the instigator, instilled doubt in me. I felt used and didn't enjoy it.

"She's not a whore, though. I hope," I said.

"Yes and no. Because you don't see her sleep with anyone means nothing. She may not be pure." Castle shrugged. "I don't think she's a virgin. Few of the girls are. Many start sex early here. When they get to the big city, some have the first opportunity alone and away from home to try something new. But I don't think she's been with an American."

Castle leaned into me and leered. I felt his recklessness, especially the insensitivity that came from his cold indifference. I smelled the beer and the tobacco on his breath, and the sweat from his body mixed with Johnson's baby powder he sprinkled liberally over himself. I knew Castle treated nothing as sacred. I knew that he had to have no fear doing what he did. His paranoia ruled him in every way. Castle stayed alive by being suspicious of everyone and of having no friends. Had he a friend, it would mean his guard might slip. One slip could mean everything would end. I supposed Castle believed he had too much life left to give in to defeat or death. He frightened me, and he knew it, something I had trouble facing and admitting. I had to do everything I could to show him that I was loose, and not worried in his presence, a difficult task. As much as I loathed the thought that I had been mislead into believing Trang special, I still had faith in what we had become and where we could be in the future, despite my lack of commitment.

"Be her first American before someone else beats you to it. Just like I might. Maybe. I sometimes get the itch. That's what I do. I take these girls and mold them to my liking. Then they are ready to provide a needed service."

John Castle leaned back, now a smug smile on his thin face. If I could see inside his head, I thought I would detect that he felt invulnerable, exalted even, intoxicated yet without being frenzied. Castle closed his eyes and for all I knew, he napped in front of me, the beer definitely working on him, perhaps some drugs taken earlier were having their effect. We were silent. Suddenly he sat up and he dragged deeply on the stub of his cigarette. After holding the smoke long, he let it out slowly and, ever thoughtful, offered me one from his pack of Pall Mall.

"Heroin?" I said.

"Yeah. It's light. I supervise the packing. I know its purity. It can't hurt. Look at me. Steady as a rock." He held his hand out. Yes. I could see, steady as a rock. I wondered how he would be later when he didn't smoke. I thought about what went on in his head and body. How fast did his heart beat, and mostly what did the drug do to his brain? Besides, drugs ruined a man's blood pressure and wrecked his appetite. I never saw Castle eat anything but sweets, mainly freshly baked pastries.

"No thanks," I told him.

I didn't exactly say that drugs, his hard drugs, scared me, but he got the picture.

"I'll stick to beer and cigarettes," I said. "That way all I'll only get a headache, and a sore throat."

He told me he wanted something else from me. He didn't think I did enough watching the laundries. He pointed to his cigarette, took one final drag and crushed the remainder under the heel of his boot. He told me what he wanted.

"I want you to work these," and he pointed to his pack of cigarettes, "into street markets everywhere in Saigon."

I made a face that plainly said, no. I could never do that. My heart felt huge in my chest. That would be crossing the line and once over, I could not be sure I would find the way back. Yes, I liked the money Castle gave me for sedentary guard duty. I liked the profit I made from selling stolen watches and cameras when I went into the countryside as a real reporter to recharge my reality batteries and forget my criminal activities. But pushing drugs would be out of the question.

"No way," I said.

"Man. Oh, man, Adam Berg" he said. "Don't play me for the fool," he shouted.

His sudden anger surprised me. His face flushed and grew strangely contorted. Then, instead of raising his voice, he whispered, that sound again, like a file on metal. Though his voice cut through me, it brought me back to the sights and sounds on the street.

"I know what you do when you go with Phuoc. You tell me H is bad. What about opium? Come on, man. How many pipes you up to? How often, man? You know it's bad for sex. You know you can't get it up after awhile? Do you want that weird shit in your life, and all those dreams? I can make your life real. I pay you to look after Phuoc and become part of him. What do you do? You tell me nothing about him, but he makes you part of him. How can you understand him if he owns you? Opium will do that. I never smoke it. Makes me too dreamy, too easy, too out of it. The more opium you use, the more ownership over you it and Phuoc will have, and the less valuable to me you'll be. The pipe will own you, man. I own you because I pay you. Just because he buys you a pipe or two, doesn't mean he's your new boss. I'm your boss! You report to me. Don't bullshit me. Not anymore. And don't judge me because of what smoke."

I looked at him in wonder. I never heard Castle say so much at once. I heard what he said, and made mental notes. True, I hadn't reported anything to him because I thought I had nothing. I misjudged his need for information, any information, no matter its quality or value. He wanted to be the judge. He wanted to decide the value of what I told him. All control freaks were like that and Castle fit the mold. That he knew about the opium didn't make me happy. Nothing that day did. My batting average dipped lower than ever.

Castle didn't know, but I still didn't have the trust of the manager at the Prince Hotel. It didn't matter how many times I went there, made my way to the basement, and paid for my pipes. The manager let me enter his opium den anytime I wanted, but he no longer prepared my pipe. He gave that job to the emaciated young man who was always there either sitting on his haunches watching everyone or scurrying around like a crab helping whoever needed it. The regulars, deep in their opium dreams, took no notice of me. We couldn't speak to each other anyway, so why acknowledge my existence. I liked it that way. I was anonymous in the basement, but I shuddered when I thought about meeting anyone from the opium den on the street. I knew that made no sense. Those men hardly were on the street, unless in the dark. All were in a deep trance, their eyes wide open, their noses running, an unlit cigarette dangling from the corner of their mouth. They didn't know who they were. How could they know me? I relaxed despite Castle leaning on me emotionally.

Castle smoked and said nothing, waiting patiently for me to respond.

"Man. I pay for my own pipes. It's only a few days a week and usually I'm alone. I am not with Phuoc. I can still get it up, by the way. Ask the girls in the laundries. I can still get up," I insisted. Though not true, I had to lie to keep the fiction alive that I still made use of, Castle's phrase, not mine, the whores he allowed me as a reward.

"Can't take a joke?" "I can't about that."

"Let's get something straight. It's time you learned you're on my payroll until I let you go. Or you leave the country. Or go to jail or die. I don't see any of those happening. You know too much. Start talking to me and telling me things I want to know about before I really get angry."

His voice now normal, he dragged deeply on another cigarette laced with heroin and waited for my reply. His eyes narrowed. He breathed harder. I could see the drug work its way into his system. I watched him relax, his tension dissipating. Despite that, what I saw in Castle, he still frightened me. My pulse beat more rapidly than normal. I sweated freely. He smiled as he watched my unease. I could tell the heroin, though mild in his cigarette, he said, had already had an effect on him but because he already smoked so many, he was high, but I hoped gently.

I changed my approach, realizing I didn't have the strength or desire to challenge Castle.

"I can't put anything over on you. You're too smart for that. Sure I smoke opium," I said, "but I only do one or two pipes at a sitting twice a week. That's hardly habitual. Hardly habitual," I repeated because I wanted to make sure he understood me.

While we talked, the sounds of the neighborhood and from the nearby traffic dipped away into a mild buzz, as if white noise with an added decibel. The noise rose and fell with our conversation. I sometimes thought we were in a vacuum. I heard Castle breathing. I could feel myself breathing. I knew Castle had me under his microscope. I understood what being in the grip of fear meant. He carried a side arm, a thirty-eight police special, polished to high black metallic sheen, fully loaded, with one bullet in the chamber for a quick shot. I carried no weapon. I grew up believing my mind was my best weapon. With Castle, I had no defense against his possible recklessness. He could be violent and had probably been often in his past. Who knew what the future would bring? I didn't want to tempt him into anything rash.

Because Phuoc wanted to know, I had asked the girls I once slept with if they knew any girls who had been beaten. I never questioned any girl unless we previously had sex. I thought to have had sex allowed me the opportunity or gave me the right to ask a few questions. I didn't want to take advantage of my position. I realized, too, they were afraid of me and that they would never say anything to Castle. They always told me they knew no one who was beaten. Yet I could not help but notice that more than one girl had bruises on her neck and face. When asked, they said, you know, drunk GI, drunk sailor, sometime wild. Just a little bit. No harm, said one girl. But pay very good, she told me.

I never directly asked any girl if Castle ever beat them. I thought that too dangerous a question. I considered it possible, but I didn't want to face Castle had it been true and it got out that I showed interest in how he lived his life. Yet, as he slept, or what I took to be Castle asleep, I noticed recent scratches on the insides of his forearms. At least they looked recent and they were scratch marks, not needle marks. I saw the broken fingernails on his right hand and recoiled, just enough to rattle my chair. *It could be anything,* I thought, and I shut my mind to what I realized it might be.

Castle woke up with a start. As if shot from a cannon. I, too, jumped.

"Stop gawking at me," said Castle.

I choked on my words, and gave a hefty cough. I rubbed my hand across my face.

"I'm not staring. I'm just curious about your arms." I paused and knew I had gone further than I wanted, further than I probably should have. He didn't care. He paused and I waited for him to reply or not.

"Oh, these." He grinned, rolled his sleeves to his elbows and pushed his forearms close to my face. I recoiled, turned my face sideways, and held my breath. I always held my breath around Castle. When I talked to John Castle, fear worked against my effort at reason.

"A girl, a very young one, scratched me when I got too rough with her. I like rough sex. Sometimes these creatures that work for me are too gentle, so I goad them into doing things they don't do normally. Then I have a good time, the kind of time I want. I call them creatures because they're there for me when I want, how I want. And it doesn't cost me a dime." He laughed. Then he continued. "I know you dip as often as you like, so wipe that critical look from your face. You're no better than I am when it comes to these women."

I agreed, but I when I was with a girl before Trang, I tried to treat her with dignity and never force her where she had not gone before. "I've been reading about those missing and dead girls," I said. I thought I must be mad to say even that to Castle. I didn't think he killed anyone, but could I be sure?

"Yeah. I read about some of them. So what. It's war. Just another dead person. Who'll miss them? Their parents? If they care, maybe. If they know where they are, maybe. They're worn out. Some are worn down to where no one cares. I don't care. After a while, they are damaged goods."

"Are any of your girls missing?"

"So far, none. The girls come and go. They disappear and reappear. If they return, I check them out personally to make sure they can still work and I rehire them or tell them to get lost. When they get some money, and you know this, many leave. Sometimes they return to their village to help their family. Sometimes they find a man. And occasionally they die from disease or are killed. Then nothing matters to them or anyone else."

He lit another cigarette, dragged deeply, and screwed up his eyes like in a gangster movie.

"Why the interest?" he asked.

"I'm thinking about a magazine story. I'm trying to learn everything I can so I have a better chance of placing it. People back home like stories about dead prostitutes and war. Exotic stories make money."

He grinned crookedly and sighed. "Still at it, huh? I thought you gave up by now."

"No. Reporting is still with me. When I see a good story, I find it hard to turn away."

"I don't know why you persist, but tell you what, anything I find out, I'll tell you first," he said.

I had two things on my mind. I had to report what I knew to Phuoc and I had to find Trang. I had not seen her for four days, a long time for us. I would give her one more day before I started to panic. Sometimes, three or four days would go by without my seeing Trang. She would go see her mother and give her money. Her absence usually didn't concern me. By going home, she refueled for her longer stays in Saigon. She would wear simple cotton pajamas. They were the comfortable kind Vietnamese wore every day. Home cooking and family gave her time to forget her work as a bar girl, something she said she had come to detest. Trang traveled home by bus through what we called VC country where Saigon stationed only a few South Vietnamese troops over the vast expanse of the Mekong delta down Highway One. The armed local civilians, though they had uniforms and weapons, had hardly any training and were the same as having no support or protection at all. Yet, Trang, as other Vietnamese, braved the journey because returning to one's roots was very important for the Vietnamese. I worried each time she went home and I worried until she returned. But I could not go to her village to find her because I would have been out of line. I had no right to reach that deeply into her private life. I could only imagine my appearing in a delta village, alone, unarmed, and speaking almost no Vietnamese. That would be a mess, impossible for our relationship to continue. Anyway, I would never make such a trip. For an American, it held more danger than for a Vietnamese. I may have been naive in understanding the Vietnamese but I wasn't stupid or a fool. I could die. My premature death did not interest me.

"You'll also tell me if Trang shows," I said.

"Maybe," he said. A wide grin crossed his face and when it did, his upper lip curled over his front teeth, exposing a missing molar, as if the entrance to a fetid cave.

I paused and started to rise. I told him thanks. Anything he could tell me about the dead women would make the story strong and I wanted him to know I appreciated his help.

Then, although I had been watching him smoke, I never really looked at his hands. Suddenly they came alive in front of me. I noticed his knuckles were rough and chapped, red as if they had been in water too long. Almost all his fingernails were broken. I thought he had been biting his nails, but then I realized they were broken and uneven, possibly from pulling or dragging a heavy load. They were not even or smooth. It seemed the condition of his fingers was not the result of his systematically chewing or picking at them. I involuntarily gave a small shudder that I hoped was not too visible to Castle's eyes. I found everything Phuoc told me to look for in Castle. Were his scratches and broken nails only the result of Castle's daily life? I was queasy and light headed. I had to get out of there and away from John Castle before he became suspicious. I got up quickly and left him. I stumbled down the street as if I were drunk, so I thought. Castle probably paid no attention to me and, just as well.

Thirteen

Two days later, another killing made the local papers. That was six days to be exact since I had last seen Trang. There was still no trace of her. The international press, too busy covering the war, as expected, ignored the deaths. Without seeing the pattern and realizing the number of dead women, they would not do a story about five or six dead whores spread over many months. That happened in every war, and no one cared. Well, not really. Family cared. Friends cared. I cared, in my way, though I could not be sure why. Faced with mounting American casualties, there would be scant room in even a tabloid or on the back page of any United States paper for a few dead Vietnamese women. One dead woman here and there, meant little to people when American soldiers were dying by the hundreds each week. But in Saigon, detective Inspector Hong Phuoc had decided he had to solve the crimes. His sleepless nights dragged on because he cared if no one else did.

The Saigon Daily News, June 11, 1967 (Page 2)

The cruel fifth or sixth death of a young woman over the last six months was announced this morning by the Saigon Police. In a sparsely attended news conference at National Police Headquarters on Tran Hong Dao, Chief Inspector Hong Phuoc of the murder-robbery squad discussed the recent death. "This death fits the same pattern as the other five or six, starting in December last year. The timings, one month apart, and the manner of death, rape, a brutal beating and strangulation, are the same for all. We have been unable to identify any of the young women who were killed. We implore the public to come forward with any information it has. Of course, we will keep anything you tell us, confidential." There were no questions. Our reporter took his notes and departed. The girl, thought to be in her teens, was buried in a simple Buddhist service. Only one Buddhist monk attended the funeral. He said he hoped they would discover her name so her soul would not wander aimlessly and restlessly for too long.

As expected, no one came forward. Phuoc knew no one ever would. Why should they, he thought, when there was nothing in it for them? There was no reward. There would be nothing but trouble should they speak up. Their neighbors might think them police informers. The pitfalls of daily living worked against people coming to the police as eyewitnesses. Anyway, many police were corrupted and out for themselves. Better to know something and keep it to yourself, than to expose yourself unnecessarily to people you didn't trust. Phuoc knew he had to rely on his own investigation using his limited Vietnamese sources, which didn't help much, and what he could glean from me, Adam Berg. At first I, too, had little to add.

I met Phuoc at the Broda coffee house, a small café near Tu Do Street, where the ever-decreasing number of Vietnamese intellectuals met to have what they thought would be free and unrestrained conversation. They understood, though, that some of their friends were police informers, yet it didn't deter their license to think and speak how they wanted. They didn't condemn the snitches and usually gave them enough information to keep their masters in the intelligence services happy. Many in the café knew Phuoc to be a detective first and a government man last. He sometimes engaged in their lively discussions about art and literature, professing a particular joy in Marcel Proust, whom he continued to read in French when he wanted to escape the rigors of life in Saigon.

"So you finally announced another death," I said.

"Yes, but I believe there are more but we have not yet discovered them. Prostitutes always die. Some accidentally, others in a fit of rage by the customers, a few from drug-addled sailors or construction workers or the occasional GI, drunk or stupid from heroin. Those deaths don't bother me because they happen from momentary madness. I use the word accidentally to describe these deaths. The ones I am after are deliberate and as I said in my news conference, cruel."

Phuoc answered me carefully, then raised his cup to his lips, and slowly sipped his espresso. After swallowing, he dragged deeply on his cigarette and exhaled the smoke through his nose.

"I have more to tell you about Castle, but I don't know where to start," I said.

I paused because I found it hard to tell Phuoc that Castle frightened me. Putting it mildly, he scared me out of my wits. I knew John Castle could do things to me, anything he wanted, that I could never do back to him. I couldn't retaliate because I didn't have the strength or will. I had the power to protect myself in certain situations when I felt threatened, but I had never had to test myself, not the way Castle had. Instinctively I knew he could go well beyond what I considered normal threats. I had to learn to live with whatever he had in mind if I crossed him. I could only guess how he might hurt me. I knew how dangerous it would be for me once I divulged most of what I knew to Phuoc. I planned to reveal much more than I had in the past and that made me sweat more than usual.

"Castle is a mess to look at and be around. I think he's using more drugs than usual. Some days he goes unshaven. His fatigues, he wears them rather than cotton slacks, look as if they came through a wringer. His T-shirts have food stains down the front."

I didn't say it, but lately Castle appeared more beast-like to me. I could see he had become more socially disconnected, probably because of the drugs. He seemed cruel without constraint and that worried me when I sat with him.

I paused to let those observations sink in and for my thoughts to further etch themselves on my psyche. I breathed in deeply before continuing because what I had to say next could seriously incriminate Castle.

But he was Castle. I was Berg. My survival came first, despite me fear.

"Several days ago when I saw him at the laundry near Skag Alley, I noticed scratches on his arms, his right arm to be precise. When he saw me looking, he folded his arms to hide the wounds. When he did, I saw his fingernails, and the ones on his right hand were broken and bloody, as if he either bit them himself, or tore them when trying to grab onto something he couldn't hold. Maybe he tore his nails when he clutched a dead girl, and she surprised him by fighting back."

A small grin crossed Phuoc's thin lips. He removed a piece of tobacco from his teeth.

"People, that is, many of my people, believe that a spirit or worse, a devil, can enter their bodies and once they do, they take over and make the person behave in a strange way," said Phuoc.

He became very quiet and said nothing. Smoking dominated his actions. His seeming impassivity in hearing what I thought to be damning evidence bothered me. Then again, it didn't surprise me as much as I thought it would, he being a Vietnamese, from a world alien to me, as mine to his.

Fourteen

Thoa Trang had not been to the Bar California for five days. Five days were much too long. Five days were unusual even for someone who regularly returned home to visit her family. I had not seen her for almost seven days. I started worrying about her with urgency. I did not want to think the worst. When I asked where she might be or if anyone had seen her, no one at the bar offered where she could be, when she would return or if I would see her again. No one believed that I cared for her. I, an American, would probably be soon gone, anyway. Another American with money would replace me and the trend would continue until there were no more friendly Americans spending their money frivolously. The Vietnamese knew they controlled their country and would be there after we Americans or any other invaders were long gone. The Vietnamese would be here forever. They were permanent. We Americans and other foreigners were transients.

When Trang or anyone who worked the bars missed too much time, they lost money and even customers. Men who frequented the bars were as fickle as the women they wanted to serve them were. Suddenly, the bartender acted as if he didn't know me. In its way, that was expected. There were times I thought he might be Viet Cong. It helped explain his animosity to me and anyone else with my skin color. Then, again, perhaps he was surly for the sake of being surly. The bar girls were equally unhelpful. I missed Trang more than I thought possible, more for herself and her gentleness than for the sex we had. Soon after starting with Castle, sex no longer posed a problem in my life. The young women were plentiful, and willing, easy to be with, and never refused. Working for Castle, allowed me to sample all the cookies in the jar whenever I wanted, though I did not overindulge.

Trang, though, presented a puzzle I had yet to solve. I talked to Phuoc, thinking that a man in his position and knowledge, a man with his wisdom, or what I thought to be wisdom, might give me some information or a way to get information. I thought, too, that he might analyze for me the state of my relationship with Trang, and her relationship with me. The day before over coffee, Phuoc refused to help me understand the meaning of what I assumed had to be love, at least some form of love, which I felt for Trang.

"You are lonely," he said. "You are far from home. She is beautiful and kind."

"Kind?" I shook my head. There had to more. There had to be something else that compelled me to be with her.

"Yes," he continued. "She's kind and you're a man who needs kindness."

I never believed I needed kindness to live, though I would consider it. Phuoc posed an interesting idea. Was he right and if so, how did he understand so much about me? Yet, when I pressed him about where she might be, he knew nothing. Sure, I understood the two had little to do with each other but I wanted them linked. No one else I spoke with told me anything. It was as if they were afraid to tell me what I didn't want to hear. No one said anything, until I talked to Lee, and as usual he had more insight than I could handle or want.

"Maybe she's here in Saigon, but she doesn't want you to know where she is."

"What does that mean?"

"She got tired of you and turned elsewhere for love." "I doubt that. How could she get tired of me so fast?"

"I've seen you when you want something. You go after it. Sometimes you succeed and sometimes you do not. With women, you don't let up. It makes you unhappy not to succeed, though most of the time your only success is with a Castle whore."

"Thanks for your vote of confidence." I was angry with Lee for speaking what could have been the truth. "Sure, it's easier to go to a laundry, find a girl, and get laid. I have less responsibility. When I cover a story, I have to do well to be paid. So, I'm aggressive. I like to think that's good aggression. But Trang is a beautiful young woman and that makes her different from a story. There's more to our friendship than my success," I protested.

"I hope so for your sake." Lee smiled and walked over to his motorbike. He mounted the machine and kick started the motor with his left foot. Then he gave me a backward wave of his hand, and wheeled into traffic.

"Lee," I shouted over the din of the traffic, but he disappeared in the heavy smog and coming dark of early evening.

The time had come for me to get off my ass and start searching for Trang, that is, if she had come to back to Saigon, as I hoped. But this much was clear. I was starting to believe and fear that Trang had gone missing. Had she died? *Inconceivable,* I thought. But where could I find her? I couldn't go to her village. I only had a vague idea where it might me. It was not the first time I thought that the journey would be too dangerous for me alone or even with a competent guide into the lower reaches of the Mekong Delta. If not careful, the trip could be my last. It could kill me. An early death didn't fit into my plans for staying alive. I didn't know where she lived in Saigon. She kept that a closely guarded secret. My already narrow search, narrowed even more into a deepening mystery.

I knew she had a connection with Castle. Many of the young and uprooted women in Saigon did because he had his fingers in most things ugly and unholy. One thought nagged at me. Could she be in a brothel, in one of Castle's many laundries? I loved that word, brothel. Using it reminded me of word games, the opening of a crossword puzzle. Was it a refined term for something ugly? Sure. It's meaning hidden in its seven letters, I preferred whorehouse. A brothel worked better in a nineteenth century novel centered on a house of ill repute. Only in novels, though, not in real life because in real life, the same results prevailed without the phoniness.

Previously Castle told me that he had been using Trang to spy on me. When he told me that, I could hardly breathe, or swallow, but I feigned composure. I wanted to strike out and smash him but that terrified me. He would hit back, perhaps knife me or shoot me. I had no stomach for physical action, especially where I might be hurt. Though my curiosity increased, I didn't give him the satisfaction of asking what she had told him about me. As much as I wanted to know what Trang told him, and I wanted to know everything, I didn't want to give Castle the satisfaction of seeing my anger and hurt. I had to protect myself from harm by hiding behind a shield that he couldn't penetrate. So, what connection did Trang have with Castle? I knew she had long ago lost her virginity, a quite common occurrence among young women fending for themselves in Saigon or anywhere else in Vietnam. Just as well. Castle loved lying with virgins. I did not. I did not want the responsibility of changing a young woman's life. There were no surprises in Trang's love making. She took no risks and she had an aversion to most sexual adventures out of the ordinary. But she made love to me as if I were her only lover. I lived cheerfully with that and did nothing to make our time together different. I enjoyed the dream.

I had to find Trang. When I did, I needed to know why she spied on me. Did Castle pay her or threaten her or her family? He had a long, dangerous reach. So I seethed, but it didn't do me much good. I whistled up a cyclo, bargained for all day, and started looking for her by driving around the city through polluted air and heavy traffic. We wove our way through people on bikes, scooters, military jeeps and the occasional taxi. We were in a hurry. Everyone else seemed to meander. My anxiety rose with each block we traversed. I wanted to be at each of Castle's establishments at once, but he had the advantage because there were brothels he controlled that I knew nothing about. I knew I couldn't possibly manage to find these other places at this late hour, so I first went to where I knew his laundries did exist. I went to the suburb of Gia Dinh. It was a distant district that I rarely visited. The ride took more time than I wanted it to, but I had no choice. We drove through Saigon and crossed a tributary, more like a stream, of the Saigon River. The brothel, behind the Le Van Duvet Temple, was, like many of Castle's enterprises, in a dilapidated villa, its walls scarred, its pastel paint peeling. Here the women, who were older than those in Saigon, catered mostly to Vietnamese Marines. Mama-san, a frumpy madam with teeth stained from chewing beetle-nut, said she knew nothing about Trang. I believed her. We left. One down with at least four to go. I wished I had a mask like the one the Japanese wore to keep the dirt and soot from my nose and throat, from coating my skin and hair. Not to complain, but I had to endure the terrible air despite my light pain and small suffering.

We stopped for a warm can of Coke and a piss in an alley. That done we went down Chi Lang, then to Vo Tanh where we made a left onto a side street outside Tan Son Nhut Air Base. We passed a little used golf course with badly manicured grass and very few players. In the distance, the men looked like Americans. Behind them, I saw a foursome of Japanese who mostly stood around scratching their heads, probably wondering about the rotten state of the course. Once past that anomaly, we went to a brothel I visited on occasion where I found the freshest, and often the most willing, women in Castle's stable. Here the girls, many still in their mid-teens, knew Trang but had not seen her in days. These girls never stayed as working prostitutes for very long. The men they catered to, mostly American military officers or high-rolling construction workers, wanted their women young, their sex fresh. Some girls even looked for permanent attachments, for six months, a year, rarely longer. The men hoped to find someone to move in with, fetch their slippers, prepare their rice, and find quality French bread and good butter with a hint of salt. Having sex on command made it easier for these men and less dangerous than heading down a dark alley with a streetwalker after curfew. There they would have some minutes of satisfaction, always too few to count, and untold danger from local gangs.

I wondered what it meant that they had not seen Trang in days. Did she visit frequently? The women giggled. A question came to me, one I refused to acknowledge. Could it be that she lived at the brothel?

"No. She not live here," said Mama-san.

I paused, thinking the worst, refusing to accept what I heard, considering something awful. I crinkled my eyes, narrowing them for meanness, and I held my breath, knowing that what I thought might be true. But how could it? How could she deceive me for so long? Had I become a dunce, something I never suspected?

It made me angry and sad. Deceit, never a part of my game, now reared its head in this strangest of lands, this oddest of wars. I hardly paused. The moment had come for me to ask the hardest question of my life, at least until then.

"Did she work here?" I said. I finally knew what it meant to have my heart in my throat.

"Yes, foolish man," said Mama-san. She grinned as wide as a western canyon, exposing broken teeth. "Only two days a week. Not more. Not less. Only two days. She very strict when she work. Trang very popular. She tell me about you. You a lucky man, Berg-San." Mama-san continued to smile broadly and she gave me a light tap on my arm that said we are friends, and if not, at least co-conspirators. I recoiled from her playful touch and shuddered. My shoulders slumped and I didn't know whether to weep, to lash out and destroy, or run and hide. I slept with whores until Trang, but they were young women with whom I had a good time without consequences. To be in love with a woman who made her money on her back, no matter the reason, and to suddenly realize she used me because of Castle, took me where I didn't want it to go. Feeling like a fool, barely described my emotional turmoil.

"You sad?" said Mama-san. "Yes, I'm sad. And confused."

Mama-san shook her head and signaled with her hands that I should leave. There were more important things than to stand around exchanging gossip with a lovesick American. I knew I had to go. I had three other brothels to check to confirm my wildest fears. Trang Thoa was a whore. Until Saigon, I had never slept with a whore. Worse, I loved a whore whom I thought loved me. Obviously, I lived in a dream world. Behind me, my cyclo driver sat on the bicycle seat probably wondering what all the jabbering had to do with anything and in American yet. I wondered, too, in a dark way. More to the point, I considered giving up the search for Trang. I thought she mattered little to me now that I knew how she really earned her living. I had become her toy in an intricate game created by John Castle. There were conflicting emotions in me which said, "Don't give up now, pursue her, find her, drag her from her mess, free her and free yourself from Castle."

I got into the worn wicker basket of the cyclo and as we drove away, I said, "If you see her, if she shows up, tell her I was here and that I forgive her. Tell her to come home. A better life waits."

I still dreamed everything would work out as the driver pedaled rapidly toward the next whorehouse. We made our way to Trung Tan Buu and then a left onto Tran Quoc Toan. We headed toward the racetrack at Phu Tho where Vietnamese jockeys' made American riders look like giants. These small men rode small horses on probably the worst track in the world that operated on its own schedule, a few days on, a few days off, depending on the whim of the men who controlled it. Castle's brothel, near a rarely used soccer stadium, served a mix of Chinese bettors, Vietnamese black marketers and other petty criminals. I didn't expect to find Trang there, but I had to look anyway. The women in this brothel hardly did any laundry. It was the crumbiest of all Castle's enterprises, but it brought in big money and served as the nearest thing to a hot sheet motel you could find in Saigon. It had six cubicles and each had a thin pallet on the floor covered by an often-washed sheet, instead of a mattress or the equivalent of a camp bed or cot. In one corner, there was a rickety chair of wood and next to it, a small plastic stool with a basin of water, a glass, and a wet towel, all to clean and to wipe away the results of sex. As if it mattered.

I never had sex in this house. That would have meant taking a chance beyond my needs. This, of all Castle's laundries, felt more like the third world than any of the others did. I knew Castle's operation well. There were other houses run by Chinese, Vietnamese, and Koreans. I understood they were more rundown than the one near Phu Tho. Here Mama-san tried to ignore me when I asked about Trang. She kept waving at me, suggesting I did not help her business when I came to check on her. She never cared for my visits even when it had been part of my job. I knew that but I didn't care. I asked for Trang and she laughed. She told me Trang never came here because Trang thought too much of herself.

"Trang, she high-class. Nose in air. Here low for Trang." She said this while gesturing with her hand under and on her nose, as if her place had a bad smell about it, which it did. That did it for me, too. I got back into my seat and the driver drove down the street. We found another alley to piss in and then bought sandwiches of French bread, Vietnamese pork pate and hot chili peppers. We ate on the roadside and washed down our lunch with warm Beer 33, the awful local brew. On our way again, we headed toward district two and the fourth of Castle's laundries.

The time was nearly two o'clock. The sun was high and hot. I had been searching for more than five hours. Though depressed about what I had learned, the driver seemed fresh and eager to continue. He was having a good day with money, lunch and beer. While we drove, I had plenty of time to think. Nothing made sense. The Far East had trapped me. *It had used me, and it was going to spit me out*, I thought. I couldn't get my mind to function without it dissolving into a pudding. I loved Trang but I didn't know that she loved me. When we were together before and after sex, I knew calm. I believed at those moments we were truly together, a pair, two people in love. I wondered if she could be two people, the one when with me, kind, tender and giving, the other when at work for Castle, calculating, working for a living and doing the worst a woman could do to herself without taking drugs.

The neighborhood took my mind off myself as the driver pedaled hard, in the increasingly dense traffic. We were now moving through a heavily populated area heading toward the Central Market and bus terminal. I told the driver where to go and fifteen minutes later, several streets and many small alleys behind the huge market square, we stopped in front of my destination, what I called laundry number 4. This brothel served anyone working in the area, including merchants and sales people from the market, mechanics and drivers from the bus terminal, men just off the buses, Vietnamese soldiers and local residents looking for quick and cheap action. Always to my surprise, the neighborhood looked like any other in Saigon. The doors to the laundry were not open. Cheap straw blinds covered the windows. The same small pool of brackish, muddy water I found everywhere, lay outside the front entrance. There were no whores, though. Instead, I could see that a large family lived inside, new residents to this changing neighborhood. I had last visited ten days ago and the brothel had been busy. Castle must have recently closed this operation down in the last week. His motivations were never frivolous. When asked for his reasons for doing something, he refused to answer or justify his actions. I would try to find out why he closed this place when I next saw him. But first, I would ask him about Trang, her role in my life and his role in her life.

I had not found Trang at the first four laundries I visited. I still believed she went south to her village and had not yet returned. I had to stay with that expectation to retain my sanity. I concentrated on my next objective. I had one more laundry to go and yet another busy precinct to pass through. Now midday, the streets were busy and would remain that way until curfew, this night at ten. Curfew changed daily and I checked the local newspapers to confirm street talk when everybody had to be in their home. After moving out of the second precinct, we moved as swiftly as we could down Le Loi. We made a left onto Tu Do past the many still dark bars where I spent so many of my nights. Then we made a right on Gia Long, a few streets from the main Catholic Cathedral, past the back of the PTT, the main post office, and toward the Saigon River. A few more streets and across the river would take me back to Gia Dinh where I started my search. After checking this next whorehouse, unless I found Trang, and I didn't believe I would, I would try to find John Castle and to get the answers to my questions.

I found the old French villa where Castle began to pimp and built the first of what would become a sizeable empire. The building with its peeling paint, broken window shutters, high, broken walls encrusted with shards of glass, and thirteen steps to the front entrance looked like a worn out prostitute. I told the driver to wait. He insisted on coming with me. We were now into our seventh hour and I think he thought we were a team. I know he wanted to see what went on inside. He would have good stories to tell his friends. Another tale could mean another free beer. I let him come with me.

Banana trees and hibiscus lined the sides of the front yard strewn with empty soda and beer bottles. These were not like lawns in America. Uneven hard-packed soil filled an otherwise empty space. An Edith Piaf song wafted its way over the walls to the street. Two American construction workers, their heavily lined faces deeply burned from the sun, lazily made their way down the steps and out the front to the avenue. The smell of cheap whiskey came from their sweat-stained shirts. Their lips, dry and cracked from too much time outside, had a satisfied smirk. I looked up to see a young Vietnamese woman in bright red toreador pants wearing a white peasant blouse standing in the doorway. With her hair cut short, she looked like a child rather than a grown woman but that is how some men wanted her when they had sex. She didn't care. Her only motivation was to make money. Through the doorway, I could see a ceiling fan turning at its highest speed to help cool the air. The young woman said hello. She knew me, and stepped aside as I entered the large front room of the once fashionable villa, formerly the home of someone very rich who had probably fled to Paris or the Riviera, their money safely in place, their life no longer under assault.

Mama-san, away for the afternoon, made sure her establishment ran without a hitch. The women, on an honor system, didn't cheat her or the customers. They were usually kinder to the man of the hour than usual because it meant a bigger tip in their own pocket. Many girls spoke some English as a necessity. Being so close to the center of town, or the center carved out by Americans and other foreigners, they had to know more than a few words of a language where most of the men, English, and where the money originated. I chose the young woman in the form-fitting, red pants to ask my questions.

I wanted to know if she knew Trang. Yes, she knew Trang. She told me most of us know Trang. "But," she said, "Trang never comes alone."

"When she come, it always with Mr. John Castle. She ride in the car with him," red pants said. "He get out first. Then she come after him out of the car. Trang carries a shopping bag for Mr. John Castle and he puts things in it from Mama-san. Then Trang, she and Mr. John Castle get in car and drive away. But Trang doesn't work here," red pants said, breathing hard from so much conversation.

Strangely, I was relieved Trang didn't work in this brothel. Worse, shocked really, I felt doubly betrayed, when I learned that she had been working for Castle as his bagman. Bagman. Bagwoman. What next? Each new revelation made me more confused. Nothing made sense. Finding out Trang worked as a whore hurt terribly. Yet she acted shy with me and pretended she knew little about sex. Discovering that Trang worked with Castle made me shudder. I hoped she did it under duress, but it sounded from what red pants said, she willing took part in what he did. Standing in the hallway of the villa listening to the flickering fan above my head, I felt a bigger fool than ever. I hated playing the fool. It reminded me too much of grade school when one bully, through the odd courage of his stupidity could dominate the life of my friends and me. What could I do? How could I fight the bully, free Trang, if she wanted freedom, and free my fears without doing damage to myself? Could I put all the pieces together to make sense? Phuoc had the detectives badge and the police behind him. I did not. I had nothing to support me. I planned to consult with him in the morning. For now, my head spun, my knees were weak, my mind a mess. I wanted to smoke some opium, but decided not to. I had to keep my mind clear. Maybe when it ended and I understood my situation and Trang's situation, too, maybe then I would allow myself more than a few pipes to take me on a new journey. I promised myself to stay clean of the lovely poppy until I had answers.

The day done, the search over, exhausted, I had the driver bring me to my apartment. I paid him for the trip and gave him a hefty tip. I knew with all that money in his hands, he would not be around for a few days. Tomorrow I would use another driver. They were everywhere and the older the better. They were reliable, and, despite their age, their legs had more strength.

Called *ong,* "grandfather," by the younger drivers, these men were more willing to work and didn't fear the police because they were too old to be press-ganged into the army if caught without papers. I had some locally brewed rice liqueur in my pad, clear, and strong. I bought a fresh loaf of French bread on the street, went upstairs, gnawed on it and sipped the drink as I did, allowing the chewy part of the loaf to take the sting out of the fiery drink. Then, though very worried about Trang, I fell into a deep, surprisingly restful sleep.

Two hours later, I awoke with a start. Is that how they describe waking suddenly, startled, unsure where I happened to be? Whatever. It is how I found myself sitting on the edge of the bed. Unable to sleep, distressed despite how deeply I thought I had been resting, heartburn from the rice liqueur eating away at me, I stumbled from bed into a cold shower. That made me laugh. I never took anything but a cold shower. I had no hot water. None existed. I knew that, yet I fantasized. Heat had no place in a Saigon apartment even when the temperature dropped to the low sixties. I was used to taking cold or mostly lukewarm showers. Only when I went those few times to Hong Kong or Taiwan, did I have the hot shower I craved. I loved hot showers, but I learned to do without for the sake of my adventure. I dried myself, drank a warm Coke for instant caffeine straight from an eight-ounce bottle. I dressed quickly in khaki trouser and a cotton shirt and headed down the block to the Bar California in search of Phuoc. I had to tell him what I learned. I wanted to unleash my most fearsome thoughts. Maybe then I could sleep.

As I entered the bar, I briefly closed my eyes. Then I opened them quickly, all in a second or two, a trick from my childhood. It helped me get accustomed to the dark and then to the smoke-filled room. Moving through the room to the back, I saw Phuoc sitting in his usual place. I maneuvered my way, and sat next to him with a heavy sigh. A waitress brought me a Japanese beer with a glass. I waved off the glass, popped open the can, and drained half without a breath. Phuoc stared at me. He saw my forehead beaded with my sweat and I knew he could feel my tension. I needed to control my emotions and tell him what I knew dispassionately. Probably that would be impossible.

I started talking about Trang. I let out all my anger and frustration about how I felt when I learned she worked as a prostitute, and, importantly, that she worked closely with John Castle. I made sure that Phuoc understood I felt betrayed.

"When I find her, I'll wring her neck," I said. "I'll break her neck," I repeated even more forcibly. She can't use me that way and get away with it. I wouldn't let her. That fucker Castle also used me and he would be next in line to feel my anger. I had fallen in love with a whore. I couldn't take her back to New York with me. Everyone would laugh and my parents would throw me out, which didn't really matter. I hardly spoke to them, anyway. I drank more beer; several cans in a row, without stopping for a breath, going for a piss only when I nearly burst. I told Phuoc everything I knew and thought I understood. He listened to me, his face impassive, his back rigid, only drinking his tea when it cooled enough for him to sip it in small swallows.

Curfew came and I think Phuoc escorted me to my apartment. I remember going inside and then double locking the door before stripping my clothes off and finding not my bed, but the pallet on the floor. I was asleep or had passed out before I knew it.

Fifteen

Many hours later, or what I assumed were many, because I had no idea when I arrived home, bright sun shone through the thin bamboo shades that covered my windows. Though still half asleep, I knew from the intensity of the sun and the noise coming from the street, midday had arrived with me still on the floor. I lay on my reed bed perspiring, the sweat running down to the small of my back. The overhead fan gave me no relief. As with all things electric in Saigon, it only worked when the fluctuating power controlled its sporadic movement. My head throbbed, pounded really, from the previous night's beer. My stomach churned and warbled unpleasantly. My mouth felt like a sand pit, dry and gritty, my taste buds already on a slab in the morgue. I tried to bury my head under the pillows, but unsuccessfully. Then the knocking started and with it, someone called me by name. *Fuck it,* I thought. *Let me alone. Please go away,* I whispered inside my head, unable to say anything because my lips and mouth seemed glued together and my throat stung from too many cigarettes. The person outside my door didn't let up. He kept calling my name. The accent was Vietnamese with a touch of British English. The repetition of my name gave the words urgency. The voice sounded like Phuoc. What did he want? Why did he come out so early? Usually, he started his day much later, and if early, he began it with his half dozen pipes of opium.

"Berg. Adam Berg. Let me in. It is I, Phouc."

The man's voice seemed far off, somewhere deep in my sleep filled brain. As I awoke, I realized the voice did belong to Phuoc. Always proper, he tried hard to be grammatically correct.

I opened the door to let him in my room. His face looked sadder than usual. In one hand, he carried a metal beaker, French press coffee maker for four cups and in the other hand, two white porcelain espresso cups.

"I think you will need this," he said. As he entered, he hooked his foot around the door and swung it shut. I could picture him outside my door, not banging with his fist but kicking the door with his foot. He poured the thick, black coffee and handed me the cup. I took a sip and ran one hand through my hair. Then I drank the whole cup, including its grinds and held it out for more. He poured me another and this time I held it in my unsteady hand without drinking, listening to the cup as it rattled in its saucer.

"I have news for you, as you would say. It is not good news. It is bad."

I looked up at Phuoc, instead of staring mindlessly into the small coffee cup. What news could he have worse than what I had learned during yesterday's tour of Castle's whorehouses?

"Please," he said. "This is not easy for me to say. This morning we found another body; a young girl killed that same way as the other women we found. Someone had strangled her, the same as the others. Purple bruises circled her neck like a chain. She had been beaten about the neck and face. Her jaw had been broken. Whoever beat her, hit her often on her breasts and badly bruised them, seriously crushing them."

Phuoc paused long enough to let what he had said, sink into my frazzled mind.

"Why tell me this? Are you looking for another story? The way the war is going, with heavy fighting along the DMZ and in the Central Highlands, I don't think I could interest any editor in the death of yet another whore."

Phuoc looked at me sadder than ever. I could have sworn his eyes were close to tears.

"Drink your coffee," he said. I did. "The woman we found is someone you know."

Now it came clear. Though I refused to admit I knew where he was heading, I knew what was coming and it scared the hell out of me.

"Tell me. Tell me quickly. Don't waste words. Just the fuck tell me."

The blood rushed to my brain. I had come fully awake. I had no doubt, what he would say next.

"We found the body of Trang Thoa dead out by the Cong Li Canal behind a garbage heap. It is hard for us to know exactly when she died but we think her death took place early this morning."

When I spoke, my voice came out as a croak, harsh, as I struggled to make sense of what Phuoc just said. I found it difficult to catch my breath. Trang dead. *God damn it,* I thought. Trang dead. I couldn't accept that as real.

"How can you be sure?"

"I saw the body myself. I know Trang so I identified her. Her body is in the morgue awaiting burial. There is no way we can send her back to her village. It is too far and too dangerous, forgetting how expensive it would be."

"Can I see her?"

"Yes, but first I have a few questions." He saw me twitch. He watched me bring my eyes to his eyes. Did I do that too quickly? What questions did he have and why?

"Do you mind?" Phuoc said. "But first, I want to warn you that you are a suspect."

"What does that mean?" I knew. The danger of what he said sank in very fast.

"You were very angry last night with what you had learned about Trang and you were very drunk. You made many forceful and threatening statements. Jealousy is a powerful motive in any death. My questions are a test. If you pass, you are free."

"I thought you were my friend."

"I am a policeman first, a friend second. I have a crime to solve. You know how the other women died. I don't think you are the serial killer I am searching for, but you could be, as you from America say, a copy cat killer."

"Bullshit. That's a stretch, man, a lousy, fucking stretch. First, I'm not a murderer. I hate violence.

You know that. I was so drunk last night that I have no clue how I got to my apartment. I vaguely remember you leading me from the bar and helping me down the street. When I arrived here, I must have passed out until you rudely pounded on my door a few minutes ago. Until then, I was dead to the world!"

I thought I heard myself shout and I saw Phuoc wince. I didn't like the sound of my voice raised to such a high level. Clearly, Phuoc's tone, veiled and openly accusatory, made me very uneasy.

Phuoc remained motionless on the one chair in my room. His only moves had been to place the now cold coffee pot on the floor near where I sat on my bed. I didn't want to be the convenient scapegoat for Trang's murder. Perhaps Phuoc wanted to use me as a stalking horse to flush out the real murderer. Maybe Phouc had new pressures applied to him finally to arrest someone for those heinous crimes. With Trang's death, the Saigon police had seven known unsolved murders, all prostitutes, including Trang. I finally had an understanding of what she did with her time and could truthfully put a name to her work. On the edge of my bed, my mind clouded with grief, anger still welled inside me. I felt awful about the death of the woman I loved. Without realizing, tears ran down my cheeks. I made no sound. Nor did I whimper. I did nothing to stop my crying. I did nothing to wipe away my freely flowing tears.

Phuoc was watching me carefully. It was as if he was waiting to see something that I was trying to keep from his all-seeing eyes.

"You know I must ask if you left your apartment last night after I brought you home."

"Didn't you just hear me? I guess not. Honestly, I don't know. As I said, I have no memory of you bringing me home. I know Trang pissed me off and I probably said things I should have kept to myself. But I didn't kill her. I loved her, man. Why destroy what I loved?"

"She was an easy target. You are a big man. She, a small woman. You knew how the others died. You had a motive and you had anger. Terrible anger. When you put the two together, they make a bad mixture."

Still too stunned by Trang's death, I didn't have the strength to move from the bed. I couldn't believe that Phuoc was putting me through a tough interrogation. It hurt to have him question me. Did Phuoc think my sweating, my uneasiness and true grief over Trang's death, were indications that I could be guilty? Phuoc knew he had me where he wanted, a prisoner, his prisoner, in what passed for my home that overlooked a noisy Saigon street. Phuoc kept talking, his voice mostly thin but occasionally overheated. I knew his tricks, so I thought. But they would never work with me. He and I had a big problem. He tried to get information from me that I didn't have. My safety valve was ignorance. There were no revelations that would come from me. It didn't matter to Phuoc. When excited, his Vietnamese accented English made him difficult for me to understand. All his self taught BBC English disappeared under the stress of his interrogation. How he talked and what he said, did not effect me. Trang dead, violently, without reason, or so it seemed, sealed the last remnant of feeling I had for Vietnam. I could leave the country without guilt about not completing whatever I thought I was doing in Saigon, in the war.

Phuoc droned on. I shut him out by raising the level of my inner voice many decibels higher than his. To keep him happy, I answered with a grunt and a nod of my head, but I gave him no information about Trang's death because I had nothing to offer. I had nothing to add to Trang's movements from the previous day when I tried to track her down. Counting the day of her death, I had not seen Trang for eight days. Phuoc knew everything I had told him.

"I need more coffee," I said.

"Go shower. Clean up. Change. I will order more coffee."

"And bread," I said. "Fresh baked, crusty outside, chewy inside.

Bread. Get the loaf with the purple stamp on it."

Phuoc rose, went to the door, handed the now cold pot to a police guard in white shirt and gray trousers, and gave his instructions. He shut the door and locked it.

I stripped and then walked slowly into the shower stall and stepped onto its tile floor. I turned the water on and, as every morning, let the rust run free to clean the pipes. Then I allowed the weak spray of almost cold water to flow over my body. Once washed, I put on a clean shirt and a pair of tan Chino slacks and went back to my post on the edge of the bed. I knew the heat would soon make me look like a used dishrag. A knock on the door told us the fresh coffee and bread had arrived. I ate and drank as if food and drink were a new experience for me. After seeing I had satisfied my hunger, Phuoc started in again, trying to break me down, seeking anything new that might come from me as I got more tired by the minute. He repeated questions as he looked for flaws or inconsistencies in my answers. I never wavered. I could see how pale his skin had become, as if, trying to trip me up, his blood turned cold while he held his emotions in check. After the second pot of coffee, we were at a standstill. I had nothing more to say. My inner tears had dried, sealed in permanent grief. I had no more time to allow real tears to flow down my cheeks. I stood and stretched. I ran my fingers around the inside my coffee cup and brought the thick, black grinds to my lips and chewed, relishing the bitterness of the grounds, wanting them to overtake my sorrow.

Morning passed into early midday. I had difficulty concentrating, yet I knew afternoon had arrived because of the siesta and its eerie quiet. We were no further along than we were when Phuoc first arrived. I felt weak, all my strength gone in the meaningless of Trang's death. I had to piss. My bowels rumbled a bad sign. I had been sitting too long. My legs were stiff from being so long in one position. I knew Phuoc wanted to make me uncomfortable. He had his methods of interrogation, those he learned from the French when he suffered as a prisoner. Keeping me, his prisoner, in a state of unhappiness was one way I believed he thought he could break me down. Ultimately for Phuoc and it was time he realized it, I had no secrets. I had nothing in me for him to break. I had so many minor discomforts that I thought sleep or a few pipes filled with opium, though not booze, would help solve my problems. Then, at least, I could get some needed rest.

After a few hours, I easily tuned Phuoc from my mind. He never gave up, though, and he rarely gave in. He was relentless in his pursuit of Trang's killer. I had done nothing wrong except to fall in love with a woman from another culture. I sensed Phuoc needed me to give in to him, and give myself up. His victory depended on how long I could stand his persistence. I refused to give in. I had to remain calm.

"You know that I'm not a killer. Look at my fingers and look at my arms. Do you see anything broken? Do you see torn flesh or scratches? Doesn't that count for something?"

"Maybe. Maybe not. You could have worn gloves. Men do strange things when they are hurt or feel betrayed. When you learned that Trang worked as a prostitute and accompanied Castle on his rounds to his brothels and seemed to so willingly, you lost your temper, found her and killed her. You used the same methods as you used before. You knew how to kill and you were getting better at it each time."

"Man! You are out of your fucking mind. Have you ever seen wounds on me that matched what the killer did to the dead women? That must count for something. When I heard about Trang, sure I was hurt, like a schoolboy. Then I started being sorry for myself. I felt like a jerk for the time I wasted, for the fool I had been because her deep black eyes brought me into what I wanted to be a new world. I got drunk instead of running around like a monkey and chasing the ghost, she had become. You saw me. You watched me get drunk and then, so you told me, out of a rare kindness

I never knew you had, you took me home, so you said, and you saw me topple into bed."

It didn't take me long to forget to remain calm.

"You could have gone out after I left you and then looked for Trang." "I was drunk. I never went out after curfew. Too dangerous. So, fuck you. That never happened."

"I am not sure you are telling the truth." I said nothing and stared straight ahead.

"You must think," said Phuoc. "It is imperative you think and tell me everything you know. Be specific. Try."

I lit another Camel and sipped my coffee. Phuoc also smoked. He didn't move his thin body, not an inch. His eyes looked straight at me as if he were intent on boring into my newly fragile soul. The air had become thick with our smoke. The day's heat didn't help. My overhead fan's wood blades moved slowly but did nothing but circulate the stuffy air already in the room. I had two windows but only one had a screen that covered its lower part. Two open windows would welcome bugs in the day and bats at night. I wanted no part of either. My breathing unexpectedly came in sharp bursts. I looked away from Phuoc. His constant, unvaried stare unsettled me. I tried desperately to collect myself. I needed all the strength I could find not to break and say or do something stupid and foolish. I had another sip of bitter coffee. I took another drag on my cigarette. Strangely, I felt at peace. I found sustenance in knowing I knew nothing. I felt relieved knowing I had nothing to fear.

My mind was now clear and it dawned on me that Phuoc wanted an American to pay for the crime. It didn't matter which American went to prison or would face a firing squad. Any American would do. Then maybe his budget would go up and his bosses would leave him alone to chase crime how he wanted. Phuoc knew almost everything about Castle's operations, including the names of his girls, their villages, the amount of money they turned over to him each day and how much money they carried home, when they could. Far from a feminist, as a middle-aged Vietnamese it never entered his mind to give a woman equal rights. Women rarely had rights and freedom in South Vietnam, but, in his favor, he believed they deserved respect. In time, he thought they could gain equality with men, but not during the war. He resented men in his own society who preferred to trample women to dust, and there were many. Phuoc had no tolerance for anyone protecting the serial killer running free in his city. I thought his questions implied I knew more than I said. Murder bothered me as much as it did Phuoc. I wondered why he thought I would protect Castle if I knew he had killed Trang. All murder was senseless. Murder spurred by madness, especially repetitive killings, when they destroyed young women barely on the verge of life, made me wonder why anyone believed in God, why anyone believed goodness had a place in the world.

I understood it would be easy for Phuoc to pin Trang's murder on me and then to link me to the other murders. I had a known connection to John Castle and I had made many appearances at his brothels. People saw me frequently in the neighborhoods where the police found the other murdered girls. Worse, I, a white American, had been deeply involved with Trang, the newest person in Phuoc's equation. I could serve as a symbol of everything wrong with the Vietnam War. I could end as Phuoc's scapegoat. Everyone thought, and rightly, that Trang and I had been intimate. Phuoc knew I had been teaching her English and a few Western ways, including giving her a short course in feminism. I got no pleasure when she walked three paces behind me, though I understood by doing that she protected herself from being insulted by angry and jealous Vietnamese men. I knew she didn't want me to lose my temper and possibly assault someone for calling me a pimp, and worse, she, Trang, my whore.

There were moments when I thought I might bring Trang to the West. I dreamed that we would start a life in Hong Kong with its mixture of Eastern and Western ways, and its facade of rich versus poor compared to the torrid life in Saigon and its war-wrought poverty. In the more buoyant Queens Road where people cared more about how they dressed and what they ate, we would have had time to decompress from war.

Now dead, Trang would never know the delights, the bright lights and tissue thin finery, though false, of life outside her Mekong Delta village, and of the polluted streets of Saigon. Did she love me? I had no idea. Would she have given up her country and family for me, especially when I had no real future? She didn't know any of that. She had no understanding of what my future meant to me. Being with Trang gave me a chance to know myself so I could project a life, however romantic and fanciful, beyond my day-to-day existence.

We did have enough moments together to know something of each other, though they were fleeting and all too short. Perhaps our love or my love, thinking she may not have loved me, had no substance. Now I would never know. I did know without doubt that none of my dreams would come true.

I watched Phuoc carefully and waited for his next move, or pronouncement, his next long pause. Phuoc, his expression veiled, imperceptibly shook his head and licked his lips. He took a deep breath and released it with a long sigh.

"I am done here," he said. Done? I wondered.

He stood and stepped back from me, reached for his jacket draped on the chair's back where he had been sitting, and put it over his shoulders like a French dandy.

"You can go. I might want to ask more questions later so do not go far from here."

With that, he turned and walked to the door.

"Where the fuck can I go?" I shouted. The blood rushed to my face. Bad enough that the heat in the room made me fell like a lump of dough, to have Phuoc's accusations meddle with my head made everything worse.

"You know damn well I can't leave the country without a visa. You have me by the balls. Until you give the word, I'm your prisoner and you know it. Some friend you turned out to be."

"I know," he said. "I have a job to do. I have my work."

His voice tired and sad, he again reminded me how he sounded when he first arrived to give me the news about Trang. Phuoc showed what I thought might be a flicker of pity for me, though I doubted it ever entered his mind. If it had, I'm certain he quickly dismissed it. I could tell he had no time for warmth or sympathy, especially for me. He had a killer to catch. He turned and departed my apartment.

Alone and free, at last, so I thought, but not really. I had work to do, a task to complete. With no one around, I whispered a pledge. I said, "John Castle I'm coming after you and when I find you, you will be mine." *Clever*, I thought but I realized I had one problem. If he didn't get me first, I just might survive. Despite my internal bluster and my fierce desire to get Castle, I did nothing then. I lay back down on the bed. All I wanted to do was sleep. Sleep would have been a perfect solution. But I had a mission to find John Castle, to get answers to my questions. As the dutiful person I always wanted to be, I got up, stuffed my pockets with piasters and dollars, changed my shirt and went out the door to the street below. Going downstairs to hail a cyclo, I realized it could be my last day on earth. Dramatic, yes, but real. The hell with it. I checked for my cigarettes and jumped into a waiting cyclo.

With Trang dead, nothing else mattered to me. I remembered how she waited for me on Nguyen Hue where the old women sold fresh pineapple, hot beef and noodle soup and fruit drinks on the sidewalk. Trang had been everyone's friend. She would tease all the people on the street and they would tease her back, especially about me. She didn't seem to care. When we first started walking that street together, I feared that those people would resent me. Maybe at first they did. Then, in time, Trang and I had become a fixture and the regulars ignored us. A jungle firefight would be welcome relief compared to what I had been going through. Phuoc and his incessant questions had exhausted me more than I realized. As I mounted the basket in front of the cyclo, I thought someone might follow me. I hoped that would be the case. If I found Castle and got from him what I wanted, it would be best for me to have backup, support from Phuoc. I told the driver where to go. Immediately we were on our way.

When I arrived at the laundry, the main one in the villa near the center of town, I saw no one and heard no voices. I went inside and could hear Armed Forces Radio playing in the back past the empty machines. I heard the news broadcast, though almost over, really, as the announcer had started the weather report. I heard young women laughing or sobbing or giggling, either all three of none of the above. Later, when I thought about it, I realized they sounded scared and out of breath. I stopped moving, fearing that the sound of my feet hitting the wood floor would announce my arrival. Then I heard Castle's voice, low, almost a growl, and very strange. His words were too precise. He sounded as if he were trying very hard to be clear in what he said, but it came out like gibberish, only as a drug addict or drunk. His mind had become, I thought, unquestionably a captive to the chemicals coursing through his body.

Upset because my emotions were out of whack, and not using my head, I pushed the door open and saw two girls, in a way I never expected. Both were half naked. I knew one, but the other was a stranger. One girl, tied to the bed, spread-eagle, her eyes filled with fear, the other strapped with a man's belt to a chair, her head lolling to the side, her jaw slack. Broad, jagged slashes of deep red lipstick smeared their small bodies and dainty faces, now grotesque, and caked with pink makeup so heavy that it looked like someone used a putty knife on their dusky skins. The two young women were sobbing and rivulets of tears ran down their faces making a gully in their made-up cheeks. Stunned, I could not move. Of course, I had to free the women, but I felt frozen, immobile, caught in a crypt run by a devil named Castle. I saw him in my mind, but that is all. Where was he? I didn't want to see him, to acknowledge his presence. I took my eyes off the two young women and saw him sitting next to the bed, a gun in his belt, a Bowie knife in his hand. He laughed. I forgot he enjoyed playing with knives. I forgot how he enjoyed laughing. Most of the time, I didn't think about the knife he carried, but I knew he had it sharpened to combat readiness. He kept sticking the point into his thumb and pricking it, drawing a drop of blood each time and then raising his thumb to his mouth and licking it dry.

Despite the still life in front of me and instead of going for Castle, which probably would have been fruitless, I rushed to the girls to free them. Even with the gags on their mouths, they were shaking their heads violently. It took me a few seconds to realize they were trying to tell me to forget them, it was no use and I should leave, get out of there, escape, flee. Fast. I couldn't read their minds nor make sense of their gestures so I ignored them. All thumbs, clumsy as usual, in those few seconds of my moving to the women, I went flying against the wall across the room. Swiftly, Castle had got up, and moved swiftly to me. He grabbed me away from the two girls, and then threw me across the room. He leaned over me as I lay on the floor, still laughing. He slapped me repeatedly across the face. A dribble of spit came from the corner of his mouth. His eyes appeared to pop from his face. Sweat beaded his forehead. Frightened out of my mind, I thought I would die. He flicked the point of the knife across my cheek under my eye. I could hardly feel the pain, his knife was so sharp, but I felt the blood going down my face and then the pain from where he had cut me. Strange, even with my life in jeopardy, I thought, though only for a moment, as if it mattered, that I would have a scar for the rest of my life.

Castle hit me again, this time on my jaw, with his fist. I reeled from his punch. Then he slammed me across my forehead, his head to mine in a crunching blow. It broke the skin and made the blood from the blow flow freely over my eyes and down my face. He kept on hitting me and I don't recall how many times he struck me before I finally blacked out. When I came to around twenty minutes later and saw the results of Castle's insane acts, I vomited on myself and at my feet, and on the ropes that bound me tightly to the chair where placed me. I throw up and cry whenever I recall the moment. I still feel sorry for myself and I feel helpless when I those memories make their return in unstoppable flashbacks. After what Castle did to me, the blows to my head combined with the intense heat of Saigon at midsummer, made my awakening from unconsciousness even more difficult than it would have been under normal circumstances. I struggled to free myself but soon gave up. Castle had tied me too tightly for me to escape. I will never forget the grotesque scene in front of me.

John Castle had cut the two prostitutes as if they were young deer he had shot and eviscerated. Their bodies, twisted, sliced and ripped were like nothing I had ever seen. Their blood had all but stopped flowing. The stink of early rotting flesh and of sudden, bodily discharge, filled the room, suffocating me with its oddly sweet odor. They were dead, so obviously, uncompromisingly and cruelly dead. They were so indecently, so inhumanely dead, that it would have been impossible to stitch them together if anyone wanted. In time, the police would discover the dead girls, neither of whom was over eighteen. One looked only fifteen. The cops would send the bodies to the morgue where someone would identify them, or not. Anyway, they would bag the bodies in canvas sacks, stuff and seal them in wood caskets, and send them to their village or home by bus for burial, if possible. The authorities would attach a note sealed in clear plastic advising the family to open the coffin at their own risk because of the brutal way their daughter or sister died. If the police could not identify either of the dead women, they would bury each in a charity cemetery on the Long Binh Road outside Saigon.

I didn't understand why Castle killed those women, especially the last two, and why he now had deviated from one a month, and dropping them in a secluded neighborhood, to this, the scene in front of me. *Blame it on drugs and his slow disintegration into insanity,* I thought. Though I was still woozy, I finally understood Castle had to be the serial killer, but with his cruel killing of these teenagers, he suddenly graduated from killing one whore a month to who knew what. Tied to the chair, the noise from the street seemed louder than ever. A swarm of black flies buzzed around the dead women. The stink from my vomit mixed with the sweetness of death's decay, made me retch with dry heaves and a fit of coughing. I didn't see Castle and wondered why he let me live. He could have easily killed me. Did he have something in mind for me that would heighten his perverse pleasure and make me suffer in ways I could not imagine? Exhaustion claimed my mind and body. I fell into fitful sleep, something I could not explain but it was probably from shock. I awoke with Castle standing over me, shaking me and slapping me on my face. It hurt particularly when he managed to hit me on the wound he had made with his knife. I didn't know how long he had been standing over me, but I felt the pain in my cheek and knew that blood flowed down it, wetting my lips, its taste like none other I knew.

"You're coming with me," he said. Though I had been beaten and cut, Castle looked worse than I did. He had not shaved for several days. His eyes were heavy from fatigue, and underneath, puffy and a sick gray, the lids drooped. His lips, dry and cracked with white crust in their corners made him seem unhealthier than usual.

"How?" I asked, my voice a cracked whisper. When he answered me, his voice came out coarse and gravelly, as if from the bottom of a cave.

"You'll see. You know, I thought you were a smart guy. But now I know you're just another dumb fuck."

He laughed. His breath smelled like sewer. Dried blood caked his shirt and combat fatigues. His broken, dirt encrusted fingernails showed blood under the nails and around their edges. Castle walked behind me, undid the ropes on the chair. Then he tied my hands behind my back and tied my ankles together. He tore apart a pair of a woman's panties and stuffed it in my mouth so I couldn't call out. He lifted me in his arms as if I weighed very little. I wanted to fight, but I was too weak to resist. He carried me out the back entrance of the laundromat, walked with me on his shoulders down an alley and shoved me into the back of a Renault taxicab. John Castle then got into the front seat and drove away.

Twenty minutes later we arrived at the brothel he ran near the Tan Son Nhut Air Base. He parked the small taxicab at the side and dragged me from the car. I hurt so much I hardly knew the new pain. My body ached from his dragging across the hard mud-packed street, but with all my other pain, it paled in comparison. People saw him but he didn't care. They were his people, to an extent. He paid some, and they, in turn, protected him. That was nothing new. It made sense that he would hide among those on his payroll.

Inside he called for Mama-san, and told her he wanted a hot bath. Mama-san and two prostitutes appeared. Castle waved the frightened women away and pulled me into a back room where I saw a big ceramic tub that he must have salvaged from a villa once owned by a rich French person. I lay on the floor in pain. He told the women to ignore me. I was his prisoner and I would soon get what was coming to me. He told her I cheated on him and that is why he had me trussed like a pig ready for slaughter.

Castle smoked pot and leaned against the wall waiting for his bath. He was ever vigilant, though I wondered how alert he would be after smoking one joint after another. In fifteen minutes, Mama-san led three other girls into the room carrying boiling jugs of water they poured into the tub. Several trips later and once filled, John Castle stripped his clothing, dropped everything on the floor and, naked, he entered the tub. Through puffy eyes, I watched Castle scrub himself clean of the blood caked on his arms and hands that had also soaked through his thin clothing onto his chest and legs. He lovingly caressed his powerful arms and chest with heavy applications of soap. He did that repeatedly and I wondered if he did it to wipe away the last two deaths. I noticed he used Tide detergent that I purchased from the PX, instead of soap like Ivory, but maybe that is all he had. It worked. The bloody water overflowed and spilled onto the floor. When that happened, Castle shouted and the women came running with more hot water to replace the run-off. Each time the water overflowed, Castle shouted, the women came running and refilled his tub. They carried rags and wiped the floor of the water.

He finished bathing. He stood and dried himself without once looking at me. He ignored the blond wood floor, now almost reddish maroon and soaked with bloody water. Castle looked at me and smiled. He changed into fresh clothing of clean cutoffs and a white shirt with two pockets and a collar that buttoned down. He rolled a heavy joint, lit it and inhaled deeply. He passed it to me and, I, too, took a very deep drag, holding the smoke long before letting it out. It helped relieve my pain. The ropes cut into my ankles and wrists. My head pounded with pain. I needed that pot to help reduce my pain and anxiety. If nothing else, I believed it worked and that is all that mattered. After finishing his joint, still smiling, he went to a cupboard and found a package of cigarettes I instinctively knew they would be heavy with heroin. He offered one to me and I refused. He didn't insist I smoke with him. For that, I gave silent thanks. I could handle the pot, but nothing much stronger. Castle removed one from the package, put it in his mouth and lit up. He had quickly moved on from marijuana to a cigarette injected with heroin. I could see the change in him as the sweet rush of H bounded through his veins. Castle gave me the finger and left the room. When he returned, his gait a shuffle rather than the usual proud bearing he usually had, the obvious results of the drugs. Two of the younger women were with him. He instructed them to take his clothing and to burn it in the in back where they usually got rid of the garbage. He wanted no evidence that could tie him to the two prostitutes he killed in the villa earlier that day.

After the women left, Castle peered at me through eyes that had become slits in his head. The lids sagged from his lack of sleep and his ingestion of drugs. I thought he might fall over but he managed to stay on his feet.

"What am I to do with you?" he said.

Of course, I said nothing. I had nothing to say, less to fight with, my strength gone from the beating I took, from my lack of food and loss of blood.

"Nothing, huh? Well, fuck you. I'm very tired, like I'm about to fall asleep."

Well, fuck you too, I said to myself, too afraid to say anything or object to whatever he planned. He had me tied as his prisoner. I couldn't resist and I would be a fool to fight. Perhaps if he slept and I did the same, I might regain some strength in the hope that the drugs would take their toll on him and give me a chance to fight back.

Castle walked to me, checked my bonds, making sure they were tight and I could not slip from them, and started toward the cot in the corner of the room but before he did, he gently patted my face on the side without the cut and again, he grinned.

"I'll take a nap. When I get up, I'll have it worked out, and if not, the hell with it," he said.

Castle giggled. The drugs made him act that way. He took a last deep drag on his cigarette filled with heroin. I had to believe he had those he smoked made with more drugs than the ones found on many Saigon street corners. At the cot, he bent to the small pillow, puffed it up and lay down. In seconds, he fell into a deep sleep, a surprisingly gentle snore coming from his mouth and nose, a bit of spittle from the corner of his lips.

Most of my pain had lessened but I was too agitated and found it impossible to sleep. When I moved my head, the cut under my eye on my cheek stung and opened each time I changed position. I needed stitches and a chance to let the wound heal. I needed water, but the gag in my mouth didn't allow me to ask for any. I hurt everywhere, my legs, my balls, my back, my shoulders, and my neck. I hurt, period. Painkillers would help. Opium would be best. But until I got free, if I were lucky, I could do nothing to help myself. I closed my eyes, hoping to rest when two young women appeared in the room. They moved slowly with awkward stealth, and quietly, too, each with an index finger to her lips to show they were quiet and I should be the same. They didn't realize I had no choice. One, so small she looked like a child, had a small cleaver, the kind used to gut a duck or cut roast pork into thin slices. The other, taller and very thin, had a clean cloth and a pan filled with water. They approached me, and the one with the cleaver whispered, "We come help you. He not a good man. We get you free." She pointed the cleaver toward Castle, and with that, she deftly sliced the ropes that tied my ankles and the ropes that bound my hands behind my back.

The girl with the cloth and pan of water started to wash my feet and hands as I rubbed them together to get back my circulation. With one swift movement, the girl with the cleaver released the tape covering my mouth and freed me of the gag. I breathed hard, but gasped as quietly as I could, fearing that I might wake Castle.

I tried standing but almost fell over, leaning on the taller woman who seemed able to take the brunt of my weight without toppling over.

"We go hurry now," said the small girl.

We started to move toward the door, a mere ten feet away but it seemed like a mile. I had never been so weak.

Outside, the door closed softly behind us, and a cyclo waited. I knew I looked like hell and the driver probably thought I had just survived a massive drunk. My clothing was bloody and torn. I was barefoot and my face slashed, with blood caked on my cheek despite the wash I had. The driver looked at me with contempt.

"Hurry, now. We go." The three of us climbed into the cyclo. "You money?" asked the small one.

I reached into my pocket and discovered Castle had taken nothing from me. I had more than enough money to pay the driver and the two women who rescued me.

Once we were around the corner from the brothel, though only less than forty feet away, I relaxed for the first time that day. The prostitutes, one on each side, held me tightly around my waist. Despite my aches and pain, and my fear of speaking because of the pain in my mouth and jaw, it felt good to be alive. The tall one kept wiping the dried blood from my face. Each time she touched me, I flinched and moaned. She whimpered in sympathy with me when she applied the wet rag to my wound and bruises.

"Why did you free me?" I asked with difficulty. The sounds that came from me were not firm or together. My words were loose and mushy. At first, I didn't recognize the sound of my voice.

The girl on my left side answered me first.

"My name Ti-Ti. Means very small." She smiled.

I could see her size. She looked like a child. "You look like a child," I said.

"GI and American much like small girl. OK, me. I hate Mr. John. He mean. He beat. I tired. Other girls tired. I no like, burn clothing. I put on pile in back. Any people need clothing wash blood and make like new."

I smiled and wondered how true that might be. I hoped Castle continued sleeping while we made our escape. I knew he had no conscience or remorse over what he had done. When we escaped, his legs were carelessly and surprisingly gently draped, so it appeared, over a long pillow the length of the cot.

"I tired taking care him," Ti-Ti said. "I not his whore. I Ti-Ti. I not do anymore what he want. I do for me."

"What do you do now? He will know you freed me. You have to keep running or go into hiding."

She looked at me and smiled sweetly. "I think Mr. John, he die soon. So me not worry. You help?"

"I don't know how, but I'll try." I didn't know. Perhaps Phuoc had an idea. Maybe the women would return to their respective villages and wait until it was safe to return. Construction workers and other civilians, sometimes those from one country or another, were always looking for full time companions. They might get lucky and find a decent man, or at least one to take care of them for an extended time. Anything was possible with nothing guaranteed. Moving swiftly through the city, with the wind in my face, I slowly came back to life. I shuddered to think how close I had come to my death. I held up my thumb and forefinger and rubbed them together. *That close,* I thought. Too close, I knew. I dug into my side pocket and pulled out a Camel. Despite the wind, I got the cigarette lit and inhaled deeply. We were heading to my apartment and would soon be there. Somehow, I knew a reception committee led by inspector Phuoc would be waiting. And I welcomed it. Thirsty and in need of a bath, I would soon arrive on my doorstep. I had to clear myself and Phuoc and his men had to go after, and finally get John Castle.

The cyclo turned the corner to where I lived and yes, as I suspected, a detachment of Vietnamese National

Police and a squad of Vietnamese military police, both led by Phuoc, was waiting for me. Phuoc sat on his haunches, despite his suit, as only the Vietnamese could, eating a bowl of noodle soup. I watched him and marveled at the speed of his chopsticks working to shovel in the slippery white noodles. The three of us, my two woman saviors and me, practically fell from the canvas basket seat as the driver, shocked to see so many armed men in one place on a busy Saigon street, came to the equivalent of a screeching halt. Half way in and half way out, I didn't move. The two women with me didn't move. I started reaching into my pocket for money to pay the driver and a dozen guns pointed at me. I heard all the safeties click off, not quite in unison, and again in the same day, feared for my life, something I wanted to overcome. I continued with my hand in my pocket, drew a large roll of piasters and paid the driver excessively for his effort. Off his seat, the cyclo driver pedaled backwards, one foot on a pedal, the other on the ground, and out of the line of fire, if that were to be our fate.

After wiping his mouth with a white handkerchief, Phuoc walked to me, put out his hand and nodded hello, the hello and the handshake both a rare gesture. I wondered what he meant. Because it wasn't hostile and I was still standing, I had to believe my life had some value. In rapid Vietnamese, the prostitutes explained everything they knew about me, about Castle and our escape. TiTi cried, whether from relief or fear, something I'll never know. The sight of TiTi crying melted everyone standing in the semicircle. It didn't make me feel better because their weapons were still primed, all pointed at me.

"What did you do?" asked Phuoc.

Still barely able to speak, I answered with a croak, "Nothing. I did nothing. I didn't kill those girls. I didn't kill anyone."

"I am inclined finally to believe you. I've looked hard into my own soul and divined that you do not have the heart of a killer."

"Thank God for that."

"Castle is out there yet and we have to find him."

"Send your men to the brothel I just came from. We left him sleeping off his drugs. Maybe you'll find him and then we, meaning me," and I smiled for the first time in the last day, "can rest easy for a change."

Phuoc issued his orders. Six cops were on their way in dilapidated Renault cars. In another rare moment of oddly religious fervor, I overheard Phuoc invoking the Buddha to help deliver Castle to his men and ultimately to him. If the Buddha delivered, Phuoc would see that Castle got what he deserved. I went up to my apartment followed by Phuoc. I dropped my clothes in a pile on the floor and entered the shower where I stayed for fifteen minutes. Soaping off the remains of the dried and caked blood proved time consuming. Though TiTi and her friend did a good job of removing most of the blood from my face, the thin wound under my eye, almost four inches running from my nose to my ear, reopened on our cyclo drive. The blood dripped and then dried on the left side of my face. The water at my feet ran with blood from my other mostly superficial wounds and eventually turned clear. I looked at the black and blue marks on my body and shuddered to think how close I came to not being of this or any world.

My desire for opium was overpowering, but I resisted. One pipe would lead to another and once I passed two, I would go to three, breaking my own barrier and find myself incapacitated for the day or more. I wanted a drink, though, and I only had several cans of warm Heineken beer on my bookshelf. I opened one and swallowed it quickly. Then I opened the other and drank that down as fast. The two cans gave me a mild buzz and took away some of my pain, but not enough of it to make a difference. I had to concentrate hard, but I managed to dress. After, Phuoc and I went to Broda for coffee and sandwiches on fresh French bread made with Vietnamese pate, cabbage, carrots and lettuce, followed by French pastries filled with and covered by butter cream. When full, I drank strong, black coffee while we waited for Phuoc's patrol to return. The day lingered. Afternoon started turning to evening. The strong coffee gave me heartburn, but at least I had some feeling that told me I still lived. My jaw hurt but I managed to gum down every bit of food in front of me.

Close to five o'clock, Phuoc's men were back with the bad news that Castle was not in the brothel, now empty of anyone. Two washing machines stood idle, their drums dry. The cops found the room where Castle had tied me down and where he had nodded off from his drugs. On the floor, they found the bloody ropes that Castle used to tie my ankles and wrists. None of the neighbors said they saw Castle, me, or anything else that was unusual. Obviously, the money Castle gave in the neighborhood paid off in the resident's silence. The police had one success. They found Castle's clothing TiTi deposited outside on the rotting pile of garbage in back of the brothel. There were no name tags or other markings on the clothing to identify it, but the blood and large size were enough to confirm that it did belong to John Castle. This new evidence meant that Phuoc no longer doubted my story, if he ever did. With Phuoc, I could never be sure of anything.

Phuoc sent other police to neighborhoods all over the city where Castle might be hiding. Instructed to ask discreet questions, to make generous threats and to hand out a modest amount of money in bribes, Phuoc hoped his men would discover Castle's hiding place. With an early curfew, we decided to stop for the day. His men would keep searching and Phuoc would meet me the next morning at eight in Broda, at the same table if possible. He had powerful superstitions and having coffee in the same place twice during an investigation was one of them.

After returning to my apartment, I had difficulty sleeping. Then exhaustion took over and I fell into deep and surprisingly satisfying sleep.

Noise from the street and sunlight streaming through my bamboo shades woke me earlier than I wanted. I lit my first cigarette of the day, inhaled deeply and coughed heavily. My jaw hurt, and my throat was still raw from the beating I took. Then I showered and shaved, and departed for Broda. Inspector Phuoc sat waiting for me and at the same table. Why would he be at any other? Obviously, I had little faith in his beliefs. He proved me wrong. Phuoc had a coffee in front of him. He had a cigarette in the corner of his mouth. Blue smoke rose in front of his face to irritate his eyes. He squinted as he leafed through a sheaf of official looking papers on the table's remaining space. I ordered coffee and several chocolate cream pastries, more than enough to give a sugar rush, to get me kick- started into the new day.

"We are out searching now. So far we have had no luck in finding John Castle."

"You'll find him. I mean, how far can he go without anyone seeing him? He'll have to surface soon and then you'll get him." I sipped my coffee and dragged on my Camel.

"My prayer is that he does not kill again before we do catch him." "What made you believe me?"

"It became clear to me as I looked at all the evidence that you had neither the opportunity nor motive. I could see no reason why you would kill Trang. I know you loved her and despite your discovery that she worked as a prostitute, I believe it was not enough for you to turn against her and kill her. There are people in my department who wished it were you. They looked forward to arresting and trying a journalist. They thought it would help to defray some of America's idealism to put a critical journalist in jail and let him rot. You are not a killer. I had to respect my instinct rather than defer to false evidence. You are now formally in the clear."

Grateful, and near tears, I screwed up my face enough to keep me from breaking down, but just doing that sent a searing pain through my sliced cheek.

"Thanks," I said. I knew my simple thanks had to be enough.

Just then a uniformed sergeant, many years older than most of the men in Phuoc's command, his shirt once white, now gray with age, his collar frayed from being washed too often, came to Phuoc's side and waited respectfully until acknowledged. Phuoc nodded and gave the sergeant permission to speak. The sergeant told Phuoc his men narrowed Castle's hiding place to a neighborhood near the Saigon River, a slum really, where he had a hovel close to a whore house owned by a sometime competitor, where he kept a store of drugs and guns, if needed.

"It is time to go," Phuoc said.

I followed him, there being nothing else for me to do, and walked with him from the dimly lit coffee shop into the bright, sunny street. We entered a black and battered Citroen. From the front seat, Phuoc immediately radioed instructions to his men for their next move. Several other equally battered police cars followed in Phuoc's wake as he pulled into traffic on Tu Do Street and headed to the Saigon River.

Phuoc told his driver where to go and we made our way slowly through the dense, smog-ridden traffic toward what we hoped would be peacefully sleeping, still heavily drugged John Castle. Phuoc raised headquarters on the radio and passed along to more men his instructions in code on the closed band. He told them to move gently and quietly into the area and to evacuate people from those houses next to where Castle slept, or, at least, where Phuoc believed John Castle might be sleeping. He told me he wanted the men to work with care not to disrupt the normal flow of life. A difficult job, but with the right mixture of threats, cajolery and well-placed rifle butts, Phuoc thought he would be successful. If the Saigon police caught John Castle with little fuss, and a minimum loss of life and destruction of property, Phuoc would achieve his goal.

I had never seen Phuoc in action, unless I counted that time when he quieted the Bar California. Usually he appeared passive and calm, almost inactive, as if he were waiting for something to happen. Well, we were in the middle of the action and Phuoc had taken command. I watched a different man at work. He told me he didn't want to waste any lives trying to capture Castle, but in Phuoc's war, where civilians needlessly died, he would do anything to win.

"I know," he said, his voice a whisper I could barely hear, "that Mr. John Castle might never live to come to trial. I can live with that. I have this strong conviction today we may see the end of Castle. He will not live out the day. I prefer that he die sooner than later. I want him to die fast, not slow. When you suffer at the hands of a torturer, you realize that it is better to die, once and fast and not experience the many deaths that torture so ably gives. I still feel the sting of the thin bamboo switch on my back and the water forced into my mouth making me gag, then vomit, my breathing labored and disabled. I feel those pains every day. That is why I seek to kill humanely, if possible."

Perhaps Castle would never make it to police headquarters. That would be the best solution. The longer he languished in jail waiting for his trial, the better the chance he would have to buy his freedom. He probably would find himself taking over the prison, what with his money, contacts, and lack of fear. Phuoc didn't want to chance that, so I knew, as he did, that

Castle might not live very long whether that day or in prison.

The driver pulled the car into an alley near the house where they thought they would find Castle. Police surrounded a square block area near the river, though they knew the perimeter would be leaky as a sieve. Phuoc knew plugging all the holes would be impossible with the small number of men he had for the operation. He did manage to surround the house where he believed Castle slept. Until the police entered the house, they would not know if they would find Castle. Filthy puddles covered the muddy street. Mosquitoes were everywhere. A foul smell pervaded the neighborhood, as if someone had just died. Mangy dogs wandered the streets, low growls coming from their throats. They had no patience for strangers, yet they did nothing more than show their fangs and bare their teeth. Occasionally a dog barked, ran to a policeman and then backed away, its tail between its legs. Children stayed back, bunched together, barely able to contain themselves, the excitement almost too much for them to bear. They behaved themselves because they didn't want a swat on the bottom, or a slap in the face.

Police brought traffic to a standstill and diverted those vehicles already inside the fire zone to other streets. These usually poorly trained excuses for real cops kneeled behind parked cars and trucks, while others stood behind the occasional concrete stanchion. Some hid in doorways to get out of the line of fire, their carbines and —16 rifles surprisingly ready, their leather holsters unsnapped, their pistols loaded and set to fire. As prepared as they seemed, their ability to act like real police was in question. Though some were combat police and better trained and better motivated than the average street cop, they had higher pay but not by much, they were far from perfect in many situations. This was one of those situations. None had any idea what waited inside the two-story house with its wire mesh fence and high iron gate. A few giggled quietly, a nervous trait found in Vietnamese men. Several smoked cheap Vietnamese cigarettes that smelled worse than their French brand cousins did. I saw a man biting his nails. Many, as if a universal habit of the Vietnamese, bit their lower lips and feigned smiles. To say how scared they were, would belittle how deeply they must have felt about the unknown. Despite being near a heavily traveled main road, and the presence of too many people who could get hurt, a sense of uneasiness was pervasive.

Standing next to Phuoc, I tried to imagine what Castle was doing. I saw him on a rumpled bed. He is gently snoring. The inevitable, oddly reliable spittle courses slowly down the side of his mouth. I wonder, how deeply is he drugged? It's a state he has become more familiar with each day, hell, each hour. Does his sleeping through the commotion outside his door mean he is waiting for us to catch him? I hoped for that to save lives, to lessen any resultant harm.

Inspector Hong Phuoc picked two men armed with M-16s to go with him when he entered the house to capture Castle. Men who have seen action in the past, call them battle tested, they wore steel pot helmets and heavy flak jackets. Phuoc knew the sound of bullets would not terrorize them. Their eyes told me they were anxious to use their weapons on something other than a wood practice target, all they had permission in last few weeks to shoot.

I stayed at Phuoc's side, not moving, watching everything and everyone, taking mental notes, just in case I might have a story. Despite my recent stupidities, journalism still drove me. I wondered what Phuoc had in mind for me. Would I trail after him like a sick puppy? I hoped he would clarify my role and it would be simple.

"What do you want me to do?" I asked.

Phuoc turned to me with a puzzled look. He pulled a Gitanes from his crushed pack of cigarettes and carefully put flame to it, inhaling deeply as he did. He let the smoke out slowly through his nose and mouth. The harsh smoke grated on me. It caused me to choke, and my eyes to tear. *Thanks,* I said to myself, not wanting to insult him or his way of life, of which French cigarettes were a big part. I stood my ground and waited for his reply. Squinting at me because the smoke got in his eyes, too, he shook his head up and down several times, a small grin crossing his lips, as if he were content with how he planned to answer.

"You have a choice what you can do. You can wait out here for me, or you can come inside when we make our move. No matter what you do, or what happens, you must stay close to me because I want you to identify Castle once we catch him. Staying close means, you cannot wander. I want you to accuse Castle in front of witnesses. I need you to present him with your version of the truth. Then I can see his reaction to what you say. Can you do that? If not, you must stay outside and well back."

"Fine," I said. I didn't like what Phuoc said. I didn't want to be anywhere near violence, especially if guns went off. Phuoc held his hand up, his palm out, and continued, this time surprisingly breathless.

"However, I would like you to come inside with me. Though I gave you a choice, I really do not want to give you the right to refuse. I want you to go first and to call Castle out, to warn him, please, to perhaps catch him off guard. That way it will allow my men the time they need to get close enough to move on him and overpower him. I want him alive when we take him. If you do that, it will be over quickly and there will be less chance of others getting hurt. A show trial will be good for my country, my police, me."

Phuoc's men were getting into place as he quietly talked to me. I screwed up my face as if I were in pain. Well, I was in pain, and damn afraid. Each time I moved my face it felt like the cut had newly opened, something was having a hard time getting used to. I was a noncombatant, for God's sake, and a pacifist, really, especially when it came to the possibility of my own pain. I had no training for war. The closest I had come to firing a weapon recently took place on a range where real soldiers practiced. Before that, I occasionally fired air rifles in carnivals at small pockmarked, fast-moving ducks and cows fashioned from pig iron. Importantly, they could not and never did shoot back, however often I hit them with lucky shots. When I covered combat, I rarely went too far to the front of the action, believing it to be a waste of my time. I had been there, close to the action, and I knew the fear from bullets and rockets flying over my head that sadly wounded too many

American soldiers. I didn't want to go home wounded, or worse, in a body bag. The thought was daunting.

"If I go with you, do I have to carry a gun?"

"It will be safer for you if we arm you."

"I know nothing about guns."

"It will not be a problem. Guns are easy to learn. I will teach you quickly. After all, it is in you best interest if you have protection. Now, and then later. You must be ready for anything."

Still uneasy, I nodded my assent. My heart in my throat, I could feel my sweat starting to roll down my back beneath my shirt. Phuoc walked to a sergeant and together, they went to a police car, opened it and removed several handguns. He hefted them one at a time and looked over to where I stood. He walked back to me, holding at his side against his thigh a well-worked, old-fashioned, police thirty- eight. In front of me, he removed the bullets from the revolving chamber, put them in his pocket and handed me the gun. I hefted it, feeling its weight in my right hand and wondered how to shoot it. Phuoc then gave me a short course on how to fire it. I thought a lot good that did, especially if I might find myself using it in the next ten minutes. Using it in the next ten minutes! I hoped not. Phuoc had me load and then put the bullets back in the weapon, and each time I emptied the bullets from the chamber, he had me squeeze the trigger.

"When you shoot, squeeze the trigger," he said. "Do not force the trigger. Do not pull the trigger. If you pull it, you will jerk the barrel and the shot will go wild. Be gentle. Your gun is your best friend. Do not forget that and you might succeed, if you have to fire."

Phuoc had me replace the six shells and then he had me rotate, really spin, the chamber the way they do it in the movies.

Despite my fear of weapons and my hatred of using them, really, the gun felt good in my hand. I didn't like that I took to it so fast. It was easier than I thought, and holding the gun in my hand gave me a strange power I couldn't understand. I made sure I turned on the safety, a small switch near the handle, and I tucked the gun into my waistband like a cowboy on a mission.

"Now, we will go," said Phuoc.

With me behind, he and four heavily armed men moved quietly to the front door of the house, not a door, but a beaded vertical curtain hanging from a curtain rod over what people used for the entrance. We were quick to the front entrance to make sure no one saw or heard us enter. How could no one know we were outside? We had been there for almost an hour setting everything up, keeping the people quite, and moving the traffic down other streets. You would have to a fool or deaf and blind not to know we were there, or, like Castle, hopefully drugged, and unable to function.

Many Vietnamese houses have two floors. On the ground floor, you first enter a large foyer. Then you go into a living room that is next to a rudimentary bathroom, if the family has indoor plumbing, a rare blessing in Saigon. Finally, there is a dining room next to a large kitchen that usually has two charcoal stoves. There are brick-lined holes, deep in the floor where the family grills their pork, chicken and fish, and even vegetables. A huge pot of rice sits heating on an upper stove where the mother cooks soup and stews. Vietnamese eat rice with every meal and the pot is always full, but here, despite the rice pot we saw, no one was home. We went through the ground floor quickly and we did not see Castle.

Phuoc motioned us to keep quiet. He pointed to the one set of stairs leading to the upper floor, where the family had its sleeping quarters, a large room like a dormitory. Here the children would sleep together on separate pallets. The parents would sleep in a small bedroom in the back. It is cleaner, cooler, quieter and safer upstairs. There is no bathroom for any purpose. If we were to find Castle in the house, he would have to be upstairs, probably in the small bedroom.

The four policemen led the way up the darkened, narrow flight of steps. Phuoc followed and I came behind, still wondering what role I would play if we found John Castle. We stumbled one into the other as we entered the large empty single room. Several doors were at either end. We had no idea where the doors went, though we guessed Castle had to be hiding or sleeping behind the door at the back of the house, in the master bedroom. I know we made more noise than we wanted. By then, it no longer mattered. He had to be there, up there, behind that closed door. He had to be, otherwise, were we there only chasing a ghost.

Bunched in the middle of the floor, we sighed as one, making certain we kept the noise we made to a minimum. Phuoc signaled two men to either side of the room. Then he told me to remove the thirty- eight from my waistband. I did without thinking, not even wondering what I had done. He reached over and undid the safety. Phuoc made sure we were not in the others' line of fire.

Phuoc whispered to me that I should go first. Castle knew me, he said. He would not shoot when he saw me enter the room. How could he shoot a friend? Why would he shoot a friend? *Nonsense,* I thought. I wasn't his friend, never had been. He beat me badly only a day ago. When under the influence of drugs, everyone was his enemy. Nobody was safe. I didn't think I had a chance but I kept going.

To calm my fears, Phuoc told me his men would only shoot if shot at first. Not great. In a split second, I had become a sacrificial lamb. Not great at all. In the spirit of good policing, the police would defend themselves first and ask questions second. But they would not shoot first. That was hard to believe, if true. I had seen trigger-happy Vietnamese cops panic and leave all sanity and good judgment behind and if I were in the line of fire, too bad. My life had little value compared to Phuoc about to complete his work, and finish the job he had been living with for almost a year. He had a plan and he would stick to it. But I didn't realize I played a big role.

I felt naked standing in the middle of the floor. Every noise sounded very loud in the hot, darkened room. I heard the boards beneath my feet squeak. How do I get rid of a squeak? Impossible. Would Castle be in the room behind the closed door? We had no guarantee. As the sudden stalking horse for the Saigon police, I would soon find out. Could Castle hear me and the sound I made as I moved across the floor? My feet were wet and sticky and the leather thongs on my sandals started tightening around my ankles, cutting into my skin. I thought anyone within twenty feet of me could hear me breathing. I wondered again, could John Castle hear me? I wished not, knowing well that wishes rarely came true.

I looked at the pistol I held loosely in my right hand. I saw Phuoc from the corner of one eye. He gestured to me with his hand to raise the gun into shooting position, which meant I had to take it in two hands, point it straight and aim for the door ahead of me. I squinted down the barrel, and for some unknown reason, I squeezed the handle, though I knew, I couldn't get very far without my finger on the trigger. Something odd came over me. I stood with a gun in my hands in a foreign city, in a strange house where every day was summer. I thought myself in a play we were rehearsing where the playwright had not yet written the end.

Instinctively, and God knows why, I squared my shoulders and moved closer to the door. I heard the police and Phuoc behind me as they followed, keeping pace, though at a safe distance, with my snail- like progress. The game was about to begin, and with it, was it my time to play the hero and end my charade? I had been a noncombatant too long. Now, armed with a loaded weapon, I found myself about to enter a new world. I couldn't believe where my thoughts were taking me. A flicker of reality coursed through me, but didn't stay long. If I took the time to worry, I would have to run.

"Castle," I called. "John Castle, are you in there? Are you anywhere?"

My voice came out like a bellow. What the hell had I done? That wasn't in the script. By calling his name, I had put myself in the line of fire of whoever might be behind the door.

No one answered, but I heard movement behind the door. Tension such as I had never known nearly overwhelmed me. My arms were like lead and my hands holding the gun, suddenly weakened. The gun had become a ten-ton anchor. I had difficulty stopping my arms from falling to my side. My mind drifted. Again, I wondered what I was doing there, there of all places, holding a gun, a loaded gun of all things, the safety off, ready to fire. I wanted to be elsewhere, anywhere but in that shabby Vietnamese house in Saigon on a hot and sticky day.

Then my trance evaporated when the door in front of me, not more than ten feet in front of me, flew open with a resounding crack against the wall, there being no door stop to break its motion.

Next came shots. Suddenly the room exploded. I knew the gun jerked in my hands, once, twice, three, then four and five times, in rapid succession, each shot piling in so close to the next shot that I had no idea the bullets came from the same gun, fired by the same man, me. I didn't know how many times I pulled the trigger but I kept firing. I saw smoke and smelled cordite, acrid and caustic, not pleasant and far from sweet.

John Castle fell to the floor, dead at my feet. Three bullets were in his chest. A fourth bullet shattered his neck. There were no screams. He didn't shout. Castle died instantly. How I became a good shot so quickly, never having fired a gun before, will forever remain a mystery. A fifth bullet struck the leg of the young women who had been with Castle in the room, a woman we had no idea who was in there with him. Other bullets penetrated the wall behind him. She said nothing but moaned quietly in shock. Thank God, I didn't kill her, too.

Bewildered and shocked, heavy perspiration burst from my body and soaked my clothing. I burned and itched with hot flushes of fear when I realized what I had done. I spun slowly on my heels like a mechanical ballet dancer winding to a slow stop. I faced Inspector Phuoc. I saw the four police looking at me as if they were seeing me for the first time. Phuoc smiled at me sadly and started walking to me. I lifted the gun toward Phuoc and pointed it at his stomach. I thought I had one bullet left, but I couldn't be sure. Phuoc stopped and didn't move any closer. He raised his arms in front of him, and opened his hands waiting for me to give him the gun. I wanted to shoot him. He made me kill a man, of that I was sure. I could finish the job he made me start. I could shoot him and then, the hell with everything. They could do with me as they wished. But I did nothing more with the gun. Everything took place so fast, including all that had flowed through my steaming mind. I looked at Phuoc as if he was a stranger and then I dropped the gun to the floor. It fell with a thud at Phuoc's feet. I let out a deep sob, a scream almost, hysterical and wailing, which still echoes in my head to this day.

I turned from Phuoc and the dead Castle, the wounded woman, and the four police. I walked, as if in a fog, unhurriedly down the steps and out to the street. Tears of sorrow and rage choked in my throat.

Just then, I felt a small tap on my shoulder. I turned slowly to see Phuoc, my sometime tormentor, sometime interrogator, and I realized, always my friend, standing to my left, his right hand gently on my back near my neck. He smiled, so rare, and I could tell his sympathy was real. After all, he had just seen me kill a man.

Phuoc watched me and said to me in a voice just loud enough for me to hear, "I knew you could do it. You see, I depended on you and you came through."

Though Castle deserved it, I had terrible trouble justifying that I had killed him out of hatred and for revenge. I suspected my troubled psyche would always carry those questions as part of me.

"Come with me," he said, kindly. "This is truly the time to savor a pipe, to allow your dreams to settle rather than wander. Come with me."

I knew where Phuoc meant, what he meant. The thoughts of smoking satisfying opium with its subtle ability to create in me soft, sweet visions helped me relax and relieve my tension. As I recalled the effect of the opium, I could feel it start to pry my soul open, enough, I hoped, to help me past the next bend in the road.

Perhaps.

Long before this unholiest of wars, wise men, sages, scholars, priests and rabbis, wrote words and prayers for each of their holiest of days. When satisfied with their words, they had them embedded in their prayer books. Before I saw the war, the death, pain and suffering it brought, and in the seeing, came to know that if a god exists, he had not made his presence felt here, not in this far off place called Vietnam. The prayer books are explicit, and detailed beyond our imagination. When read alone or with a congregation in unison, the words create their own soaring power. They are about who will love, who will die, who will live beyond his years before death. Those words are also about who will die by weapons in the hands of evil men, who will die because they are hungry or thirsty. Because they evoke an era thousands of years ago, they talk about death by strangling and even by stoning, primitive compared to how we now live, yet relevant, real to our time of war and to the women who recently died in Saigon. And through it all, those words refer to the tranquil, the troubled, the humbled and the exalted.

I had to learn so much the hard way, and that my striving for perfection, even briefly, had little chance for success. My hubris was thinking I could have it all—love, success, money, a fine meal, strong drink, and pipes of warming opium. In that tawdry house, in a moment of anger and irrationality, I saw everything disappear. I knew many memories would remain, tucked away in my psyche only to emerge unexpectedly when I least wanted. I knew it would take a very long walk for me to forget everything I had seen, and everything I had done. I wondered did I have the strength to start down that new road.

The End

About the Author

Photo: Eileen Douglas

Ron Steinman was with NBC News for 35 years. He was a writer on the Huntley-Brinkley show before going to Saigon as bureau chief in 1966. He served as South East Asia bureau chief based in Hong Kong and then London bureau chief during the "Troubles" in Northern Ireland. He was Washington producer for Today and he had other senior positions on Today, Early Today and in the news division, often covering politics. He is currently a partner, producer and writer at Douglas/Steinman Productions where he directed the documentaries, "Luboml: My Heart Remembers," "My Grandfather's House," and "the Dance Goodbye." He is the author of "The Soldiers' Story," "The Soldiers' Story: An Illustrated Edition," "Women in Vietnam," "Notebooks," a memoir, and "Survival Manual," a memoir.

Author's Note

Dear Reader,

I hope you enjoyed reading Death in Saigon as much as I enjoyed writing it. Please do me a favor and write a review on amazon.com. The reviews are important and your support is greatly appreciated.

Thank you,
Ron Steinman

Inside Televisions First War

A Saigon Journal, Inside Television's First War, recounts Ron Steinman's tenure as bureau chief for NBC News in Saigon. It is an intimate and deeply personal recounting of many of the Vietnam War's most difficult and harrowing days. These include the huge American buildup of troops, the famous hill battles in the Central Highlands, heavy fighting along the DMZ, the siege of Khe Sanh, riots against the government in the streets, Buddhist monks burning themselves to death in protest of the government and the Tet Offensive, the centerpiece of the book, when Hanoi attempted to take over South Vietnam but failed.

The book also recounts the personal story of Steinman's romance with Josephine Tu Ngoc Suong, his future wife, and her near fatal accidental shooting. During this period television news learned to cover the war with correspondents and camera crews working alongside the troops, giving people at home an intimate view of what war was really like.

Dubbed the living room war, people at home watched it unfold on TV over dinner and in their living rooms, something, until then that had not been possible.

The Soldier's Story

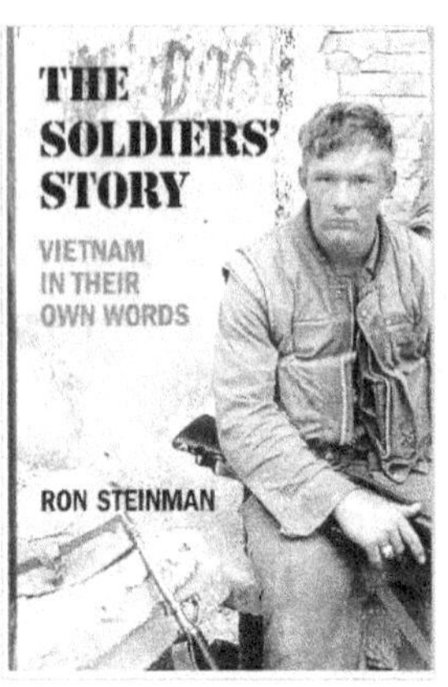

Most history-minded Americans have discussed the Vietnam War, becoming familiar, at the very least, with the names of such pivotal events as the Siege of Khe Sanh, the Tet Offensive, and the Fall of Saigon. But to grasp the full impact of this agonizing conflict, the human costs of an infernal war that raged for ten years and took more than 58,000 American lives, one must hear about it from the soldiers, sailors, and airmen who experienced the fighting and endured.

In The Soldiers' Story, veteran journalist Ron Steinman gathers the candid reminiscences of seventy-six men who survived combat in Vietnam. Not a military analysis or political study, this oral history vividly conveys the hardships, friendships, fears, and personal triumphs of Marine, Army, Air Force, and Navy veterans-each of whom shares memories that have lingered to this day.

It is a valuable frontline record of battle-torn Vietnam from the perspective of those who lived it first-hand, giving us a window into the horror, intensity, and raw courage that the war engendered

Women in Vietnam

In *Women in Vietnam*, veteran journalist Ron Steinman collects the testimony of sixteen remarkable women who served, and provides an unflinching account of this crucial and long ignored part of the war. In powerful first-hand accounts, we read of their experiences on the front lines, on the bases, and in the cities, towns and villages. All these women served with honor, without complaint, and with distinction.

Women in Vietnam is a unique historical document and a powerful record of extraordinary accomplishment. As a significant tribute to the women serving in Iraq, there is a fresh essay from Ron Steinman about their accomplishments and heroism in that different war in an equally far off land that helps put in perspective how these women today also serve with honor and without complaint.

The Soldiers' Story: An Illustrated Edition

Veteran journalist Ron Steinman gathers candid reminiscences from seventy-six men (including Senator John McCain) who lived through the brutalities of combat in the Vietnam War. A Soldiers' Story provides a vivid and gripping oral history of the fear, fellowship, trauma and triumph of these Marine, Army, Air Force, and Navy veterans. Complete with maps and battlefield photographs, these indespensable first-hand accounts provide a unique front-line record of Vietnam - from its surreal horrors, to the comradeship and courage forged in battle.

From the jungles of Southeast Asia to life back in the United States as veterans of an unpopular war, A Soldiers' Story also includes complete and updated biographies of the brave men who are profiled. This is a book that goes beyond the military and political implications of Vietnam, to the truth of what the war cost - and who actually paid the price.